You Still Love Me

Copyright © 2012 Regina Edwards Drumm
Cover Design by K. Leah O'Connor
Cover background photo by Dan Sullivan –
www.redbubble.com/people/lonestar
All rights reserved.
ISBN: 1-4679-7038-7
ISBN-13: 9781467970389

You Still Love Me

Regina Edwards Drumm

2012

Dedication

To my family, friends and writing buddies, I couldn't have done it without you. Your support and encouragement kept me going. A special thank you to my husband, Bill. You are my hero in real life and I couldn't love you more. You always supported me and never complained about hours on the computer or a messy office. You even provided inspiration for my heroes. And thank you to my family who always knew I could do it and are my biggest fans. I love you all.

chapter 1

THE STREETS WERE quiet. Just the way newly appointed Sheriff, Ethan Kirkpatrick, intended to keep things. Nice and quiet. He unfolded his six-foot-four frame from his patrol car and stretched, flexing the muscles in his shoulders and back, working the kinks from his body. He ran his fingers through his short, dark, curly hair and grabbed his Stetson.

With no time to hit the Wal-Mart in Cotton Wood or Flagstaff, he headed for the local drug store on Main Street in Oak Creek, hoping they would carry the items he needed. He was finally getting settled in his new job and home in Arizona and needed to pick up a few personal items before heading back to the station.

He meandered up and down the aisles, searching for the items he needed, when he overheard a couple of women gossiping. He shook his head. Did he hear them correctly? A whorehouse outside of town? No way, and not so nice and quiet. That's what he got for eavesdropping. Unable to help himself, he wandered over in their direction.

"Good afternoon, ladies." He tipped his hat to them.

"Hello, Sheriff," they cooed in unison.

"Lovely day," he replied, starting to walk past them.

The older, gray-haired woman leaned over and whispered something in the middle-aged, dark-haired woman's ear, then cleared her throat. "Umm, Sheriff?"

"Yes, ma'am." Ethan turned to face her.

She leaned toward him and lowered her voice. "I know you're still new here, but what do you plan on doing about that whorehouse outside of town?"

He had heard them correctly, he thought with dread over what these busy bodies expected him to do about it. Maybe he should have driven into flagstaff after all. "Whorehouse, ma'am?" He raised an eyebrow.

"Those women who live on that ranch outside of town are not respectable." The dark-haired woman pursed her lips.

"How are they unrespectable, ladies?"

"Well, there are all these men and boys that work on their ranch, and busloads of women show up all the time. Obviously, they are doing shameful things there." The gray-haired woman gave him a 'you know what I'm talking about' kind of look.

"Are you ladies talking about The WWC Dude Ranch?"

"Yes, that's the one!" they squealed in unison. "You should know the Mayor also strongly disapproves of that ranch."

They had to be kidding. It was a dude ranch. Men working on a ranch seemed pretty normal to him. He composed his thoughts. He caught her implication by mentioning the Mayor. Even though he had been appointed Sheriff, eventually he'd have to run for re-election if he wanted to keep his job.

"I'll take your concerns under advisement and send a patrol car out to check things over. I assure you, if something 'unrespectable' is going on, I'll put a stop to it."

"Thank you so much, Sheriff. Someone needs to close that brothel down." The gray-haired woman shook his hand, a smug look of satisfaction on her face.

"My pleasure." He smiled, tipped his hat and headed to check-out. Being in a small town was going to take some getting used to. He was more familiar with the city where you blended into a crowd, not a small town, where apparently, everyone knew your business. Still, he couldn't help but shake his head at their concern. An escort service maybe, but an actual brothel? He expected something like this in a big city. Lord knew escorts were easy to come by. But a brothel in this quaint, church going community?

Ethan decided it wouldn't hurt to swing by the ranch, if for no other reason than to settle his own curiosity. Besides, as the new Sheriff, he wanted to assure the upstanding citizens of Coconino County that he took their concerns seriously, even if he wasn't crazy about their busy-body ways. He needed to prove himself and win them over. What better way than to either address or squash their concerns about the ranch.

The ranch in question was located between Flagstaff and Sedona. He had passed by it several times on his way between the two cities. He had chosen Sedona as his new home because he was tired of the fast pace, hustling and bustling of big cities his previous job had taken him to. Now he wondered if he should have opted for the anonymity that city life provided.

Thank God they didn't live in Texas or he really might raise an eyebrow. He laughed to himself as he walked to his car thinking about Dolly Parton in the movie 'The Best Little Whorehouse in Texas'. "Look out chicken ranch, here I come."

ೂ✿

The buzz of activity swirled around Jessica Montgomery as she waited for the bus filled with new arrivals to finish unloading. She watched with pleasure as her guests followed the flagstone pathway, through the wrought-iron gate, leading to the park-like setting of The WWC Dude Ranch.

Jessica's gaze swept over a barn-wood fence that helped lend itself to the old rustic charm surrounding the courtyard. Split rail fences, wagon wheels, an abundance of vibrant flowers like pink and purple penstemon, and yellow zinnias, complimented the old fashion water pump gurgling out water in the massive area.

A young man ran into the courtyard, tipping his hat to the ladies as he made his way up to her. Jeremy Evans was already too handsome for his eighteen years. At six feet tall, he towered over her petite five-foot-five frame. Jessica hoped he wouldn't leave too long of a trail of broken hearts. The worried expression in his deep brown eyes did not go unnoticed.

"Aunt Jess, we have a problem," he blurted breathlessly, as he wiped the sweat dripping from the auburn hair sticking to his forehead.

"What is it, Jeremy?"

He leaned in close and whispered so the guests wouldn't hear. "Someone spray painted on the outside of the stables. You need to come read it."

"Read it? Just tell me what it says."

"Please, Aunt Jess, just come and look at it," Jeremy pleaded, his cheeks growing red as he kicked at the dirt.

"That bad?" She raised an eyebrow. "Alright, lead the way."

She followed him through the courtyard, across the driveway to the stables. They rounded the side of the barn and she stopped dead in her tracks. Across the red barn in big black letters, someone painted the words 'whorehouse'.

"Damn it all."

"What are you going to do, Aunt Jess?"

A big sigh escaped her lips. She really didn't need this right now, especially since their guests had just arrived. "I'd like you to grab a couple of the other guys, get some paint, and paint the side of the stable. There should be a couple of gallons in the storage barn."

It seemed like all she did lately was fix problems like this. It was growing old.

"That's it, Aunt Jess?"

"Yep, that's it. They're just stupid words. Now, I've got guests to take care of. Thanks for telling me, Jeremy."

He reached out and stopped her with his hand on her arm. "Are you going to tell Mom, or do you want me to?"

She frowned at the thought. "Don't worry. I'll tell your mother we had another visit. You just make sure it gets painted before any of the guests see it." She turned on her heel and headed back toward the lodge.

Jessica blew the air from her lungs. She dreaded telling Laurie about the latest development. She wasn't surprised by the words painted on the barn. One more incident to add to the growing list. So be it. Graffiti never hurt anyone.

As she walked across the driveway, her eyes roamed over the ranch. A feeling of great pride washed over her, and she sighed contently. When she looked at the massive structure, she felt warm and safe, like being wrapped in her grandmother's afghan.

"Miss Jessica!"

She turned to find Joe McCaffrey striding toward her. He still commanded respect in spite of his sixty-five years with his broad shoulders, and muscular arms still rock solid.

"Hey, Joe, what's going on?"

He came to stand in front of her. "I saw the barn," he said, running his hand through his dark brown hair that had only begun to show signs of gray.

"Nice touch, don't you think?" Her voice dripped with sarcasm. Joe was more than just the foreman on the ranch. Head wrangler, Mr. Fix-it, Veterinarian, and substitute dad were a few of the other roles he had assumed.

"I see we have new arrivals. I'll make sure it gets painted quickly."

"Yes, we do, and that's not something they need to see."

Aside from her father, he was the only other man she trusted completely. He had come to her ranch looking for work, not because he needed a job, but because he needed something to fill his days. His beloved wife Evelyn had passed away from cancer, and his children lived around the country. She truly felt he was an angel sent to watch over her.

Joe's dark brown eyes twinkled as he smiled and patted her arm. "Don't you worry your pretty little head over it. I've got you covered."

"Thanks, Joe." She smiled back at him.

She continued on her way back to the lodge. One by one, she watched as their visitors stepped through the gate and filled the courtyard. If the smiles on their faces were any indication, they appreciated the handsome picture that stood before them.

With a smile of her own, Jessica flipped her long blond ponytail back over her shoulder. Sweat trickled down the back of her neck in-spite of her light, pink, cotton skirt and white short-sleeved blouse. She still hadn't quite gotten used to the Arizona heat. Watching her guests, she thought about how far the ranch had come in the last year and a half. It had been run down when she arrived, but hard work, a lot of elbow-grease, and perseverance brought it back to its original glory. She couldn't have done any of it without the help of her best friend.

Laurie Evans came to stand beside Jessica, auburn curls bouncing around her shoulders. Smiling from ear to ear, she also took in the expressions of their guests as they stood looking around the courtyard. "Who would have ever thought we'd be running a successful dude ranch that caters to women only?"

Jessica chuckled. "I guess it takes a couple of women who have been stressed out, over-worked, under-appreciated, and rejected to understand what their fellow suffering sisters need."

Boy did they understand.

Jessica climbed onto a bench that surrounded a mosaic tile fountain in the middle of the courtyard and cleared her throat so she could be heard over the bubbling water. "Ladies, Ladies, may I have your attention please?" She clapped her hands together, and the chattering women focused on her. "Welcome to The WWC Dude Ranch. I'm Jessica Montgomery, hostess and owner of the ranch. We are all so pleased you decided to join us for the next week." She waved a hand around the courtyard, indicating the staff who stood ready to cater to their every need.

"We would like to review a few things with you. First, let me introduce Laurie Evans, Activities Director. If there is anything you are interested in doing or something special you need, please let her know. Laurie, take it away."

Laurie stepped forward to address the women. "Thanks, Jess. Ladies, if you check the schedule being handed out, you will see we have lots of outdoor activities; a variety of seminars and classes; fun things like hayrides and campfires every night; and of course, relaxing spa treatments. This vacation is all about making your experience here everything you hope it will be. If you need anything or have questions, please don't hesitate to ask me."

The women applauded.

"Thanks, Laurie," Jessica continued. "As you can see, the scenery here is quite luscious." She smiled and looked toward the group of cowboys standing together on the opposite side of the courtyard, which caused the women to roar with appreciation.

"Should you decide to indulge in any extra curricular activities, please remember this is a respectable establishment. I expect you all to behave in a similar manner by being courteous of your fellow guests and my staff."

She hated addressing this issue, but one never knew what might happen when a bunch of mostly single women on vacation and hot virile cowboys got together. She wanted to make sure the women understood that the cowboys who worked for her were not part of the package deal, contrary to what people in town thought. They made her so self-conscious, she felt obligated to utter the disclaimer.

"Now, please, go and enjoy yourselves. Again, welcome to The WWC Dude Ranch." The ladies clapped and started giggling and whispering as they made their way to their rooms, escorted by the staff.

Jessica had chosen the name of the ranch. While the official name was The WWC Dude Ranch, she and Laurie knew it really stood for Wayward Wives Club. It seemed rather appropriate, all things considered.

Laurie wasn't just their Activities Director; she was a small shareholder in the ranch. Jessica hadn't been the only one blindsided by heartache. Her best friend was only too eager to join her on the ranch, ready to build a new life for herself after a messy divorce.

"Hey, Laur, I'm gonna head to my office. There is a mountain of paperwork on my desk that I had better take care of."

"Okay, I'll make the rounds and check on our guests. We'll catch up later."

"Sounds good." Jessica headed into the lodge and made her way to her office.

As she stepped through the door, a wave of cool air from the A.C. greeted her over-heated body. She slumped down in the plush executive chair. The cool fabric felt good against her skin.

Her mind wandered as she looked around her little sanctuary. The colors of the office reminded her of sunsets in the desert. Her spirits were always lifted when she entered, except for today.

Jessica sorted through the mountain of mail on her desk. The ranch was doing well, but there were still a lot of extra bills from the restoration to pay.

As she leaned back in her chair, her gaze froze on the large thick envelope lying on her desk. She hadn't prepared for its arrival quite so soon. Her hands shook as she opened the envelope, knowing full well what the contents were. She slid the documents out, and then read the cover letter. The finality of the words hit her hard.

God, what had happened to her life? How had she gotten here? She closed her eyes tight, wincing at the heartache that came as memories flooded back.

"Happy birthday to you...happy birthday to you...happy birthday dear Jessica, happy birthday to you...."

While forty candles blazed brightly on top of her birthday cake, her family and friends stood around her laughing and smiling. Before making a wish, she paused, waiting for the customary ending of the song, *"...and many more!"* Instead, she heard her husband whisper those awful words, *"I want a divorce,"* in her ear.

Her perfect life hadn't been so perfect after all.

She tried to shake the memories from her head as she focused on the scenic pictures of the Grand Canyon that adorned the walls, along with statues of horses on wooden shelves. She let out a har-rumph as she stared at bookcases filled with texts on business management, dude ranches, and equine husbandry. A lot of help those books were. Lately she questioned whether she really knew what she was doing or just kidding herself.

Her gaze shifted to her large oak desk that held pictures of her family back home. It was days like today she wondered if she had made the right decision by moving to this small town. She missed her mother, brothers and sisters. Perhaps her siblings would let her nieces and nephews visit this summer.

The door of her office swung open with a thud against the wall, startling her from her thoughts. Laurie, usually even-tempered, stormed into the room. "Jessica Montgomery, you cannot ignore this any longer."

"Ignore what?" She attempted to blink back the tears that had started to form.

Laurie stopped abruptly in front of the desk when she saw Jessica's face. "You're looking awfully nostalgic, my friend." She sank down into one of the leather chairs. "What do you have there?"

Jessica wiped a tear from her cheek with the back of her hand. "It's final."

"What's final?" Laurie looked puzzled until Jessica held up the final divorce decree. "Oh, that. I'm really sorry. I know it still hurts."

Brushing the remnants of tears away, Jessica took a deep breath and let it out in a swoosh. Giving the papers a good shove, she pushed them back in the envelope and tossed them aside. "Well, now that the divorce is final, that chapter of my life is closed. Alone again, what a surprise. I guess it's time to move on to bigger and better things."

John wasn't worth it; she needed to let go of the pain. He was the past. She had a new life now, one she loved very much, minus their recent onset of problems.

Laurie stood up and walked around the desk, offering her friend a hug of support. "You're not alone."

"Thanks for always being there for me." Jessica sniffed.

"What are friends for? Are you feeling better?"

"Yeah, no, but I will. So, what's up?"

"I've got a bone to pick with you. Jeremy told me about the barn. Guess what else happened?"

Jessica was on her feet, a pit forming in her belly. "Something else happened?"

"Yes, Mike was out riding and noticed the fence for the horse corral was down. The horses are gone. I sent Joe with a bunch of the guys out to round them up."

"Shit. Just what we need. Those horses had better be okay. We've spent a small fortune on them and can't afford to replace them." She walked around to the front of her desk. "I should go help."

Laurie held her hand up to stop her. "Joe and the guys can handle it."

"Damn it, we can't afford to have anything happen to those horses. I can't sit here and do nothing."

"That's exactly why you can't ignore this anymore. What you need to do is stay here and fix this."

"Fine. What do you want me to do?"

Laurie placed her hand on Jessica's arm. "What if someone had gotten hurt? Expensive animals are missing, so it isn't harmless anymore. It's starting to get expensive, and I'm not sure we can handle the price it might cost us if something happens to one of our guests."

The worried look on Laurie's face conveyed how serious she felt about recent events. "You're right, but I can't afford to hire guards, and we certainly don't want our guests to think it's unsafe here."

"Call the Sheriff."

"And tell him what? If he's anything like the rest of the people around here, he probably won't take me seriously. He'll think I'm a hysterical, overreacting woman and won't give any credibility to our problem."

"That may be, but if you file a report and something else happens down the road, it will be on record."

"I don't know, Laurie. Maybe having it on record would only give him a reason to close our 'whorehouse' down. Let's try to handle this ourselves. I promise I will think of something." Jessica walked over to the window and stared out. She was damned if she did and damned if she didn't.

Laurie grabbed the phone and handed it to her. "Jessica Montgomery, call the sheriff. Now."

chapter 2

"THE WWC DUDE Ranch." Ethan read the sign swinging in between two log beams. "Now is as good a time as any to check it out."

He slowed his patrol car and turned down the long, curvy drive of the ranch. As he reached the end of the pine tree-lined driveway, he couldn't believe what loomed before his eyes. A magnificent log and stone lodge stretched for what looked to be forever. With its peaks and valleys, tall log columns and covered porch, the huge lodge was impressive. He was immediately drawn to it. The porch, filled with rocking chairs spaced among pots bursting with flowers in full bloom, beckoned for someone to come and sit a spell.

It was not at all what he had envisioned. This was no Chicken Ranch. Shaking his head, he laughed to himself and started to hum the little ditty. If the owner of this ranch looked like Dolly Parton, he was in big trouble.

Ethan parked his car and decided to wander around behind the building toward a row of barns. He wasn't sneaking around, but he didn't want to announce his arrival, either. He wanted to see more of the place and what he might catch a glimpse of before he met the owner.

To his surprise, he wasn't surprised at all. Wranglers off in a distant corral worked and cared for horses; a few cowboys instructed ladies on horseback; a few more women batted around tennis balls on one of the tennis courts. There was nothing suspicious going on.

As he rounded the back of the lodge, he came to a fenced-in pool with a wrought-iron gate. Several women leisurely lounged by the pool, sipping fancy umbrella drinks. This was as good a place as any to make his presence known. As he entered the gate and walked across the paved patio, he felt several pairs of eyes follow him. He'd received his fair share of attention before, but these women looked ready to pounce.

He tipped his cowboy hat. "Afternoon, ladies." His usually deep voice came out more like a whisper. The top button of his shirt had suddenly become too tight.

"Afternoon, cowboy," they chimed in unison, then giggled.

He swallowed hard and looked around for a place away from the hungry stares. An auburn-haired woman holding a clipboard was giving instructions to some of the ladies. Hopefully she was someone of importance, and could be of assistance to him.

"Excuse me, Miss, I'm Sheriff Kirkpatrick. I was looking for the owner of this ranch."

The woman turned at the sound of his voice. "Sheriff? Oh, my gosh, Ethan Kirkpartick? I must be dreaming." She threw her arms around him. "After all these years, I can't believe you're really standing here in front of me."

Ethan tipped his head back to study the woman, blinking to make sure he was seeing her clearly. His brows shot up, surprised to see her. "Laurie Evans? What on earth are you doing on this ranch?" he asked, returning the hug.

"I work here. Why are you on the ranch?" she inquired.

"I'm the new County Sheriff, and I stopped by to meet the owner."

"So, you're the new guy, very interesting. You don't look like a Sheriff." She looked him up and down.

"I'm off duty." He couldn't help but notice the smirk she was trying hard to contain.

"You said you wanted to meet the owner. So, she did call you."

"No one called me. Is there a problem?"

An odd twinkle entered her eyes. "Oh, that means you don't know who the owner is." The smirk tugged at her lips.

"No. I haven't been around town long enough. I was on my way home and thought I would stop by and introduce myself." It wasn't a total lie.

"Gosh, it's so good to see you. Cowboy or Sheriff, you're a sight for sore eyes." She hugged him again. "Come on; let me introduce you to the owner."

Once they were inside the lodge, he followed her down several corridors until she came to a closed door. She stopped to knock. He heard a muffled 'come in' from behind the door.

"The Sheriff is here to see you," Laurie said, stepping into the office.

As he moved into the room, Ethan noticed the smirk on Laurie's face was no longer being concealed. He blinked, taking a minute for his eyes to focus on the person sitting behind the desk.

Good Lord, it wasn't possible, it was better than Dolly Parton. His heart slammed into this chest at the very site of her and he was a goner. In a heartbeat, he was transported back in time.

Jessica was on her feet and around her desk in a flash. "Did you say Sheriff? Who's the cowboy...." She stopped dead in her tracks when her eyes landed on the man who followed Laurie thru the door. She had to be imagining things. She rubbed her eyes to make sure. "EJ?"

"Jessie!" Ethan crossed the room in three long strides and picked her up in his arms.

"EJ, put me down." She batted his arm, still in shock. It had been twenty years since she had last seen him.

Ethan set her down, but didn't let go, as his emerald green eyes sparkled down at her. "Still as beautiful as ever."

She ignored his comment and forced a smile. Her racing pulse echoed in her ears. After all this time, was he really standing in front of her, here on her ranch? "Why are you here? How are you here?"

He just kept smiling that perfect smile of his. "Do you want the 'why' or 'how' first?"

She wanted to smack it off his face so he didn't look so damn charming. "Let's start with the how. Wait a second. Laurie, didn't you say something about the Sheriff?" She looked Ethan up and down in his Dockers and button down shirt. Her eyes grew big as the realization hit her. She stumbled back. "No, not you!"

"Yes, me." He grinned at her. "I'm the new Sheriff."

"You can't be. What happened to the FBI?"

"I retired."

She couldn't believe her ears. "*You* gave up the FBI? No more saving the world?"

He frowned. "It takes a toll on you after a while. My cape was getting a little worn out. So, being that I'm too young to officially retire at forty-four, I started looking for a slower paced job in law enforcement."

"How on earth did you end up here?" More importantly why the hell was he on her ranch? One question at a time she told herself. She shoved her hands in the pockets of her skirt to keep them from shaking. Now, if she could keep her knees from buckling, she'd be doing swell.

"I worked on a case out here and got to know Sheriff Pribil. When he decided to retire, he called me and wanted to appoint me as the new Sheriff of Coconino County. I had to take it. I fell in love with this place the summer we spent here. How about you? How'd you end up moving from Upstate New York to Arizona?"

"Divorce. So why are you here on my ranch?" She wasn't about to tell him she had come here for the same reason, a summer that she would never forget as long as she lived. Her jumbled nerves couldn't handle anymore idle chitchat with him. Did he think he could just waltz back into her life after twenty years like nothing had ever happened between them?

"Ahhh, yeah, why I'm here," he paused. "I feel kinda stupid now."

"Why?" She stepped further away from him and crossed her arms over her chest, as if distance would make dealing with him easier.

"Some women at a local store were gossiping about your ranch. It was stupid."

"Let me guess. They think I'm running a brothel?"

His brow shot up. "You know?"

"Let's just say it's a small town, and I found out shortly after opening the ranch that I'm not real popular around here. Even the Mayor has vocalized his feelings regarding my ranch. Trust me, they aren't positive ones. I think he's helped influence the town's opinion. Most of the women turn and walk the other way, and the men just sneer. They have no idea what I'm trying to accomplish on this ranch. Instead, they sit back and pass judgment."

Laurie, who had stood quietly in the doorway, stepped forward. "Tell him what's been going on, Jessica."

Ethan looked from one woman to the other. "Something going on I should know about?"

"Nothing I can't handle," Jessica responded through clenched teeth, shooting Laurie a disgusted look.

"Aunt Jess! Aunt Jess!" Jeremy ran into the room and screeched to a halt when he saw Ethan. "I'm sorry to interrupt, but there's been another accident!"

"What happened?" Laurie shrieked and grabbed her son by the shoulders and patted him down.

"Mom, I'm fine." He pushed her hands away. "It's Scott. A wheel fell off the wagon, and he's hurt. You've gotta help him!"

Jessica stepped back. Seeing the panic-stricken look on Laurie's face was too much. The seriousness of the situation hit her hard.

Ethan grabbed Jessica's arm and pulled her toward the door. "Come on."

All three took off at a run behind Jeremy. They found one of the wranglers sitting on the ground, doubled over, holding his leg, and moaning. Jessica and Laurie ran to his aid while Ethan went to the wagon to inspect the wheel. Another wrangler unhitched the horses before they tried to pull on the broken wagon.

Jessica touched the cut that bled down the side of Scott's face then turned to feel his leg. She winced at the bone almost protruding through his skin. "He has to go to the hospital. His leg is definitely broken."

"I'll take him. Jeremy, come help me." Laurie looked Jessica right in the eye as Jeremy and another wrangler helped Scott up. "Will you please tell him now, before someone else gets hurt? What if it had been Jeremy or one of the guests? You couldn't live with yourself if that happened. It's up to you, Jess. We can't afford to lose this ranch, not now. We have too much invested."

Laurie led the guys away, leaving Jessica to stare after her. Her hands trembled, and her legs still shook. She wasn't sure if it was because of the accident or Ethan's presence. Either way, the adrenaline was flowing through her body. One thing she did know; Laurie was right. What if it had been Jeremy? It was bad enough one of her employees had gotten hurt. She could never live with herself if something happened to someone she loved.

"Jessie, what the hell is going on here? The bolts on that wheel were tampered with." Ethan stood in front of her, hands on his hips.

She looked up into his green eyes, ones she had gotten lost in so many years ago, and could hardly think straight. "It's nothing. Really," she whispered as her throat tightened.

He grabbed her by the shoulders. "It didn't seem like nothing to Laurie. She was pretty upset. Why don't you want to tell me? I'm the damn Sheriff. If for no other reason, Jessie, do it for your best friend."

She closed her eyes tight. Why was this happening? Why her? More importantly, why him? Why did he have to be the one standing before her? Why did he have to be the one offering to help? Anyone, but him.

Looking up at Ethan, she saw a man she knew genuinely wanted to help her. There was no denying his law enforcement career was stellar, and if anyone could help her, he could.

"Okay, fine. I'll tell you, but not here." She turned and headed back to her office in silence. This was not something she wanted to discuss out in the open. There was no need to upset the guests or her employees with a public discussion of the trouble around the ranch.

Ethan quietly strolled along beside her. She felt so awkward and uncomfortable next to him, a feeling she had never experienced before where he was concerned. He, on the other hand, was his usual relaxed and charming self, like nothing had ever happened. Damn him.

They returned to her office, and she quickly went behind her desk to sit. She felt better with the large object between them and motioned for him to take one of the chairs in front of the desk.

He broke the silence first. "So, do you want to tell me now?"

"Alright, I'll tell you." She leaned back in her chair. "It started about two months ago. It was nothing major, just little things."

"Like what?"

"One morning, we found garbage strewn all over. I thought maybe some wild animals had gotten into it. Another morning, our mailbox went missing. Another morning, the ranch sign was down. It was all annoying but harmless stuff like that. I thought it was probably a bunch of mischievous kids thinking they were funny."

Ethan leaned forward. "That can't be why Laurie is so upset. What else?"

"Well, people in town started gossiping about the ranch, saying I ran a whorehouse."

"That's what those women said to me. Why do they think that, Jessie?"

She raised an eyebrow. "Have you looked around?"

"Yeah, it's a great place. No chickens running around here."

Jessica burst out laughing. "I can't believe you remembered that. Oh, the irony of it all!"

She looked at him, thinking back. In college, they'd performed in 'The Best Little Whore house in Texas'. She had played Miss Mona, owner of the Chicken Ranch, while he had played Sheriff Ed Earl Dodd, Miss Mona's love interest.

He laughed along with her. "Why do you say that?"

"EJ, haven't you noticed something missing?"

"No, this place is incredible." He flashed her that smile again. "Male guests."

His smile faded instantly. "Okay, I'm not laughing anymore."

She couldn't help chuckling at his reaction. "Relax, it's not illegal."

His chest deflated as he let out his breath. "Thank God!"

"I must admit I haven't done anything to help the situation. You really can't blame the people here. I keep to myself so they don't really know me, and going to church hasn't really been a priority on my list. I've been a little short on faith. So, I'm not surprised they don't understand what kind of place this is."

"So what kind of place are you running?"

"It's a ranch for Wayward Wives."

"Excuse me?" His voice squeaked out an octave higher.

She laughed again. "Settle down. It's a ranch for women who have suffered a divorce, lost a spouse, wives who need a break from their demanding families, or any woman who just needs a place to go where she can rejuvenate and feel good about herself. I cater to the woman's soul."

"No whorehouse?"

"Nope, just a retreat for women." She saw him relax against the chair. "Now, I'm not going to lie to you. There are some very fine-looking cowboys working here, but that was just the luck of the draw. I hired them because they know how to work on a ranch; their looks are just a bonus. We are all consenting adults here. I neither encourage nor discourage extra curricular activities. You do remember the movie *Dirty Dancing*, don't you?"

"Jessie!"

"Oh, don't give me that appalled good Irish-catholic boy look. I know better. Men do this kind of stuff all the time, and you know it. I'm not so naïve to think it would never happen."

"So, the townspeople think the men who work here are boy toys for your lady guests."

"Basically."

"Sounds like they are."

"They most certainly are not," she snapped. "While, yes, there is no doubt they are eye candy, I have made it very clear to my staff that if anyone—employee or guest—does anything that makes them feel uncomfortable or wants them to do something inappropriate, I want to know about it. I assure you, I won't tolerate anyone being mistreated or disrespected."

"Okay, I believe you." He raised his hands in a sign of retreat. "So, what else has happened? Laurie wouldn't get all riled up about missing signs or mail boxes. There has to be something more."

"There is."

"Well, out with it!"

"Recently, someone painted 'whorehouse' on the side of the barn and broke some fences allowing the horses to get loose. It still seemed pretty harmless. Expensive, but harmless, until today."

"That wheel falling off was no accident, Jessie."

"No, I'm afraid it probably wasn't."

"This is serious."

She sighed. "So it seems."

Ethan stood and looked down at her. "We need to find out who's doing this."

"We? No! I don't need you to solve my problems."

"Apparently, you do."

She was on her feet in defiance. "This isn't any of your business."

"Damn it, Jessie!" Ethan leaned over, planting both fists firmly on her desk, and stared straight into her eyes. "I'm the Sheriff in this county. Someone got hurt today right in front of me because somebody doesn't want you running this ranch. That makes it my business. Whether you like it or not, I'm investigating."

"Fine. Whatever," she huffed and folded her arms across her chest in disgust. "Just tell your guy to come see me when he gets here. Make sure it's someone who knows how to be discreet. I don't want my guests or staff to suspect something is up."

"I know how to be inconspicuous."

"You!" She looked him up and down. "There's nothing inconspicuous about you. You're not investigating anything."

"Yes, I am."

She came around her desk to stand toe to toe with him, unintimidated by the fact he towered over her. "You can't. You run the station. You can't be out in the field investigating. You belong behind a desk, shuffling papers and barking orders."

Ethan scowled at her last remark. She didn't care. She absolutely, positively, did not want Ethan Kirkpatrick on her ranch any longer than necessary. Her nerves were already too jumbled to deal with him for even a minute longer, never mind an extended period of time.

"I beg your pardon? Think again, sweetheart. I'm handling this matter myself, and you don't have a choice in the situation. If the perp is someone local, they most likely know a lot of the deputies. I don't want to take a chance and scare them off. Since I've only been here a few weeks, not too many people in town know me yet, plus I'll be out of uniform."

"You still have a station to run."

"I'll put the Under Sheriff in charge and check in with him every day. If there is a problem, he'll know how to reach me."

"Whatever will the town biddies say?" she asked, her tone laced with sarcasm. "Cavorting with the enemy?"

"Don't worry about them." He winked at her. "I know how to charm the ladies."

She harrumphed. "Yes, you do." Unfortunately, no woman was immune to his charms, no matter how hard she resisted.

"I am doing as they asked." He lowered his voice mimicking the women in the store. "I'm undercover trying to get to the bottom of the 'shameful' things that go on here."

She pursed her lips together and frowned at him. "Fine, have it your way, but you better be discreet. I can't afford to have my guests upset. So far I've been able to avoid that."

"You won't even know I'm here."

"I wish," she muttered under her breath.

"I should be going."

"Yeah, you probably should."

He looked down at her, taking a step closer, their bodies almost touching. "I'm sorry it's under these circumstances, but it's great to see you."

"Yeah." She wanted to shake off the hand that rested on her arm, sending warm tingles through her. She tried to step away from him, but the desk impeded her ability to put distance between them.

"I'll see you tomorrow." He leaned over and kissed her cheek.

She clutched the desk for support. "Do you know the way out?" She choked the words out.

"I can find it. Have a good night, Jessie. I hope Scott is okay."

"Thanks. You, too." She watched as he left her office, then walked around her desk and fell back into the chair. Well, this was a hell of a situation, in more ways than one.

༺༻

Jessica waited up in the living room of her personal suite in the lodge. It wasn't huge, but it had an eat-in kitchen, living room, and three bedrooms in case she had family or friends come for a visit. She had been trying to read a trade publication as a way of removing Ethan Kirkpatrick from her thoughts when someone tapped lightly on her door.

"Come in." She uncurled herself from the big, comfy, navy chair she was sitting in and stretched.

Laurie stepped into the living room. "Hi, I'm glad you're still awake."

"How's Scott?"

"He has a compound fracture. He'll be out of commission for a while."

"Sit, please. Is it bad?"

Laurie sat down on the sofa across from Jessica's chair. "Bad enough. The good thing, the doctor said, was it's a clean break. Since he's young and fit, he'll heal in no time, but Scott's worried about keeping his job and the medical bills."

"I'll talk to him tomorrow and ease his mind. The ranch has insurance to cover his medical bills. I'll find something for him to do so he doesn't have to worry about earning a paycheck."

"What did Ethan have to say?"

"Thanks a lot for that mess."

"What? Laurie smirked. "What'd I do?"

"First off, you could have told me he was here instead of marching into my office without warning and him in tow. What were you thinking?"

Laurie grinned sheepishly. "I thought you would enjoy the surprise."

"Laurie! How could you?" Jessica exclaimed, smacking her forehead. "After what happened between us, how could you think seeing him would be an enjoyable surprise?"

"My God, Jess, that was over twenty years ago. You both moved on. At least I thought you had."

"Yeah, well, you don't just forget when one minute you're planning a wedding and spending the rest of your life with someone, and the next minute you're alone crying your eyes out."

"You were kids when that happened. I know he broke your heart, but you both moved on and married."

"He did more than just break my heart."

"You can't be serious. You really need to let go of the past. It's time to move on."

"Laurie, what happened can never be undone. I have to live with that every day for the rest of my life."

"I understand that, but Jess, that accident wasn't Ethan's fault, and you know it."

"Like hell it wasn't. He was the cause, the fall was the result."

"That's not fair. He didn't know."

"He didn't give me a chance to tell him. He was more concerned about ditching me and joining the FBI. He told me there was no place in his life for a wife; it would only hold him back. How could I tell him after that?"

"I know, hon, but you're still not being fair. He's here now. Give him a chance."

"Life isn't fair. He may be here now, but how long does he plan on staying? All the men in my life have left. Why should this time be any different? So please forgive me if I chose to depend on myself. Isn't that we help women do, be self sufficient?"

"Yes, but Jess…"

"But nothing."

Laurie laughed. "Girl, you've got issues. You need to get yourself some therapy."

"You're a fine one to talk, Miss 'Hasn't Had a Date in Five Years'," Jessica shot back, grinning as she threw a pillow in her friend's direction.

"I never said I didn't have my own issues." Laurie caught the pillow and tossed it back. "I'm being more selective this time around. No need to repeat past mistakes."

Jessica sobered. "Speaking of past mistakes, thanks for forcing me to tell Ethan about our problems."

Laurie's smiled faded, too. "Something bad happened right in front of him. He's the Sheriff. It's not like he was going to ignore it. Jess, this is getting worse. At least with Ethan, you'll know he's on your side and not one of those judgmental townspeople."

"I know, but now he plans to stick around and investigate this himself."

"Really, now?" Laurie raised an eyebrow.

"Do not go there."

"Why not? You're a free agent, and I didn't see a ring on his finger, nor did he mention a wife."

"That doesn't mean anything. Besides, I'm not about to forgive him, or as you pointed out, repeat past mistakes."

"I think I could forgive him anything." Laurie sighed dreamily. "You have to admit he is as fine as ever. Did you see how rock hard his body still is? My Lord, watching his muscles ripple gave me goosebumps, and he certainly hasn't lost any of that Irish charm."

"Since you're so enamored, you can deal with him."

"Oh, no. You're the owner of the ranch."

Jessica threw Laurie a quelling look. "You wanted him here; you can deal with him."

"Okay, you win, but you'll be wishing it was you."

"I doubt that very much."

Laurie stood to leave, and Jessica walked her to the door. "Thanks for taking Scott to the doctor's. I don't know how I'd handle this without you."

"What are friends for? Just remember, Jess, I was there after Ethan left. I know what you went through. I was there then, and I'm here now. Just go easy on him. He's a good man. I'm sure his intentions are honorable."

She smiled. "I promise I'll try to go easy on EJ. I know he's only trying to help."

"Maybe with Ethan around, we'll start feeling safe here again."

"I hope so, Laurie. I sure hope so." She hugged her friend goodnight.

chapter 3

JESSICA STOOD AT the front desk of the lodge, stretched and rolled her head around to loosen the kinks in her neck. She had hardly slept last night. Visions of the ranch and Ethan Kirkpatrick kept flowing through her brain.

"What a mess," she mumbled out loud, staring blankly at a stack of papers.

"Perhaps I can help."

She looked up to see a tall, extremely well-built cowboy in jeans and a dark green t-shirt with a black Stetson sitting low on his forehead, standing before her. She blinked, not exactly sure if her sleep-deprived brain was playing tricks on her.

"Excuse me?"

The cowboy moved to stand before the desk. "Allow me to help."

She frowned. "Oh, it's you." After all these years, she still couldn't believe he was here on her ranch.

Ethan flashed her a big smile. "Well, good morning to you, too."

God how she hated the way his eyes sparkled when he smiled, and the way that t-shirt made them look an even darker green. "I'm sorry. Good morning." She reminded herself of the promise she made to Laurie. "What are you doing here?"

"Investigating your problem like we discussed."

She couldn't stop staring at the muscles bulging beneath the tight, cotton, t-shirt. Damn he did look good. Laurie was right again. The years had obviously been kind to him. Too kind. On top of everything else, she didn't need to find him attractive in any way, shape or form.

"Uhhh, Yeah, right. So, why are you dressed like that?"

"You told me to be discreet." Ethan waved his hands in front of himself. "You didn't think I would show up in uniform did you?"

She didn't know what she expected. "Dressed like that, you would be anything but discreet. And people think I'm running a whorehouse. Go figure."

"Pardon?"

"Never mind. So what's your brilliant plan?" She was trying hard not to let his appearance unnerve her. He was, after all, only trying to help, whether she wanted it or not.

"I thought I could take Scott's place. With him out of commission, it would seem logical that you would get someone else to fill in. Not that many people know me as Sheriff yet, and most of your guests are from out of town. Perhaps if I could develop a trust with the other guys, I might learn something. As an employee, people wouldn't think too much of my presence."

"That makes sense."

"Believe it or not, the FBI did train me on how to blend in."

"If you say so." She shrugged, finding it difficult to believe he could blend in anywhere. "Let me give Laurie a call. She'll show you around the place and where you can stay." Jessica picked up the phone and called Laurie. The conversation was brief, and she was not pleased when she hung up.

"You don't look very happy. What's wrong?"

"Nothing." She forced a smile and motioned toward the door as she walked from behind the desk. "It looks like I'll be the one to show you around."

They stepped outside into the warm Arizona sun. It was early so the morning was still pleasant. "Where shall I begin?" She started to walk across the courtyard toward several red and white barns that sat off to the side of the lodge.

Ethan quickly fell into step beside her. "Tell me about the ranch. How big is it?"

"We own seventy-five acres. As you can see, we have several barns. We have forty horses for riding and twelve draft horses to pull the wagons and such."

"You always loved your horses. You must be in heaven."

"It is nice having one of my own and lots of space to ride."

"Do you remember the first time you took me riding at your grandparents? I was sore for a week."

"Yeah, you weren't very good, but you learned." She smiled at him, then quickly looked away. She wasn't going to do this. No walks down memory lane. In spite of the good ones, the bad ones were just too painful.

"How many guests do you have?"

"If all the rooms are booked, we can accommodate up to seventy-five women. We have twenty-five private rooms and twenty-five doubles."

"Doubles? I thought this place was for women only."

"Yes, sometimes friends come together and share a room."

"Oh. How many people do you employ?"

"Right now, thirty-two. There are twelve women and twenty men."

"Wow, that's a nice size staff. Certainly not enough men to satisfy seventy-five women, but still, a decent size staff." Ethan laughed.

The deep rich sound echoed in her ears. "Yeah, they get awfully tired trying to keep up with demand." She chuckled back, trying to move past the memories. "We have housekeeping, horse handlers, cooks, maintenance, spa personnel and then specialty instructors. You'd be surprised how many people it takes to keep a place like this running. I probably could use more."

They walked to one of the corrals where a few horses grazed. Jessica stood up on the fence and whistled. A chestnut mare with a black mane and tail trotted up to the railing and nuzzled her. She pulled a carrot from her pocket.

"Who is this lovely lady?" Ethan asked, stroking the mare's nose.

"This is Sadie."

"I'm assuming she's yours."

"Yeah, she's my girl." Jessica rubbed her cheek against the horse's soft velvety nose and then fed her a carrot. "What else can I tell you about the ranch?"

"Okay, so if I'm a guest here at the ranch, what is there for me to do?"

Jessica gave Sadie one last pat, and hopped down from the railing and walked toward the barn.

"Let's see, if you like physical activity." She gave him a quick sideward glance to see if her words would get a reaction, and wasn't disappointed by his raised eyebrows. "You can choose from horseback riding, tennis—we have four courts—, hiking, mountain biking, nature walks and swimming. We have one indoor and one outdoor pool. We also have hayrides and campfires in the evenings. There are yoga classes and a fitness room."

"Wow, what don't you have? What if you're not into getting physical?"

It was her turn to raise an eyebrow. "For those looking to relax, we have art classes and a first rate spa. We also offer self-esteem seminars. My goal is to contract with experts and have them come to the ranch during special weeks to address self-improvement issues."

"You've got it all covered. I'm impressed."

"Thank you. I've worked very hard on this place." She took a deep breath, trying to slow her racing heartbeat. She was anxious to get back to the business at hand, not provide scenic tours. "Okay, so here is one of the stables where we keep the riding horses."

"Nice place," he said, giving the inside a long look. "I wouldn't mind being a horse here."

"If you're going to take Scott's place, you should know he handles the draft horses and wagons. They're in another barn. Follow me." Her knees shook as she wiped her sweaty palms on her jeans, trying to keep her emotions under control. Being around him again after all those years was unnerving her.

"Sure thing, boss."

She looked at him and caught his little smirk. She stopped in her tracks and spun around. "Do you even know anything about horses?"

"You taught me well."

"That was a long time ago."

"Let's just say, you'd be surprised what I learned to do as an undercover agent. I won't let you down. Promise."

"Right, I've heard that one before."

"Jessie, don't do this. I'm not going anywhere this time."

"I don't know if this is such a good idea."

"Do you have a better one?"

"Fine, come on." She led Ethan to where the draft horses were kept.

"Holy horseflesh, Jessie, I see you went for the little guys." Ethan walked over to one of the stalls and patted the neck of one very large horse. The dapple-grey gelding made Ethan feel like he was standing in a hole.

"Too much for you to handle?" She could only hope.

"Not at all. They are beautiful."

"We have four Clydesdales, four Belgians, and four Percherons. They are all very gentle." Jessica stroked one extremely large nose that butted her in the shoulder, knocking her into Ethan.

Ethan steadied her on her feet. "Yeah, I see that."

Jessica quickly pulled away. "Duke is a bit of an attention hound. You'll figure out their personalities once you get to know them. We keep the wagons and harnesses in the smaller barn next door."

"Did you fix the wagon that was tampered with?"

"No, you'll need to take care of that, if that's not a problem."

"Not at all. Maybe I can get a few clues from the wagon." He raised an eyebrow. "Is there anything else, boss?"

She rolled her eyes. "You'll be responsible for coordinating the hayrides. We try to have at least one every night. Sometimes we only need one wagon, other times more. I try not to put more than twenty people on a wagon."

"Sounds easy enough."

"Oh, and in addition to caring for these guys, you might have to help out with the other horses. If we have a great demand for lessons or trail riding, the chores get behind. You'll need to help pick up the slack."

"I'm good at shoveling manure."

"I bet you are."

"Am I sensing some hostility here?"

"Sense whatever you like."

Ethan reached out to grab her arm. "Jessie, it's been twenty years."

She looked down at the hand that seared a hole through her flesh. "Yes, it has."

"People make mistakes; people change."

She stared blankly at him trying to keep her emotions hidden. "Yes, they do."

"We both moved on. So, what's the problem?"

"Sometimes those mistakes cause irreversible damage."

He scowled. "What's that supposed to mean, Jessie?"

"Nothing. Forget about it." His nearness caused too many memories from the past to wreak havoc with her feelings.

He threw his hands up in the air. "What's the matter with you? You obviously meant something by it, or you wouldn't have said it. What aren't you saying?"

"Nothing. I have a ranch to run and you have a job to do. I'd appreciate it if you would remember that. I told Joe, my foreman, about your arrival. He knows why you're here and will cooperate with you. Now if you'll excuse me, I'll ask Scott to show you to the employee quarters." She turned and headed across the yard toward Scott and some other employees, leaving Ethan to stare after her.

Her legs shook as she walked away from him. It may have been only twenty years for him; to a shattered life, it felt like yesterday. She fought back a tear. Why did all the men in her life leave? She wasn't about to give EJ the opportunity to do that again.

No. She wasn't going to do this.

She was being overly sensitive because her divorce was final, and her last memories of EJ weren't pleasant ones. She didn't need a damn man in her life to make it meaningful. She had plenty of meaning in her life, plenty. She marched back to the lodge as quickly as her shaking legs would carry her.

Ethan stared at Jessica's retreating back. She wasn't the woman he remembered. He knew he had hurt her, but why was she so reserved and distant. At moments, the old Jessie had appeared, but then just as quickly, she'd disappeared. He could see it in those beautiful eyes of hers. There was pain in them, pain that wasn't just from him. What had happened to her?

All he wanted to do was help her. What were the odds he was here on her ranch? Memories from the past flooded him. Wonderful memories of years gone by made him wonder why he'd made the choices he had. If only he could go back and undo some things, he would. Hindsight was twenty-twenty, that was for sure.

God she still looked good. The memories filled with both love and regret flooded his heart. How he would love to take her in his arms and make everything right for her. Maybe this was fate stepping in. Maybe he could make up for some of the hurt he'd caused her. He wasn't a bad guy; he had just been young and stupid. Now he was a grown man who had learned many of life's lessons.

Perhaps this was his chance to right some wrongs.

chapter 4

"Laurie, I arranged for two wagons for the ladies." Ethan finished harnessing the team of horses. "They're all set."

"Thanks, Ethan. I'll let them know we're ready."

"Have you seen Jessie?"

"No, why?"

"She was upset with me this afternoon. I know she's not crazy about having me here."

"You seem surprised by that fact."

"Yes and no."

"Ethan, I know you were married once. You must realize a woman never forgets, at least not when it comes to affairs of the heart."

"Never forgets? Oh, for the love of God, Laurie, that was a long time ago. I didn't expect her to forget, but I thought perhaps forgive might be an option."

"You weren't just some college boyfriend for God's sake. You were the love of her life and supposed to be married. Did you really think she would be all hugs and kisses when you drop in out of the blue? I don't believe her last memories of you are fond ones, ya big goof, even if it was a long time ago." She smacked his arm playfully.

"We were kids, and I was stupid," Ethan offered a lame defense.

"I'm not the one you need to plead your case to, even though I *am* the one who had to pick up the pieces. It wasn't pretty I might add. Give her some time. It's not like you're leaving town anytime soon, are you? I really think you two need to talk."

"You're right. With a little bit of time, maybe she'll talk to me. I have no plans to leave, not this time." He smiled to himself. Things would be different. "I'll go bring one of the wagons around."

"I'll get the ladies."

Ethan hopped up onto the wagon just as Jessica rode up on Sadie. The sun shined down upon her, casting a yellow hue. Her sun-kissed skin glistened and golden hair cascaded around her shoulders like a cape. Her cheeks were rosy and full lips beckoned to be kissed. He shook his head to remove the thoughts before he started to drool like a fool. Give her some time before you ravish her, he reminded himself.

"Are you sure you can drive this rig?" she asked.

"Nervous I can't handle the mighty beasts?"

"A little bit."

"Is that why you're on horseback instead of the wagon?"

"Perhaps."

"A little faith, Jessie, that's all I'm asking."

Faith. He wanted her to put her faith him? Not any time soon. "I'm sorry. I told you I was a little low on faith."

"Ouch, another blow to the midsection." He grabbed his stomach as if he had been punched. "I guess you don't practice what you preach."

"I didn't ask you to come here to solve my problems. You're free to leave anytime you want, unless you think you want to stick around and rebuild that faith again." She turned Sadie around and rode toward the lodge where everyone was gathered.

"Women," he harrumphed.

He rubbed his forehead. What did she want from him? So he had made a few mistakes in his time. Back then he and Jessie were kids and he was joining the FBI. What kind of husband would he have made? Not a very good one. He certainly hadn't been a good one to Kim. He hadn't been a good father, either. He wasn't proud he had put his career first and family second. Now he was paying the price for that choice in more ways than one.

He pulled the wagon up in front of the lodge and hopped down. Jessica stood on the front porch, watching the activities as the women lined up at the wagon. He happily helped each and every one of them up onto it. This job wasn't so bad after all.

He couldn't help but glance at Jessica. Was it his imagination or did the more he assisted the women, the stiffer she stood on the porch? The ladies certainly didn't hold back on flirting. He laughed at something a voluptuous redhead said. He looked up to see that Jessica had turned away, arms folded across her chest.

Was he getting to her? A smile crept across his lips.

"Okay, ladies, let's go enjoy an evening ride." Ethan hopped back up onto the wagon seat and flicked the horses into motion.

The wagon lumbered down the drive and off onto a trail. Ethan noticed Jessica had mounted Sadie and was following alongside, chatting with some of the guests.

A few of the women started to sing. Ethan couldn't help himself. He had to join in. His rich tenor voice was a melody all on its own, and it wasn't long before he realized he was singing by himself. When he stopped, the women moaned their disappointment.

Jessica cantered past his wagon. He chuckled to himself. Apparently, she didn't enjoy his voice as much as the other women.

He couldn't help notice how beautiful she looked with her long loose curls flying behind her like a flag, her jeans conforming to her shapely butt. Her figure was fuller than he remembered which only made the curves more inviting.

He thought about what Laurie said. What was it going to take to get her to forgive him? What had happened after he left? He knew he had hurt Jessie, but she had obviously moved on with John, so what was the problem? There was obviously a piece missing to the answer of that question.

It was dusk, and they didn't want to go too far before dark. Ethan flicked the reins and the horses picked up a little speed.

He looked back to check on his passengers, and then up ahead where Jessica had ridden off to. One minute he watched as she raced down the trail, the next her horse reared and veered sideways. A scream echoed in the distance as she flew from Sadie's back.

Ethan snapped the reins and raced the horses in her direction. He leaped from the wagon and found Jessica lying on the ground. He dropped to his knees beside her. "Jessie, are you okay?" He gently lifted her up into his arms. His heart pounded in his throat with fear.

"EJ?" she moaned.

"Yeah, babe, I'm here. You're okay," he whispered as he brushed her hair away from her face. A large gash along with a bump had formed on her forehead, as blood trickled down the side of her head.

She raised her fingers to touch the welt and winced. "What happened?"

"You fell off your horse." Ethan cradled her in his arms and tried to calm his racing heart. She had scared the hell out of him. "Does anything else hurt besides your head?"

"No. I'm good. Sadie!" she frantically called out and tried to rise.

"She's fine. Just lay still." Lord she felt good in his arms. He had forgotten how soft and tiny she was.

Laurie, who had been riding on the second wagon, came running up to them with several of the women following. "I heard a scream. What happened? Is she okay?" she asked, dropping to the ground next to them.

"She hit her head."

"Sadie. Go get Sadie," Jessica insisted.

Laurie looked up at him. "Would you mind? I'll take care of her."

Reluctantly, he let her go. A few yards, away the horse minus her saddle munched on the leaves of a bush. He led the animal back to the group and tied her to the rear of the wagon. He returned to where Jessica had flown from Sadie's back and found the missing saddle. When he picked it up, he noticed the girth swinging back and forth. He placed the saddle down on the wagon bed to examine it.

"Damn it." With long purposeful strides, he quickly returned to Jessica and Laurie. "Laurie, I need to see you for a moment."

She left Jessica with a few of the women fussing over her. "What's the matter?"

"The girth on Jessie's saddle was tampered with."

"What!"

"It appears it was severed. The cut looks like it was deep enough that Sadie's moves when she ran must have pulled it the rest of the way apart. Somebody isn't playing games anymore. They deliberately tried to hurt her."

Laurie covered her face and began to cry. "I knew something like this was going to happen."

Ethan wrapped an arm around her shoulder. "It's okay. Don't worry. I'll find out who's behind this. I promise. Now let's get Jessie home."

Laurie lifted her head and sniffed. "I'm so glad you're here."

He returned to Jessica who was now on her feet. Swooping in like a bird on its prey, he scooped her up into his arms like she was light as a feather and cradled her against him.

"EJ, put me down," she whispered through clenched teeth. "I can walk."

He tightened his grip around her. "Like hell you can."

"What will my guests say?"

He flashed her a wide grin. "What a lucky woman."

"Damn it, EJ, put me down. I'm fine." She struggled to free herself from his arms and winced as a pain stabbed at her head.

"Nope, I'm really enjoying the feel of you in my arms." He felt her body tense. She wouldn't dare make a scene in front of other people, so he decided to enjoy it while it lasted. He walked to the back of the wagon and lifted her up so she could lie down on some hay.

"Ladies, would you please take good care of our hostess?"

"Sure thing, Ethan." They all clamored together. "What happened?"

"Something spooked her horse, and she fell off. I really thought she was a better rider than that. Perhaps she just wanted me to come to her rescue."

Jessica shot daggers at him as the women went crazy over the idea of being saved by him. He chuckled, pretty sure she wanted to slap him silly. He had forgotten how much fun it was to tease her.

Ethan drove the wagon back to the ranch and stopped in front of the lodge. He quickly hopped down and moved to get Jessica.

"Please." She held up her hand to stop him. "Don't carry me. I've had enough attention for one night," she said through gritted teeth. "I swear I can walk just fine."

Ethan stepped back, bowed and waved his hand, motioning for her to pass. Jessica shuffled by him.

"What's going on?" Laurie had hopped off her wagon and came to stand next to him, as Jessica limped up the stairs muttering to herself.

"She's just a little riled up, that's all."

"What did you do?"

"Who, Me?" He tried to feign innocence.

Laurie stood with her hands on her hips. "Yes, you. What did you do to her?"

"When I carried her back to the wagon, I told her I liked holding her in my arms."

"Ethan James Kirkpatrick! You're a cad."

"You wound me." He tried to give her his best dejected face.

"I said you needed to talk to her, not push her buttons."

"I can't help it. They're begging to be pushed."

"Ethan, she's been through a lot over the years. She puts on a good show, making it on her own and not needing anybody, but I honestly don't think she could take losing anything more. You know I love you, but if you hurt her again, I'll hurt you back."

"Don't worry, Laurie. She's safe. I would never hurt her again. I won't make that mistake twice."

Was she safe? Maybe from him, because he swore he would never cause her that kind of heart ache again, but what about the person who was causing her problems? The thought of her being hurt again made him sick. He hadn't expected to feel the way he did, especially when she was in his arms. He liked the way she felt next to him. That probably wasn't a good thing, considering her current feelings toward him.

After all these years, Jessie still stirred up those old feelings in him. He chuckled to himself. Who was he kidding? Those feelings had never really left; they had just been tucked away deep inside. He returned the wagons and horses to the stable and bedded them down for the night.

Adam, one of the guys who helped out in the lodge and stables, walked into the barn. "What's going on? I thought I heard people talking about an accident."

The young man was tall and lean with, shaggy, black hair. Ethan didn't know him well, but he seemed okay. He was certainly always willing to help-out.

"Jessica fell off Sadie."

"No way, she's a good rider."

"I thought so, too. I think something scared Sadie and Jessica took a header."

"Is she hurt?"

"Just bruised."

"Is there anything I can do? Need any help with the horses?"

"Thanks for the offer, but I'm done. I'm headed over to the camp fire. How about you?"

"Yeah, me, too. I'll walk with you. I hope Miss Jessica is okay."

"I think she will be."

"Sounds like it was a good thing you were around."

"I'm sure anyone would have helped her."

After Ethan closed up the barn, the two men made their way to an area with an outdoor fire pit behind the guest rooms. He smiled, admiring the Adirondack styled chairs and benches arranged around the campfire. She had certainly brought a little piece of home with her.

A few of the other cowboys tended to the fire, and a large group of women lounged chatting. He saw Jessica standing off to the side, leaning against a chair, watching her guests.

Ethan quietly walked up to her. "Are you feeling better?" He lightly brushed his fingers across the bump on her forehead and down her cheek.

She pushed his hand away. "I'm fine. Thanks for asking."

"We have to talk."

Her gaze remained fixed on the group of women. "About what?"

"You didn't just fall off Sadie. You know you're a better rider than that."

"So what happened?"

"The girth was cut. It wasn't an accident that you fell."

"Great."

"Jessica, this is serious. I dusted the saddle for prints; we'll see what we get back." He placed his hand on her arm. "You scared me half to death."

She finally looked up at him. "Then I hope you're as good at your job as you say you are and quickly figure out who's behind this." She gave him a half-hearted smile, and then pulled away to join Laurie who sat in a chair near the fire.

"Okay, if that's the way you want it." He watched as she said something to Laurie and laughed. Okay, maybe he didn't deserve her faith right now, but he was determined to earn it back. Laurie was right. A little bit of time was all he needed.

He strolled over to join Scott, Jeremy, Adam, and the other cowboys. One of them had a guitar and began to strum a melody.

"Ethan, sing us another song," a middle-aged blonde yelled out.

Another woman agreed. "Yeah, Ethan, sing us another song."

"I don't know, ladies," he drawled.

"Oh come on, please," they all chimed in.

"Okay." He sat down on a bench, and the cowboy handed him the guitar. He softly strummed and began to sing "Shameless" by Garth Brooks.

Jessica pursed her lips and narrowed her eyes, seething as Ethan, oozing charm, crooned to the women.

Laurie leaned over. "I didn't know he could play the guitar and sing."

"Neither did I."

"The ladies sure do love him."

Jessica watched in disgust as her guests got all dreamy eyed listening to him. "So I see."

"You would think these women were back in high school the way they are mooning over him." Laurie chuckled.

"You would think he could have picked something besides a love song. Doesn't he realize that men caused the majority of these women's problems?"

"Lighten up, Jessica. Just because they may or may not have man troubles doesn't mean they've given up on love and romance. What woman wouldn't want to be romanced by the likes of Ethan Kirkpatrick? We all have our fantasies, especially when it comes to hunky cowboys."

"Oh, please." Jessica huffed.

"What about you? You've given up on love?"

"The last thing I need in my life is a man. I think my track record proves that. What about you, Miss 'No Date'?"

"I haven't given up on love and romance, but right now I'm enjoying my independence. Keith was so controlling, he made me dependant on him. It feels good to stand on my own two feet, answering only to myself."

Jessica patted Laurie's arm. She knew the hell her friend's life had turned into before the divorce. "My point exactly."

"Jess, I know it hurts right now, but give it some time and you'll be ready to love again. My God, you're only forty-two. Too young to remain alone."

"We'll see."

"You may see sooner than you think."

"Excuse me?"

"Ethan has stared at you the whole time. I think he might be a little bit smitten with you again."

"For the love of God, Laurie, would you please stop going down that road? It's been well traveled and is now closed."

"Closed or just in need of repair?" Laurie raised an eyebrow. "You loved him once, why not again?"

"That was twenty years ago."

"Between the two of you, I am so sick of hearing about how it was twenty years ago. By the way you're acting, you'd think it happened yesterday."

"You know exactly why I'm not over it. So, could we not discuss EJ, or any man, for that matter? Let's just enjoy the evening."

"Aren't you just a little bit curious why fate happened to bring you two face to face again after all these years? Come on, Jessica, what are the odds Ethan would end up being the new Sheriff in Coconino County and coming to your rescue?"

"He has <u>not</u> rescued me from anything."

"What are you really upset about? Is it what happened when he left or because you still have feelings for him that you don't want to admit to?"

"You need to stop reading so many of those philosophical articles." Jessica crossed her arms over her chest. "In case they haven't told you, you're not Oprah and Dr. Phil has his own show."

"As long as you're sure you don't want him for yourself, would you mind if I got reacquainted with him?"

"Knock yourself out."

After Ethan finished the song, he handed the guitar off to one of the other cowboys and then slowly approached Jessica and Laurie.

"Ladies." He tipped his hat.

"Ethan, you were wonderful." Laurie crooned. "I didn't know you could play the guitar and sing."

"I'm a man of many talents." He smiled down at her.

"I bet you are." She batted her eyes at him.

Jessica needed to get out of there before she gagged. "If you two will excuse me, it's late and I'm tired." The two of them fawning over each other was something she didn't need or want to see.

When she stood up to exit stage left, a horrific pain pierced her temple. Her hands clutched her head, and a moan escaped her lips. She felt her knees buckle and had no control to stop her fall.

Ethan's strong arms swooped out and caught her before she hit the ground. "Jessie!"

Laurie surged to her feet. "What's wrong? Do you want me to call the doctor?"

"I knew she wasn't okay from her fall."

"I don't need a doctor or a scene, just rest. I saw Cindy when I got back, and I'm fine. Besides, I don't want the guests to think there is something wrong." And she needed to get out of Ethan's arms as soon as possible.

"Who's Cindy?" Ethan asked.

"She's our nurse and lives here on the ranch," Laurie answered.

"Okay, but I'm still concerned. Do you have blurred vision? Nausea?" He bent to pick her up.

Jessica batted his hands away. "No, I only have a headache."

"You should still have help to your room in case you pass out or something."

"I am perfectly capable of walking. Laurie can help me if it makes you feel better."

Laurie slipped an arm through Jessica's. "We'll *both* help you." Together she and Ethan assisted Jessica back to her wing of the lodge and into the bedroom.

"Thanks. I'm fine. Seriously, you two can go." She offered them a weak smile and sat down on the bed. "Thanks for helping me back. I'm gonna go to sleep."

"Laurie, I need to talk to Jessie alone for a minute," Ethan said. "Do you mind?"

"I'll be right outside the door if you need me." Laurie winked at her then slipped out the door.

Jessica frowned. Sitting on the bed alone with Ethan made her feel extremely uncomfortable.

"Jessie, I mean it. This is serious."

"I'm fine. It's a stupid bump."

"I'm not talking about your head. Someone tried to hurt you today. No, they *did* hurt you today."

"I'm fine."

Ethan took her chin in his hand and forced her to look up at him. She swallowed hard, trying to ignore the heat of his fingers on her skin.

"You're not fine. Do you realize you could have been hurt worse, or even killed? Jessie, someone targeted you. You were on <u>your</u> horse with <u>your</u> saddle."

A tear trickled down her cheek, and Ethan wiped it away with his thumb. The gravity of the situation washed over her like a tidal wave slamming into the shore.

"EJ, I can't lose this place. It's all I've got. Do you understand me?" She grabbed the front of his shirt with both fists. "You have to find out who's behind this and make them stop." She couldn't hold the tears back any longer. "It's my life, EJ," she muttered. "I can't fail at this, too. Please, I can't fail again."

Ethan pulled her into his arms and let her cry into his shoulder. "I'll find them, Babe, don't you worry."

Her tears flowed even harder. She hated the familiar way he talked to her, and she hated needing him. Most of all, she hated how good it felt to have his arms around her again.

Just for a minute, she wanted to feel like it was all going to be okay. She closed her eyes as exhaustion moved in and the world swirled around her. Ethan laid her back on the bed and covered her with a blanket. Defenseless to his charms, and in a dream-like state, she reached up and pulled him down, her mouth seeking his. She kissed him softly at first, and then the hunger took over as she devoured his lips.

Ethan lay down next to her. Her hands caressed his face then slid down his arms and across his back. She could feel his strength. She needed his strength. He was warm and solid and would make all the hurt go away.

She was drifting, drifting into darkness. The last thing she felt was the warmth of his lips on her cheek as she began to slip into a much needed sleep.

Ethan softly whispered her name and she moved closer to him; his warm breath tickled her neck as his hands caressed her back. Her eyes snapped open. Good Lord, what was she doing?

She bolted up right. "Get out."

"Huh?" He sat up next to her.

"I mean good night." She gave him a half-hearted smile.

"Good night?"

"Yes." She shoved him off the bed. "You need to go." The bewildered look on his face said it all. "I'm sorry, I really need to rest." She rose from the bed and pushed him toward the door.

He went to speak but closed his mouth except to mutter "Good night."

"Yep, see you in the morning." She gave him one final push and closed the door behind him. She fell against it and let her breath out, trying to slow her heart rate that he always seemed to get racing. She had rendered him speechless. Of course she had. She practically ate him alive and then shoved him out the door. Poor guy. He was trying really hard to help her, and that might be more dangerous than whoever was trying to sabotage her ranch.

"Nice going, Jess. Real nice going."

chapter 5

Jessica opened one eye and winced. She raised a hand to her head and tried to move her body. Everything hurt.

"Did anyone see the bus?" she muttered to herself.

She slowly stretched, first her legs, then her arms, trying to cause the least amount of pain. She sat up and closed her eyes tight. It felt as though an entire marching band beat inside her head.

"Why me? What did I ever do to anybody?" She forced her body out of bed and held her head with both hands as she made the trek into the bathroom. In desperate need of a hot shower and three aspirin, she shuffled along as if she were eighty.

The warm water felt good as she rotated her shoulders and neck, trying to loosen the tightness in her back. The shower did little to help her head, but her body felt better. Hopefully the aspirin would kick in soon, and the marching band would cease playing. She really hated the base drum.

She finished her shower and pawed through her dresser drawers, quick and simple today. She pulled out a pair of khaki cargo shorts, pink printed t-shirt, and threw her hair into a ponytail.

Grabbing her make-up bag, she stared at her reflection in the mirror. She touched her lips with gloss and suddenly remembered the kiss she shared with Ethan and the look on his face when she'd abruptly kicked him out. She must have hit her head pretty hard to let her guard down like that. Weak and vulnerable, it was disgusting. She'd practically devoured him. Maybe if she was lucky, she could avoid him this morning. She sighed and gently applied a dab of cover-up to the bump and gash on her forehead.

A knock sounded at her door. "Come in," she yelled and then winced, as she walked from the bedroom.

"Good morning, Miss Jessica, how are you feeling?" One of the housekeeping staff poked her head in the door.

Maddie Lamson was middle aged, probably in her mid to late fifties with short red hair and big green eyes to go along with her outgoing personality. She still had a slender athletic build and the energy to go with it.

"Like I got hit by a bus, but I'll be just fine. I'm moving a little slow, gotta work the kinks out."

"Are you sure? Can I get you anything?"

"No, I'm gonna head out and see what is going on."

"Well, don't over do it. Make sure you get some rest."

"Oh, Maddie, you're such a sweetheart for worrying."

She had joined them on the ranch about six months ago and was always fussing over Jessica, very much the mother hen. As a single mom of four, with a loser husband who'd walked out on them, Jessica discovered Maddie could relate to what she was trying to do at the ranch.

Jessica gave her a quick hug and headed out.

The ranch was already a buzz of activity when she reached the great room of the lodge. Guests headed in different directions while the staff did their best to cater to their needs. She watched a small group congregating in the entryway, preparing to go for a hike and another one headed out for a bicycle ride. It was business as usual.

The aroma of fresh coffee and bacon wafted through the air. She breathed in deeply and her stomach grumbled loudly. Perhaps breakfast should be first on the day's agenda.

Her nose led her toward the dining room. Jessica stopped abruptly when she spotted Laurie on the other side of the room, speaking with Ethan. From the look on her friend's face, she was serious about getting reacquainted with him. Her smile couldn't be any wider as she stared up at him.

Jessica couldn't argue that he made a fine-looking cowboy. Nor could she blame Laurie for wanting to reacquaint herself with the likes of him.

So why did seeing them together like that cause a pit in her stomach?

Ethan looked up and smiled at Jessica, tipped his hat, then left the room. Good. Perhaps he had finally gotten the message to leave her alone. That was exactly what she wanted, wasn't it? She rubbed her temples. He made her feel like she didn't know if she was coming or going.

She walked over to Laurie. "Is everything going okay?"

Laurie turned. "Jessica, how are you feeling?"

"A bit of a headache and a little stiff, but I'm fine."

"I know Cindy said you were okay, but you probably should go see a doctor. You could have a concussion. I'm sure Jamie Anderson would see you."

"I'm fine. I don't feel sick or anything, just a bump and a little sore. Any problems I should be aware of?"

"No, actually everything is running smoothly."

"Oh? When I saw EJ speaking with you I was afraid something else had happened."

"No, he was simply checking in."

"I see." Jessica raised an eyebrow at her. "He was checking in with you."

Laurie smiled and looked down at her feet. "Perhaps."

"That's nice."

"You are okay with it, right? You said you weren't interested, but if you are, I won't…."

"Of course I'm not interested. I think twenty years makes him free game."

"Ummhmm." Laurie cocked her head and studied Jessica. "Sure you're not interested."

"Just be careful, he's a heartbreaker. I'm going to go check on Sadie to make sure she's okay." Suddenly, she wasn't hungry anymore. What she needed instead was some fresh air.

"Okay, but be careful. Who knows what could happen next."

"I will." Jessica headed to the stables. What did she care if Ethan was checking in with Laurie? She simply didn't want to see her best friend get hurt.

When she reached the corral, she found Sadie leisurely grazing with the other horses. She whistled, and the horse quickly trotted to the fence.

Jessica climbed over, much to her body's displeasure. "Hey, girl, are you okay? Let me check you over." Sadie stood perfectly still as Jessica ran her hands over every inch of her. She wanted to make sure her beloved horse had escaped the fall unharmed.

"She's doing fine. Can we say the same for her owner?"

Jessica stiffened at the sound of his voice. She turned to find Ethan leaning against the fence. Her pulse started to race. Why did his presence make her so nervous?

Her gaze drifted to his booted feet and moved up his jean clad legs. Boy, did he know how to fill out a pair of jeans. Her eyes shifted upwards, roaming over his chest. The muscles rippled as he moved. She sucked in her breath. It should be against the law to wear a t-shirt when you have a build like that.

She had to get a grip. "I'm fine. Did someone already check her over?"

"I did, last night."

"Are you sure you know what you're doing around horses?" She couldn't help notice the spark in his green eyes when he smiled, the same eyes that had once entranced her.

"You're not the only one who loves horses and knows a thing or two."

"Aren't you full of surprises?" She walked back to the fence and climbed over it, wincing as she did.

"I certainly try." Ethan stepped behind her to help her down on the other side. As he eased her to the ground, his large, strong, hands roamed over her butt and slid up over her hips. His long fingers spanned her waist as he gently set her on her feet.

The warmth of his hands penetrated her clothing. Why did he always feel the need to touch her? He made her weak in the knees when he did, and she hated it. Composure, she didn't want him to know he affected her that way, especially after she ravished him last night.

While his hands still spanned her waist, she turned to face him. The length of their bodies practically touched. She was beginning to feel more than the warmth of his grasp. "Ethan," she said, looking down.

"Okay, okay." He stepped back and held up his hands. "I thought after last night...."

She silenced him with her finger to his lips. She was the one who'd pulled him in for a kiss and then pushed him away the moment he complied. She couldn't blame him for being confused; she was confused herself. "Last night was a mistake, and I'm sorry."

His gaze fixed intently on her. "It sure didn't feel like a mistake."

She stepped away from him, not ready to discuss her actions last night any further. "Have you made any progress in your investigation?"

"I've had a chance to spend some time talking with the other guys. Since this person obviously knew which saddle was yours, I thought it might be an inside job."

"Good heavens! I hope not. I'd like to think I have a pretty loyal staff."

"You would be correct in thinking that. So far, everyone only has great things to say about both you and Laurie, and they seem to love working here. You take pretty good care of them."

"I try to. They're like family."

"That's what they said. They feel like this is a big extended family for them. I must say, I am pretty impressed with how loyal they are to you. Word traveled fast through your staff that you fell off Sadie last night.

"Oh, great. I guess it was stupid to think I could keep this quiet."

"They seem to have come to the right conclusion about it not being an accident. Your staff isn't oblivious to what's been going on, Jessie."

"Just what I need, a smart staff. I can't afford for this to get out to my guests. It would ruin us. I'm sure they are wondering enough on their own."

"Your staff knows that. They aren't going to say anything."

"That's reassuring. Did you get the prints back from my saddle?"

"Yes, we found yours, Jeremy's, Scott's and Adam's. All people who would handle your saddle."

"I trust all of them, which means you're no closer to figuring out who's trying to get me to close my doors."

"I'm afraid not. If it's not one of them, then this person is from outside the ranch. Someone could have been lurking around, spying on you, and watched to see which saddle was yours."

"How special, a peeping-tom." Sarcasm tainted her words. Sadie butted her in the shoulder with her nose and snorted. "I agree, girl." Jessica reached up and scratched her ears. Sadie snorted again.

"I'm going to do background checks on everyone, just to be safe. You never know what's in someone's past or an enemy who might be out for revenge."

"I'm not sure whether to hope you find something or not."

"I'm still fishing around, but I think there are a couple of guys I can trust, and I may enlist their help patrolling the place."

"Please be careful. I don't need anyone getting hurt."

"Too late for that."

"You know what I mean. Hey, how'd you get the guys to open up so easily?"

"My charm."

"Cute. If they were women, maybe."

"Like I said, your staff is loyal to you. They heard I was quick to help you. I guess I earned some brownie points. Plus Joe has been very helpful, and I guess if Joe thinks you're okay, then you're in."

"It's nice to know they care."

"I should probably get back to work. I don't want it to look like I'm hanging out with the boss." He flashed her yet another brilliant smile.

"Yeah, you wouldn't want that." She tried to smile back. She'd actually been enjoying their conversation. Why did he have to pick now to listen to her and back off? And why did that bother her so much?

Good Lord, he had her feelings all mixed up. Her divorce being finalized, seeing him again, the problems on the ranch, needing his help and then the way he made her insides feel when he touched her, it was too much. Distance, she needed to keep distance between them, and she would be fine.

⁂

Ethan prepared the horses and wagons for the evening hayride. Hopefully, tonight would go much better than last night. He pulled the wagon up in front of the lodge and hopped down to greet the ladies. Mike and Aaron drove the other two teams of horses and pulled them up behind him.

"Hey, Ethan, ready for tonight?" Laurie bounced down the steps of the lodge to stand in front of him.

"As long as it's not a repeat of last night."

"I sure hope not."

"I had to add another wagon. We're at full capacity. It looks like hayrides have become quite popular."

"Is it the hayride or the driver?" Laurie joked with him.

"I'm sure the women who joined us last night told the rest, and they're just here to see if there will be any more problems."

"Well, they certainly saw you rush to Jessica's rescue. Perhaps they're looking to be rescued themselves." She laughed and elbowed him.

Ethan rolled his eyes. "I doubt that."

"Don't be surprised if someone falls off a wagon. Do you mind if I ride up front with you?" Laurie inquired.

"No, not at all. Hop on up." Ethan grabbed Laurie around the waist and hoisted her up. He then moved to the back and assisted the rest of the ladies up on the wagon.

Ethan returned and hopped up on the wagon along side Laurie.

"Have you seen Jessica today?" she asked.

"Not since she stopped by to see Sadie this morning. How about you?"

"I haven't seen much of her, either. Maybe she wasn't feeling well after taking that fall."

He was ready to head out when he saw Jessica approach the wagons. She headed toward him but then stopped when she looked up and saw him and Laurie sitting together. He smiled at her and tipped his hat. She frowned at him and walked to the other wagon. He couldn't help chuckling.

"What's so funny?" Laurie asked, looking in the same direction.

"Looks like Jessie doesn't want to join us. Oh, well, her loss." Ethan flicked the reins, and the horses moved forward.

"So what's your story, Ethan? Why are you here?"

"I got divorced, retired and took a great job here. I knew some people in the area from past assignments and got appointed to the position."

"I know that part, but why at our ranch? Why are you so determined to help?"

"Because you need me."

"*She* needs you," Laurie clarified.

"I know she does." He flicked the reins so the horses would pick up their pace.

"But?"

"But, she doesn't want to." Ethan shrugged. "She obviously doesn't want to need any man. That damn stubborn pride of hers won't allow her to."

"Do you blame her? You practically left her at the altar for the FBI, and her husband left her for a younger woman. Can't say I would have much use for your species, either. How would you feel?"

"I don't blame her and believe me, I've regretted that decision every day of my life, but sometimes you can't handle things on your own. I just want to help her, maybe make up for some of the hurt I caused her."

Laurie looked back at the wagons following them. "Why should she let you?"

"I'm the Sheriff, and it's my job to protect and serve. Besides we meant something to each other once upon a time. That should count for something."

"Do you really regret leaving her?"

"Yeah, I do. It was the biggest mistake of my life."

"But you married someone else."

Ethan turned to look at her. "Just because I got married doesn't mean I picked the right person."

"What about your daughter?"

"I love my daughter to death, but Kim wasn't the one I was meant to spend the rest of my life with. We obviously got divorced for a reason."

"What are you saying, Ethan? Do you still have feelings for Jessica?"

He ran his fingers through his hair and sighed. "Laurie, somewhere deep inside I never stopped loving her. Seeing her again and how I felt when she got hurt made me realize that. It made me realize a lot of things, like I don't think I want to lose her again.

Maybe that's why I wasn't such a good husband to Kim and allowed work to come first."

"If you still loved Jess, why didn't you try to get back together with her before now?"

"Look how she is toward me. Do you think she would have been receptive back then? Besides, when I finally came to my senses, she was already taken."

"She's not taken anymore, and I'm assuming you're older and wiser now." She laughed and elbowed him playfully.

"I am, but Jessie has made it very clear she wants nothing to do with me. What makes you think she would even want to rekindle things? She obviously loved John or she wouldn't have married him. I'm sure she's over her feelings for me or at least the loving ones. She hates me."

"Yeah, you're probably right. She and John had such a great relationship that he went and found someone else. That's a tough love to get over."

"Laurie!"

"Ethan, he wasn't her soul mate. You two are more alike than you know. She was all about her career, just like you. Obviously she and John weren't destined for forever. Sounds a lot like you and Kim."

"That still doesn't mean she has feelings for me."

"Oh, she still has feelings for you, trust me."

"What makes you think that?" Ethan asked, hoping there might be a chance for him to reconcile the mistake he had made so many years ago.

"Have you seen the look on her face when any of the women flirt with you? Just to see what she would do, I asked her the other day if she minded if I reacquainted myself with you. Her mouth said no problem, knock yourself out, but the look on her face said 'keep your paws off him'. You forget I probably know her better than she knows herself. Did you catch the expression on her face when she saw me sitting up here with you?"

Ethan laughed. "Yeah, she didn't look very happy. Do you think she's jealous?" Ethan was afraid to hope that he might have a second chance.

"Green, my dear. She was green. Unfortunately, she's in some serious denial."

"Okay, so she's green. That still doesn't mean she's going to give me another chance. She's too damn proud to admit she still cares and needs or wants me around."

"I never said you weren't going to have to work to win her back. I'm sure it will take lots of groveling and pleading. It isn't going to be easy, but if you're a good boy, I just might help you." Laurie punched him in the arm and laughed.

"I'm always up for a challenge, and she's worth it."

"Please don't make me regret this."

"Don't worry, I won't." Ethan flicked the reins and smiled with renewed hope. He knew taking the job as Sheriff would change his life, but he never dreamed he would be reunited with the one woman who had never really left his heart. He could only hope that somewhere deep inside her heart there was a piece still left for him.

※

As usual, the evening hayride was followed by a campfire. Jessica really wasn't in the mood to be sociable, but after last night, she thought she should stick around so her guests wouldn't get suspicious. She slowly made her way throughout the group.

An older woman in her mid-sixties approached her. "Hey, Jessica, how are you feeling tonight?"

"Much better. Thanks for asking, Elaine."

She had become the mother figure of the group.

Melissa Wilkinson, another guest, came to stand next to her and smiled shyly. "Hi, Jessica."

"Hi, Melissa, how are you doing? Have you spoken with your husband yet?"

"Yeah, I finally called him last night. I think he actually misses me. I hope this trip will help him appreciate me more."

"I'm sure it will. Remember, you're still newlyweds, and it takes time to adjust to each other." Jessica knew Melissa was in her early twenties and still had a lot to learn about relationships. She had certainly learned a lot over the years and from the seminars on the ranch.

Elaine patted Melissa's arm. "That's right, honey. You know these men have to be trained."

"Yeah, I know. I just wasn't prepared for the change in him. For some reason he thought he was marrying June Cleaver. Catering to his every need is a bit much."

"Stand your ground. Make sure you let him know this is a partnership and you have needs, too." Jessica reminded her.

"The seminars have really helped me a lot. I think we'll be having some long discussions when I get home."

"Good."

"Thanks for opening this ranch, Jessica." Melissa hugged her and left to join some of the other women.

Jessica continued to converse with the ladies and then relaxed in one of the Adirondack loungers. The evening was cool in the desert, but the fire warmed the air. She made a point to sit on the opposite side of the campfire away from Ethan and Laurie. Three was a crowd. Not that it mattered, considering all the women who came out to listen to him strum a few bars on his guitar.

It had been a long day. Her body ached and watching Ethan and Laurie together didn't exactly help her disposition. It wasn't that she didn't want Laurie to be happy, but if Laurie dated Ethan, that would mean he'd be around a lot more. That was something she wasn't ready to handle. She prayed he would hurry up and figure out who was trying to sabotage her ranch. He was, after all, former FBI. How hard could it be to crack this case?

Deep in thought, staring into the dancing flames of the campfire, she didn't notice the person who came to sit beside her.

"Penny for your thoughts."

She jumped at the sound of his voice. "Oh, EJ, I didn't see you sit down."

"Obviously. Penny for your thoughts?" he repeated.

"They aren't worth a penny." She sighed.

"I doubt that. How are you feeling? You look tired."

"I'm a little sore, but nothing I can't handle. I guess I am tired. I hadn't really stopped to notice until now."

"Maybe you should turn in. It looks like the crowd is starting to thin."

"That's because you stopped singing. Maybe I will call it a night." She stood up to leave, and he joined her. His tall, muscular body towered over her.

"Let me walk you back to your room."

"That's not necessary." She took a step sideways away from him.

"Actually, I had something I wanted to talk to you about."

"You can't do that here?"

"It's a personal favor."

She raised an eyebrow at him. "Oh, alright. Come on." She headed back to the lodge. "So what's on your mind?"

"Well, my daughter wants to come for a visit."

"You have a daughter?" How had she missed that bit of information? She felt a painful twinge in her heart thinking about him with a family.

"Yes. She's fourteen, and she wants to come here and spend the rest of the summer with me. I haven't seen her in a while. Between the move and settling into my job, I haven't had a chance to send for her."

"Sooo?" Was he trying to tell her he was going to bail on his investigation and get someone else to step in for him?

"Well, since I'm staying here and working on your case, I was hoping maybe she could also stay here. The bunkhouse isn't appropriate, so I was hoping she could stay with you or in a guest room near you."

She raised an eyebrow at him. "You want me to babysit?"

"I wouldn't call it that. I will keep her with me during the day as much as possible. She's a good kid."

"If she is with you, how are you going to investigate? She shouldn't be in the middle of that."

"Yeah, you're right. It was a stupid idea."

Jessica saw the sadness in his eyes as he lowered his head. How could you fault a man for wanting to spend time with his child? "Hey, of course she can stay with me. You are here because of me. It's the least I can do." She was going to regret this later, she was sure of it.

"Are you sure? I know you have a job to do as well. I promise she will be well-behaved and won't be any trouble."

"It will be like having one of my nieces here. Don't worry. We'll make it work." They had arrived at her private suite, and she stopped at the door.

"Thanks, Jessie." Ethan moved in closer to her and lowered his head. "This really means a lot to me."

His voice had grown softer, and Jessica swallowed the lump in her throat. His nearness was clouding her already confused brain, and she was finding it hard to breathe. "Sure," was all she could spit out.

He braced an arm on either side of her and leaned in even closer, backing her up against the wall. "Jessie, I was young and stupid. Please forgive me. I never meant to hurt you the way I did."

"But you did." She wanted to run, but his body blocked any chance of escape. She prayed that her knees would not give way beneath her.

"That was a long time ago. People make mistakes, but that doesn't mean they don't care.

"Things happened."

"What things, Jessie? Tell me what happened after I left? How can I fix it?"

"It doesn't matter now." Her voice grew soft, her words seemed barely spoken. "You can't fix it."

"Apparently, it does matter because you can't seem to forgive me."

"Just forget about it." The memories were sneaking back. She felt the pit grow in her stomach as the emptiness crept its way back into her heart. She had lost so much. She wasn't sure her heart could handle losing anything more.

"So much pride," he whispered, brushing the back of his hand against her cheek. "Don't you teach the women here to forgive and move on? You say forget about it but, obviously you can't."

"Forgiveness is one thing, but forgetting is another."

"I've never asked you to forget. I could never forget what we shared. I'm asking you to forgive me and for us to move on."

"I did move on, but that didn't turn out so well, either. Maybe I'm just the type of woman men like to leave." The tears slid down her cheek. All of her insecurities came crashing down on her. "They all leave. One way or another I'm left alone."

Ethan wiped the tears away with his thumb. "Don't ever say that. Men are jackasses. They don't know a good thing when they have it."

She tried to smile. "Does that mean you're a jackass?"

"First rate all the way. I am sorry, Jessie. I hope someday you can forgive me because I have no intentions of leaving you again. Not when I know you still love me." He leaned down and kissed her lips quickly before she had a chance to protest, then left her standing in the hall.

"Damn it, EJ," she whispered and hurried into her suite. Closing the door, she leaned against it, touching her lips. The kiss had been soft and gentle. She didn't want him to be soft and gentle and caring. She wanted to stay angry with him. If she was angry, he wouldn't slip back into her heart. Did he really mean what he said? He had no intentions of leaving her again? No. The men she loved never stayed in her life. She couldn't risk her heart again. The feeling of loss and devastation crept around.

Sleep. She needed sleep so she could think clearly. She groaned, remembering what she had agreed to. "What am I going to do with his daughter?" She touched her fingers to her lips once more. "Better yet, what the hell am I going to do with him?"

chapter 6

STROLLING ACROSS THE courtyard, Jessica stopped by the tennis courts to check on a couple of her guests who were taking lessons. Alicia Jones was working with Eric, the tennis instructor. Standing behind her with one arm around her waist while the other ran the length of her arm, he showed her how to serve the ball. Alicia waved and gave Jessica a thumbs-up.

Eric's dark tan complemented his blond hair and blue eyes. The fact that he filled out his shorts nicely, didn't hurt, either. Tennis lessons with Eric were as popular as the hayrides with Ethan.

Jessica shook her head and chuckled. Allie Litman and Beth Mitchell walked over to the fence where she stood. The two friends had come to the ranch to escape stressful jobs as stockbrokers.

"Hi, Ladies. How's it going? Improving your game?" Jessica inquired.

"We wish." Beth looked toward Alicia. "It appears some of us require more one-on-one instruction than others."

"She's defiantly the teacher's pet. Wouldn't mind playing that role," Allie joked.

Alicia was a leggy red-head with some very large assets. Jessica made a mental note to speak with Eric about his behavior during group lessons. He needed to give each student equal attention.

"You know what they say about divorcees?" Beth whispered.

"Hey, now," Jessica chided. "I'm one of those divorcees."

"I'm just kidding, but it does appear Alicia is recovering rather well from her divorce."

"Now, that's a good thing. Remember, she was very low on self-esteem when she arrived."

"Low on self-esteem? Her?" Allie laughed. "I should be so lucky to have her self-esteem problems."

"Any plans after your tennis lessons?" Jessica inquired.

"Yeah, we're taking riding lessons this afternoon with that little cutie-pie, Mike." Beth elbowed Allie who nodded.

"Ladies, he's too young for you."

"We know, but he sure is sweet on the eyes." They all laughed.

"Enjoy your day and behave!" Jessica called out as she headed to the stables.

Not feeling overly chatty this morning, she was eager to be on her way. Actually, there really was only one person she didn't want to see or talk to. Her hand instinctively went to her lips as she remembered the kiss Ethan had placed on them.

Damn him. He was starting to get to her. She didn't need or want that to happen. She had been doing just fine on her own these last couple of years until someone started to mess with her ranch. She hoped a ride on Sadie would clear her head and by the time she returned he would be off doing chores or investigating.

"Good morning, Aunt Jess," Jeremy greeted her at the stable doors.

"Good morning. Is everything quiet?"

"Sure is. Can I do anything for you?"

"No, I thought I would take Sadie out for a ride."

"Let me saddle her up for you. Ethan has already been here and checked your saddle. He wanted to make sure it was safe for you to take your morning ride."

"Thanks, Jeremy." He was such a fine young man. Laurie had done a good job. Okay, she guessed Laurie's ex had helped a little, very little.

So, Ethan had already been by to check on her. At least she knew he was being thorough. Jessica walked outside and watched the other horses grazing in the corral. She spotted Ethan hosing down one of the Percherons. A chuckle escaped her lips as she watched him try to give the giant horse his bath.

Goliath hated baths.

She couldn't help herself, she had to go and goad Ethan just a little bit. He seemed to be capable of doing anything except give a horse a good scrubbing. Okay, maybe Goliath was an exception, but she couldn't help wanting to show him he wasn't invincible, and she wasn't helpless.

"Too much to handle?" She walked up to stand a few feet away so she could avoid the hose.

"Not at all." Ethan smiled at her through clenched teeth as he struggled to hang onto a ton of horseflesh. Goliath yanked his head up hard, pulling the lead out of Ethan's hand, making him drop the hose. The horse trotted toward the open gate in an attempt to make his escape.

"Hold on, big fella." Jessica ran toward the horse and grabbed his lead. "Whoa, easy now." The horse immediately stopped for her. "What's the matter, boy? Don't want a bath today?" Goliath nuzzled her shoulder, and she stroked his large velvety nose.

Ethan walked up to her. "I can take him."

"He doesn't want a bath today."

"Oh?" He raised an eyebrow at her.

"Nope. Good luck." She smiled and handed him the lead and walked away chuckling. Jeremy walked out of the barn with Sadie.

"Here she is, Aunt Jess." He handed her Sadie's reins.

"Thanks, Jeremy." She swung herself up into the saddle and trotted out the gate and down a dirt path. She desperately wanted to look back to see if Ethan had Goliath under control, but she didn't dare.

It was a warm morning that would segway into a hot day. She wanted to get her ride in before the heat became unbearable. She loved her morning rides. They were so peaceful and allowed her time to reflect on things. Riding, no matter when she did it, was a release for her. It always had been since she was a child visiting her grandparent's farm. She felt free when she rode, like things weren't as bad as they seemed.

Lost in thought, the hoof beats thundering up behind her startled her. She turned in the saddle and groaned. No, no, no. This was her time alone to think, and he was one of the things she needed to think about.

"What are you doing? Don't you have work to do? What about Goliath's bath?" She frowned at the intruder.

"You said he didn't want one, and I am working."

"Oh, really? And what job might that be?"

"I'm protecting you." Ethan flashed her a grin.

"Protecting me? I don't need a babysitter out here."

"How do you know? The last time you went for a ride you ended up with a big bump on your head."

She frowned, knowing he was right. "That doesn't mean anything."

"I'm not leaving, so you can either show me around the ranch and enjoy my company, or we can head back to the barn. It's your choice." He sat defiantly on his horse.

"Fine." She turned back around in her saddle and squeezed Sadie forward.

They rode a distance in silence. Jessica kept wishing he would get bored and return to the stables. Perhaps if she ignored him, he'd give up and let her be. After their kiss last night, she was slowly coming unraveled.

Ethan wasn't about to turn back. They were out here alone, and this was his chance. Maybe he could get her to talk to him, tell him what had happened after he left. He had to get through to her somehow.

Ethan spoke first. "How's your family?"

"Fine."

"Your parents doing okay?"

"Mom is doing okay. My dad passed away about three years ago."

"Jessie, I'm so sorry, I didn't know. What happened?"

"Massive heart attack. It was a huge shock to us all."

"You must have been devastated. I know how close you two were." He looked down at the ground. He should have been there for her. She was the apple of her daddy's eye. Another man she had loved and lost. He was beginning to understand her hurt.

"Devastated would be accurate." Her throat tightened as her voice cracked. "I miss him a lot."

"I'm sure you do." He couldn't imagine the loss she must feel. "How are Sean and Michael? I sure miss those guys."

"My brothers are doing fine, and so are my sisters." Her answer was kurt.

"Any nieces and nephews?"

"Would you believe nine?"

"Nine! Wow, I bet get-togethers are crazier than ever. I always loved when your family hung out together. I'm surprised you moved away from all that. I know how much your family means to you. You must miss them."

"Yeah, I do. The kids are great. Never a dull moment with that crew."

Did he sense the tension starting to leave? She actually answered him with more than a few words. Her family meant everything to her. He had no idea about her father. A twinge of pain stabbed his heart over the devastation she must have felt. Damn he wished he had been there for her. He wished he'd been there for a lot of things.

"Do you see them often?" he asked, wanting to keep their conversation going.

"I'm hoping they will come for a visit. The kids would love the ranch."

"I'm sure they would. I remember how much fun we used to have on your grandfather's farm, never lacked for something to do."

She chuckled. "We found our share of trouble, didn't we?"

He almost fell off his horse. She actually had a smile on her face.

"If your grandfather ever knew the things that went on, he would have beat us."

"Oh, I think he knew a lot more than he let on. No matter how sneaky Sean and Michael thought they were, he was on to them. Now, us girls, we were his angels. We did nothing wrong."

He loved her smile. Her eyes lit up, and her face was radiant.

"Angels my butt. Sneaky she-devils are more like it. So, how come you didn't have any kids to add to the chaos?"

Her smile disappeared.

"Because I can't."

"Oh, I'm sorry." Great, just when he was making progress, he stuck his foot in his mouth. Change the subject, fast. "How did you end up on a ranch in Arizona?"

"I saw an ad in one of my travel magazines about a dude ranch for sale just outside of Flagstaff. After receiving divorce papers for my fortieth birthday...."

"What? No way, he did not ask for a divorce on your birthday."

"Yeah, he did."

"What a charmer."

"Yeah, he already had a replacement for me. So, with my perfect life in shambles, I decided to pick myself up and start over. I quit my job as Vice President of Operations at Rochester General Hospital, packed my things and called Laurie."

"I almost fell over when I saw her. I can't believe you two are here together. Although, I really shouldn't be surprised, you two were practically inseparable."

"Laurie's divorce wasn't much better than mine. She was only too eager to pack her things and join me."

"What's her story?"

"Interested in her?"

"Interested in her ex-husband."

"Excuse me?" Jessica gave him a sideways glance.

"I sensed from her that perhaps her ex-husband wasn't very nice."

"To say he was controlling is an understatement. Laurie was crazy in love with him and eager to please. Then his 'expectations' of her got a little ridiculous. Ever see 'Sleeping with the Enemy'? Anyways, after she had Jeremy, she didn't dare leave."

"Sounds like a great guy."

"Once Jeremy went to school, she realized what Keith was doing to her. She wanted a life outside of him and he wouldn't allow it, so she gathered up her nerves and left him."

"What about their son?"

"There was a nasty custody battle. She won, but last year when she moved here to be with me, Jeremy opted to stay with his dad until he graduated from high school."

"So it was his choice to come here for the summer?"

"Yeah, that went over like a lead balloon."

"I can't imagine her ex was real pleased about his son spending the summer with a bunch of women."

"Keith was ticked. Thank goodness Jeremy is eighteen and can make his own decisions."

"I'm sure that's something else that must please Keith."

Jessica turned and looked at him. "Ethan, what are you getting at?"

"I was wondering if Laurie's ex-husband was mad enough to make her life miserable and pay your ranch a visit."

"Keith? I don't know, Ethan." She shook her head in disbelief. "I never really thought about Keith doing anything like this. Besides, that doesn't explain why I was targeted."

"Who encouraged Laurie to leave Keith?"

"I did."

"Who asked her to move here?"

"I did."

"Who is encouraging women to do exactly the opposite of what he thinks a woman should do and probably filling his son's head with nonsense? I saw 'Sleeping with the Enemy,' and he tracked his wife down."

"Alright, alright." She held her hand up for him to stop. "I get your point. I suppose you're right, he probably wouldn't like me very much."

"Nobody is above suspicion, especially possessive or ex husbands."

"Great, all our hard work down the drain because of men. They're what put us here to begin with."

"Jessie, you've done an incredible job. I'm very impressed, and your hard work is not going to go down the drain. I won't let it."

"Thanks. We never expected our idea for the ranch to take off. I guess there was a need for it. I probably shouldn't be surprised by that."

"You have a lot to be proud of. John was a fool to leave you."

"You're kind to say that, but I suppose I have to take some responsibility for the demise of my marriage. He wanted to adopt kids, and I wanted a career. I guess he got tired of waiting. Perhaps his young perky bride will give him the children he wanted."

Ethan reached over and grabbed Sadie's reins to stop her. "Jessie, I'm really sorry about that. You would have been a great mom."

"What's done is done."

"Is it?" He held her chin in his hand and gave her a searching look. "I'm here now."

"But for how long?" she whispered, then pulled free of his grasp and nudged Sadie forward. They rode in silence for a few minutes. He was making progress. She had actually opened up to him. He wasn't giving up yet.

"You know, it was tough leaving when I joined the FBI. They put me through some very serious training."

"Sure didn't look tough. You left and never looked back."

"It wasn't an easy decision."

She reined Sadie in and glared at him. "It was the only decision for you, and you know it. All you cared about was playing super hero and saving the world. Rescuing people is what you do best."

"That's not true, Jessie."

"What? I believe you informed me there was no room in your life for a wife."

"That was true. Training was hell. I had to be at the top of my game. There was no room for distraction, no room for error. After I finished the academy, I joined NSS—the National Security Service. Intense doesn't even touch the training we went through."

"I see." She looked away from him and urged Sadie forward again.

It was clear she really didn't want to hear this, but he needed to tell her everything. "Jess, we were kids. I was young and stupid. I had no idea what I was getting into…" He paused and looked at her. "…or what I was giving up."

"What are you saying?"

"Obviously, I was right. I made a terrible husband and didn't do much better in the parenting department. Kim got tired of being alone."

"I see."

"No, you don't see. Did you know I came back for you?"

She swung around in the saddle again to gape at him. "You what?"

He saw the shock on her face. Were those tears forming in her eyes? It was apparent that no one had told her he had come home to see her. Probably just as well for her sake.

Still he couldn't help repeating, "I finally came to my senses, and I came back for you."

"Why? Why would you do that?"

Was that anguish he saw in her eyes? "I came back because I should have never left you in the first place. I realized how much I loved you and how empty my life was without you."

"But you left again without a word."

"You had already moved on and were engaged to John. I figured you were finally happy, and better off with out me, so I just left."

Tears slid down her cheeks. "We would have waited for you. All you had to do was ask. I would have understood."

He was completely confused. "We? I don't understand."

"It doesn't matter now," she choked out.

"What happened, Jessie? Why won't you tell me?" He reached over and grabbed Sadie's reins to pull her closer.

"Please don't. I can't, Ethan." The tears were now streaming down her cheeks. She yanked the reins from his hands and kicked Sadie forward, heading back to the barn, leaving him in the dust.

He let her go. She was obviously keeping something very painful from him. Why wouldn't she tell him? He had made progress today until he put his foot in his mouth. He'd just have to be patient, at least for now. Maybe now that she knew the truth, they could move forward.

Jessica rode up to the stables and hopped off. She led Sadie into her stall and laid the saddle over the door. She grabbed a brush and started to brush Sadie as a means to control her emotions. He had returned for her. She didn't know if that made her feel better or worse. If he had only asked her to wait instead of just leaving, things would have turned out so differently. She wiped the tears away with the back of her hand.

"Hey, Miss Jessica." Adam leaned on the door of Sadie's stall.

Jessica jumped. "Adam, I didn't know you were here."

"I didn't mean to scare you. Can I put Sadie's saddle away for you?"

"Yes, thank you."

"Sure thing." Adam took the saddle from the door and headed to the tack room.

Ethan entered Sadie's stall and walked up behind her. "Are you okay?"

She closed her eyes tight at the sound of his voice. "I'm fine." She opened them and continued brushing Sadie.

"Are you sure?" He leaned up against her and covered her hand with his.

Her throat constricted, and her voice was a mere whisper. "Really, I'm fine." Her heart raced from his closeness, and she was positive he could hear it beating. She kept thinking about him returning for her.

"Maybe I need some help."

His breath tickled her ear and neck. Jessica closed her eyes as wonderful sensations coursed through her body. Her heart ached, and she wanted him to make it feel better. What was she thinking? She wasn't, that's what her problem was whenever he was around. She wasn't prepared to let a man back in her world. And she most certainly wasn't ready for this particular man to show back up in her life. She had to gain control.

"Don't you have something to do?" She ducked under his arm and slipped away from him, walking around to the other side of Sadie.

She opened the stall door and went to fetch some grain. Standing over the barrel, she was lost in thought surrounding Ethan and the past. He had totally blown her away with his revelation.

"Jessie! Look out!"

She looked up in time to see Ethan running toward her, hurling himself in her direction. He caught her around the waist, knocking her off her feet. They crash landed into a pile of hay.

"What the hell! Get off me." She pushed at his shoulders. His entire body lay on top of her.

Green eyes met blue, their breath mingled together. She pushed at his shoulders again, but he only stared at her. Before she knew what was happening, his lips brushed across her lips.

"Forgive a fool." His words came in a breathless whoosh.

Light as a feather at first, then more demanding as his kiss consumed her. His tongue pushed her lips apart so he could gain entrance. Her mind swirled. Feelings she buried years ago rushed to the surface, slamming into her like the waves crashing into the rocks. Her arms wrapped around his neck, and her fingers weaved into his thick, curly hair.

She was doing it again, allowing him to get to her. She turned her head away from him, breaking the kiss and pushed with all her might. "Please, get off me."

Ethan rolled next to her.

"What the hell was that about?"

He sat up and looked at her. "Are you okay?"

"Yes, no, I'm fine except for being tackled by you. What were you thinking?"

"About that crushing down on your head." He pointed to the large bale of hay that lay near the feed barrel.

"Ohhh. Where the hell did that come from?"

"It fell from the loft. Stay here."

"Where are you going?"

"To see why that fell."

Ethan scrambled up the ladder to the loft. Jessica stood and brushed the hay from her clothes and picked it out of her hair. She touched her lips, more concerned about the passionate kiss they had just shared than the hay bale that almost landed on her head.

How could she have let that happen? She couldn't let him back into her life, not now, maybe not ever. She felt that ache in her heart again. It hurt for what she had lost and what she could lose. Nope. She wasn't ready for this, she wasn't ready for him to leave her again. She couldn't depend on anyone but herself.

"Jessie, is everything all right?"

She felt his hand on her shoulder and turned to look at him. "I'm fine. Can you tell me what the hell just happened here?"

"When I followed you out of Sadie's stall, you were standing over the feed barrel. I saw some hay float down around you. When I looked up, I saw the hay bale teeter and then fall, almost on your head. Sorry I pushed you so hard."

"I'm not sure which is worse…" She looked him up and down. "…getting hit on the head with a bale of hay or body slammed by the likes of you?" She smiled, trying to make light of the situation.

"I didn't hurt you, did I?" He reached out to touch her.

"No, I'm fine. Thanks for pushing me out of the way, I think." She raised an eyebrow at him.

"Jessie, I don't think that was an accident."

"What did you find?"

"Nothing, but it just seems too calculated that it should fall in the exact spot you were standing at the exact moment you happen to be at the feed barrel. Come on, Jess, you know better."

"EJ, that means the person was here with us. How can that be? I didn't see or hear anyone."

"Looks like we have a phantom saboteur. It is possible he could have gone out the loft window. It opens above the roof of the tack room."

"Are you trying to tell me that whoever is doing these things is either sneaking around my ranch like a ghost or is one of my own people? I don't like the thought of either."

Ethan nodded. "You've gotta be careful, Jessie. Promise me you'll be careful. This is the second time you were targeted."

"Better me than someone else?" She offered him a half-hearted smile.

"That's not funny. I know what you're saying and I understand you don't want to see anyone get hurt, but I don't want to see you get hurt again."

"Hey, what's going on?" Adam walked into the barn along with Aaron. "I thought I heard voices. Is anything wrong?"

"No, we're fine. Did you guys happen to see anyone else outside?" Ethan asked.

"No, although I wasn't really looking. I was putting away Miss Jessica's saddle. How about you?" Adam turned to Aaron.

"No, I didn't see anything, either."

"Oh, okay. Thanks, guys." Ethan put his arm around Jessica's shoulders and started to walk out of the stable. "I'm gonna find this person, I swear to you, I will."

"I know you will. I'm heading back to the lodge."

Ethan stopped her with a hand on her arm. "About the kiss."

She looked up and searched his green eyes, for what, she wasn't sure. A lot had transpired today. "Another mistake. I've gotta go." She turned and headed out of the barn.

"Jessie, wait."

She stopped and closed her eyes tight. She couldn't do it, she just couldn't do it. She opened them and then ran across the grass heading toward the closest entrance to the lodge.

chapter 7

THE DINING ROOM was loud with chatter, as guests filed in for the evening meal. The wait staff was busy taking orders, and the smell of bar-b-que chicken and corn on the cob filled the air. Jessica's stomach grumbled as she walked around the dining room, trying hard to forget about the afternoon, in more ways than one. She made her way around the tables, chatting as she went. Even though her guests were only there for a week, she enjoyed getting to know them. Connecting on a one-to-one level was important, and she hoped they would return.

She stopped to see Allie, Beth and Elaine. "How were your riding lesson's, ladies?"

"Fantastic, Mike is an excellent instructor," Beth said.

"He most certainly is," Allie concurred and winked at Beth.

"Ladies, I don't want to hear about any wild escapades," she gently scolded with a smile.

"Don't worry, Jessica, I'll keep these wild ones in line," Elaine assured her.

"I'm glad someone will keep an eye on you two."

"Who us?" Beth and Allie chimed together, trying to act innocent.

"Enjoy your evening, ladies." Jessica laughed and moved on. Her heart went out to Elaine. Marital issues could usually be resolved, divorce you eventually move on from, but losing the love of your life was something you could never really get over. Death was a permanent heartbreaker, something she knew too well.

She stopped at another table to visit and was engrossed in a conversation with a couple of the women, when the whole table stopped talking. She knew without even looking that Ethan was standing behind her. Ignoring him in front of her guests wasn't an option, damn him. She slowly turned around to stare at his smiling face.

"Evening, ladies." He tipped his hat and smiled even wider.

"Evening, Ethan." They all cooed.

She rolled her eyes over the reaction he invoked from the women. Shameful, these women were just shameful when it came to him.

"EJ, did you want something?" She regretted the question as soon as she asked it.

"As a matter of fact there is something I want. You."

The women at the table let out ohhs and ahhs.

"EJ." She wanted to smack that Cheshire cat smirk right off his face. That got just the kind of reaction she was sure he'd been looking for.

"Ladies, settle down. I want to <u>speak</u> with you, Jessie, if you have a moment."

"Now?"

"If it's not a problem?"

"Okay. Excuse me, ladies."

"Take your time, honey. I know I would," Alicia called out.

Ethan walked away from the table, and Jessica followed. He led her outside onto the patio. The sun was setting and the sky was spectacular with streaks of pink and orange decorating it.

"I never tire of these sunsets." He stared up toward the sky.

"Me neither. It's one of the things I love about this place." She leaned on the wrought-iron fence that separated the patio from the pool area. "So what did you want to talk to me about?"

"My daughter." His arm brushed against hers.

"Oh." His closeness was distracting her. The feeling of his skin touching hers sent warm tingles through her body.

"I wanted to let you know that she arrives tomorrow."

"Tomorrow!" Jessica's head snapped around to look at him. "So soon?"

"Is that a problem?"

"No, I guess not." She was so not ready to deal with his daughter.

"I really appreciate you allowing her to stay with you. She's kind of young to stay in a room alone."

"Not a problem. We'll do girl stuff."

"I can't thank you enough. Like I said, I haven't been the greatest of dads, and the fact that she wants to come and spend some time with me means the world to me."

"I'm sure it does. We'll make sure she has a good time here."

"Thanks. Will I see you at the calf roping contest?"

"Absolutely."

"Great, then I'll see you in a little while."

"Yeah, sure."

Ethan leaned over, kissed her cheek and quickly slipped away before she had a chance to protest. This was getting to be too much. He was wearing down her walls, walls she wasn't ready to let crumble, and now she had to entertain his daughter. This ultimately meant she'd have to spend more time with him.

She still couldn't help but think about what he said during their ride. He had come back for her. Damn him to hell. She would have preferred not to know that he had come back. Things might have turned out differently and that broke her heart.

"Hey, what are you doing out here?" Laurie walked up behind her. "What a beautiful sunset."

"Sure is. I was talking with Ethan."

"Really now." Laurie raised an eyebrow. "Sunsets and Ethan, nice combination."

Jessica rolled her eyes. "He needed a favor."

"I bet he did." Laurie tucked a long curly strand of auburn hair behind her right ear.

"Laurie! He wants me to babysit."

"Him?" Laurie turned around and leaned her back against the fence.

"No! His daughter. His daughter wants to spend the summer with him. Since he's here on the ranch investigating our problems, she needs a place to stay. She's going to stay with me."

A smirk tugged at the corners of Laurie's mouth. "Testing out your stepmom skills?"

"I don't think so. He seemed rather pitiful, and I couldn't say no. He is here trying to help us."

"Are you softening up toward him?"

"No! Stop pushing. Believe me, the faster he figures out what's going on; the faster he is off my ranch. Besides, weren't you the one who said she wanted to reacquaint herself with him?" Jessica crossed her arms in annoyance.

"What's got your knickers in a knot tonight?"

"Did you know he came back for me?" Jessica moved to sit in one of the chairs on the patio.

Laurie joined her. "Came back for you when?"

"After he finished all of his training, he came back for me. He said he realized his mistake."

"He told you?"

"You knew?" Anger erupted from her. "You knew and didn't tell me?"

"Whoa, hang on sister." Laurie placed a hand on Jessica's arm. "I just found out. He told me the other night, and I told him the two of you needed to talk."

"I'm sorry. I just can't help but think about how different things could have been."

"Even if he had told you when he came back, it wouldn't have changed anything. The accident had already happened."

"I suppose you're right. If he came back, why didn't he just ask me to wait to begin with? We could have waited to get married, but he never gave me a chance to tell him."

"You know what they say, you don't know what you've got until it's gone. There's something else bothering you."

"Why do you say that?"

"I know you too well. What else is going on? Was there another accident? Jessica!"

"Alright, alright. A hay bale almost fell on my head today in the barn."

"What? Are you okay?" Laurie reached over and grabbed Jessica's arm.

"I'm fine. EJ pushed me out of the way in time."

"Thank God."

"It was just a freak accident. He didn't find anything."

"Ethan doesn't believe that, does he?"

"No, he thinks that either someone is lurking around here like a ghost, or it's somebody who works here."

"Oh great."

"Yeah, neither are appealing. He's been gathering prints and running background checks, but so far nothing suspicious has surfaced."

"What else happened?"

"Nothing." Jessica rose to her feet and walked away from Laurie.

"Jessica." Laurie rose and followed her.

"Ya know, it is really annoying that you know me so well. EJ kissed me."

"You let him?" A huge smile spread across Laurie's face.

"No, I didn't let him. It just happened. When he attempted to save my life, he body slammed me into a mound of hay. We were nose to nose and it just happened."

"I knew it." Laurie gave an arm pump, emphasizing that she was right.

"You knew what?"

"I had a feeling there were still feelings between you two. You can deny it all you want and you can profess to still be angry with him, but there is still something between you."

"You're not mad? I know you said you were interested in him. I'm so sorry Laurie, I swear I didn't mean for that to happen. I would never hurt you."

"Jess, you're my best friend, and the two of you belong together. I knew that the minute the two of you set eyes on each other again. I was only trying to make you jealous, so you would see you still care."

"Why you brat! You're a hopeless romantic, stop playing matchmaker." She laughed. "I'm going to get ready for the calf roping contest. You know how much the women love being helped by our wranglers." Jessica patted Laurie on the arm and walked away.

"I'm right and you know it," Laurie shouted after her.

"See you later." Jessica waved as she walked away.

❧

The ladies were directed into various lines, where wranglers were ready to show them how to rope some calves. This was something new they had started to do and it was a hit. The few calves they used were borrowed from a neighboring farm because they grew up to be cows. Horses were one thing, but Jessica wasn't prepared to handle cattle. She promised the owner that none of the big brown-eyed creatures would be hurt.

After directing the women, Jessica climbed up on some bleachers. They had set them up next to the corral, so those who weren't participating could still watch.

"Evening, ladies." Ethan leaped up on the bleachers and found a spot next to Jessica.

Jessica was ready to jump off the bleacher when he practically sat on top of her. His thigh brushed against hers, and the musky scent of his cologne tantalized her senses. "Why do you have a guitar? Do you bring that thing everywhere you go?"

"Laurie thought it would be entertaining if I played my guitar. I guess the ladies enjoy it."

"Swell." Leave it to Laurie to come up with this brilliant idea.

"Awww, what's the matter, Jessie? Don't you like my singing?"

"I guess it's okay." She considered getting up and changing her seat, but the contest started and she didn't want to miss any of the action.

She was very lucky to have the staff she did. The wranglers were patient in their attempts to show the women how to throw the rope. They were also very good natured about the flirtation that went along with the lesson. It was all in fun.

First, Allie gave it a go, but missed. Then it was Beth's turn. She came closer, but still missed. Even Melissa got up and gave it a try.

"Okay, girls, let me show you how it's done." Elaine stepped up and took the rope from Mike. She swung the lasso over her head a few times then tossed it. Bingo, right around the little calf's neck. The women roared with admiration.

"Thank you, thank you." Elaine took her bows.

"It looks like we have a winner." Jessica stood up and yelled.

"What does she win?" Someone called out.

"A date with Ethan." Jessica looked down and smiled at the shocked look on his face. The women hooted. "Just kidding, but she does get the VIP treatment at the Spa." The women awed their disappointment.

With the contest over, everyone moved back to the campfire area.

"Ethan, how about a song?" one auburn-haired woman called out.

"Yeah, Ethan, sing something for us," an older brunette encouraged.

"Ladies, your wish is my command." He sat down on a bench next to Jessica. A cheer went up from the women as they crowded around the campfire. Jessica harrumphed. What had she done by allowing him to come here? The women would be mighty disappointed when his job was finished and he left. Yes, left. Eventually he would leave again.

"Ladies, I want to play a little tune for someone who is special to me. It's by a couple of guys you might have heard of called Rascal Flatts."

The women cheered again.

"It's called 'My Wish' and it goes something like this." He began to strum his guitar.

Jessica couldn't believe her ears. This was one of her favorite songs. She wondered who that special someone was. Was it Laurie? Could it be her? There she went again. She was letting him into her world, and that was very dangerous for her heart.

The women hung on his every word. His tenor voice was smooth and enchanting, too enchanting. He was weaving a fantasy of the dashing cowboy entrapping his love in his musical web. She couldn't afford to get snagged in that web.

The women clapped and cheered when Ethan finished.

He leaned in close to Jessica, his voice a soft whisper that tickled her ear. "I meant that for you. I only want what's best for you."

"A little late don't you think?"

He took her chin in his hand so she had to look at him. "I thought I was doing the right thing for both of us. I'm sorry that I was wrong."

He quickly rose from the bench, leaving her to contemplate his words.

She hated how sincere he sounded. She didn't want his apologies. They made her want to forgive him.

※

The kitchen was organized chaos as the cooks prepared to fill the breakfast buffet. Pans of scrambled eggs, bacon and fresh fruit were carried past Jessica, but she barely noticed. Exhaustion from a restless night's sleep was winning out. She was getting quite tired of being haunted by EJ in her dreams.

She found the coffee and poured a cup. "Ummm." Closing her eyes, she inhaled deeply, letting the aroma tantalize her senses.

"I don't think I have ever seen such a sensual reaction over coffee before."

Jessica opened her eyes to find herself standing toe to toe with Ethan. "What?" What the hell was he doing in the kitchen, couldn't she go anywhere without him popping up?

"I said I've never seen that kind of a reaction to coffee before. The look on your face was rather…sensual."

She was speechless. Her brain was reeling. Ethan…sensual. Those two words should not be used in the same sentence.

"Hello, are you okay?" He waved a hand in front of her.

"Ah, yeah, I'm fine. Just need coffee to wake up and get going." She walked into the dining room, waving to some of the women already seated for breakfast. He followed close on her heels.

"I wanted to let you know Chrissie should be arriving here shortly. I sent one of the ranch shuttles to pick her up at the airport."

"Chrissie?"

He raised his brow at her. "My daughter."

"Oh, right, your daughter. I'll be ready. Just let me know when she gets here."

"Dad!"

"I guess that would be now." Ethan waved to a young girl who came running across the room. Ethan caught her in his arms, picking her up and swinging her around. "Hey, Sweet Pea, how are you?" He kissed her cheek.

"I'm great now that I'm here."

Ethan hugged her tight and then placed her back on the floor. "Jessie, I'd like you to meet my daughter Christina. Chrissie, I'd like you to meet Jessie, she owns the ranch."

"Nice to meet you." Christina stuck her hand out.

Jessica shook it. "Nice to meet you, too." A small twinge of pain stabbed her heart as she stared at the young girl with the long dark curly hair and green eyes. She was the image of her father. Jessica wondered what their children would have looked like.

"You're going to stay with Jessie in her suite. Dad is working on something top secret for her, so I have to stay somewhere else. I hope that's okay."

"That's fine as long as I get to spend some time with you."

"Absolutely, Sweet Pea. I promise we'll spend lots of time together."

"How about we get you settled, and then we'll take a tour of the ranch," Jessica offered.

"That sounds like a plan. I'll grab her bags and bring them."

The threesome made their way down the halls that led to Jessica's suite. Ethan deposited Chrissie's bags in one of the spare bedrooms.

"You can unpack later. Why don't we show you around?" He grabbed Chrissie's hand.

"Sounds great, Dad."

"You don't mind do you, Jessie?"

"That's fine."

"We're not taking you away from anything, are we?"

"Nope." Not that she was thrilled about spending more time with him, but it was better than dealing with his daughter on her own. That would come soon enough.

"What would you like to see first?" Ethan asked.

"I don't know." Chrissie shrugged shyly.

"I bet she would like to start with the horses. Perhaps we can pick out one that is hers to ride while she is here."

"That would be so cool. Thanks." Chrissie smiled.

"Well, alright then, let's go." Jessica opened the door and ushered them out.

Ethan placed his hand on her arm and leaned over. "Thanks, you were great," he whispered.

"No problem," she smiled and whispered back, then followed him out the door.

The threesome took a leisurely stroll out to the stables. Chrissie was in awe of the horses. Jessica noticed that wasn't all she was in awe of, judging from the way her eyes scanned every cowboy who swaggered by. Lord help her, she wasn't sure if she was ready to chaperone a teenager.

"Your horses are beautiful."

"Thank you. Did you see one that you fancy?"

"I don't know." Chrissie shrugged.

"Do you know how to ride?" Jessica asked, realizing she had no idea if the child even knew how to get on a horse, much less ride one. They walked through the stables and out to the corral.

"Dad taught me."

"She's pretty good at it," Ethan said, puffing up his chest.

"That's good. How about Lilly?" Jessica walked over to a beautiful Bay with white stockings who trotted up to the fence when Jessica approached.

"Hey, girl, I have a new friend for you." She stroked the horse's velvety nose who whinnied her answer. "Chrissie, meet Lilly. She's a good girl. I think you will enjoy riding her."

"Hi, Lilly." Chrissie walked over to the horse who nuzzled her shoulder.

"I think she likes you." Jessica patted her neck.

"She's great." Chrissie reached out and stroked the horse's nose.

"Good. How about we see the rest of the place?" Ethan interjected.

"Sure, Dad." Chrissie walked over to him.

"Why don't the two of you go on a head? I will meet you back at the suite. We can have dinner there if you want. I'm sure Chrissie will be tired and want to unpack."

"Dinner at your place? Sounds good to me." Ethan winked at her.

"Great." She gave him a half-hearted smile. What had she just done, inviting Ethan back to her suite?

"I'll see you two later."

"Thanks, Jessie." Chrissie waved good-bye as she headed toward the tennis courts with her dad.

chapter 8

JESSICA WATCHED THE pair leave. She had a sinking feeling in the pit of her stomach. She just knew there was going to be trouble. Having Ethan's daughter under foot meant that Ethan would be under foot. Was it too late to move Chrissie to another room or maybe with Laurie? No, that would be too obvious. Besides, Laurie had a teenage boy. Jessica had promised Ethan she would look after his daughter, not that she owed him anything. Being here on the ranch was purely his idea, not hers. He could have assigned someone else to the case.

Dealing with Ethan was one thing, but the essence of her problems was the person trying to sabotage her ranch. She thought about what Ethan had said after the hay bale almost fell on her head. It was either someone on the ranch or someone who was slipping in and out like a ghost.

She couldn't bear to think of one of her employees doing these things. She was a good boss, at least she tried. They were her family, and she hoped she had always treated them that way. So why would they do this to her? But the thought of someone slinking around her ranch undetected was even more alarming. This was her home, and she wanted to feel safe again. She wanted her guests and employees to be safe here. Right now, that wasn't the case.

Jessica headed back to the main lodge thinking she might actually make dinner herself. She never cooked much anymore; there really was no reason to. Most of her meals were eaten in the dining room with her guests. She supposed they could have eaten in the dining room, but she didn't want to overwhelm Chrissie. A public display with Ethan also wasn't on her list of things she was prepared to deal with. There would be plenty of time for that during his daughter's stay.

Eating in her suite would give her time to get to know the girl and learn more about her. She needed to know what she should be prepared for. So far, Chrissie seemed like a very sweet fourteen year-old, one that loved her daddy very much, in spite of what he said about his parenting skills.

Jessica returned to her suite and started to prepare a grocery list when a knock sounded at her door. They couldn't be back yet, she wasn't ready.

"Come in," she called out from where she sat at the kitchen table.

"Hi Miss Jessica, I was stopping by to check on you."

"Oh, Maddie, I'm so glad to see you. Could you do me a huge favor?"

"Sure, what do you need?"

"I'm making dinner here tonight, and my fridge is pretty bare. Would you mind terribly getting a few things from the main kitchen for me while I take care of some other things?"

"No problem, where is your list?"

"Maddie, thank you so much." Jessica walked to the door and handed her the list. "I really appreciate your help."

She wanted to get the table all set and make sure Chrissie's room was ready for her. For some reason, she was suddenly nervous about making dinner for Ethan and his daughter. Why should she care so much? It wasn't like she was trying to impress him.

It wasn't too long before Maddie knocked on the door again, returning with the items Jessica needed to prepare the evening meal. "Thank you again, Maddie. I want dinner to be special."

"Not a problem, Miss Jessica. What's all the fuss? It doesn't have anything to do with that new cowboy who seems to be dogging your every move?"

"What? He's not dogging my every move."

"You might not realize it, but I've caught him watching you."

Jessica swallowed hard. "Really?"

"Yes, dear, really. Who is this guy anyway? He isn't some guy you just hired off the street, is he? We don't need any crazy stalkers around here."

Jessica laughed. If she only knew. "You know me better than that. Actually he's an old friend from college. He's new in town and needed a job. That's all."

Maddie laughed. "Sure wish I had friends that looked like him. He sure is easy on the eyes."

"Looks aren't everything. His daughter will be staying with me until he can get settled. I thought dinner in tonight would be better than taking his daughter to the dining room."

"Those ladies can get a little racy, might not want little ears to hear some of the talk."

"My thoughts exactly, at least until I get to know her better."

"Well, have fun. If you need anything else, just call. Don't do anything I wouldn't do." Maddie joked and slipped out the door.

Special? Did she say she wanted dinner to be special? No. She could handle this and still keep her distance.

☙☙

Jessica made the finishing touches to the table when there was a knock at her door. Ethan poked his head in, shouting a cheerful "hello" before he and Chrissie came strolling through. The pair laughed and chattered away.

"Hi, honey, we're home," Ethan joked as they walked into the kitchen. Chrissie headed to her room to change her clothes. Ethan walked over to where Jessica stood at the stove and inhaled deeply the aroma of her cooking. "Did you miss me?"

Jessica shook her head. "Were you missing? Hadn't noticed." She tried to hide a smirk.

"You're no fun." He frowned at her.

"That's because we're not playing house." She grabbed her glass of Pinot Grigio and took a big sip. She wasn't much of a drinker, but she did enjoy a good glass of wine every now and then. Tonight, it wasn't about pleasure, it was about settling her nerves. She had to remind herself that Chrissie was not their daughter and this was not their home.

"Sure feels like that," he whispered in her ear.

His breath on her neck sent a tingle down her spine. She was right; this was a horrible mistake on her part. She sidestepped him just as Chrissie came into the kitchen. That was a little too close for comfort. She did not need Ethan's daughter getting the wrong idea.

"Why don't you two go wash your hands? Dinner will be ready shortly." Jessica grabbed the bottle of wine and poured another glass.

"Yes, ma'am." Ethan winked at her and tickled his daughter as they joked on their way to the bathroom.

Jessica placed the dishes of food on the table and sat down to wait. Her guests soon emerged from the bathroom and raced to the table.

"Ummmm...boy does that smell good, I'm starved." Ethan smacked his lips together in anticipation.

"It's my specialty, Chicken Parm with angel hair pasta. Hand me your plate, and I'll dish it up for you."

Ethan and Chrissie both handed over their plates and then eagerly dug in.

"So, how was your afternoon? Did you see all of the ranch?"

"This place is so cool, Jessie. Thanks for letting me stay. There is so much to do."

"You're very welcome. I'm glad you have a chance to spend some time with your dad."

"I can't wait to ride Lilly tomorrow. Dad promised we could go for a ride in the morning. Would that be okay?"

"Sure it would."

"This is going to be so great. Dad said you knew each other in college. Was he as much of a dork back then as he is now?"

Jessica was caught off guard that Ethan had told his daughter they knew each other back then. In fact, she was surprised he had mentioned that time in their lives at all.

"Yeah, we've known each other a long time." She tried to keep her composure.

"So was he a dork?" Chrissie twirled spaghetti around her fork.

"Hey! Be kind to your old man," Ethan said.

Jessie dabbed her napkin at the corners of her mouth then smoothed it out in her lap. "Actually, he was every girl's dream of the perfect guy." She could feel herself starting to relax. The wine must be kicking in.

"Dad? Ewe, that's just plain gross." Chrissie laughed.

"It is, isn't it?" Jessica laughed with her. "He thought he was all that and then some."

"Hey now! Still sitting here. No need to throw insults."

"Sorry," they said in unison.

"Wait a minute, I didn't think I was all that."

"Oh, you did, too. Quarterback of the football team and a hotshot Short Stop on the baseball team pretty much says it all. He even had brains to boot. Can you imagine a total jock who got straight A's? The girls were lining up."

Ethan cleared his throat and looked directly at Jessica. "They may have been lining up, but I believe I was taken."

"You were taken, Dad? What was your girlfriend like?"

"Dessert anyone?" Jessica grabbed her glass of wine and downed the contents.

"No thanks," Ethan and Chrissie answered.

"So, Dad, what was she like? Was she like Mom?"

"Yes and no, she was very smart and funny."

"Was she pretty?"

"Of course she was. Do you think 'Mr. All That' would date an ugly girl?"

"Oh, Dad. Tell me more. Were you guys 'the couple' on campus?"

"You could say that."

"Are you sure nobody wants any dessert?" Jessica was being completely ignored. Why was he going down this road? It was so unnecessary. She refilled her glass.

"What did she look like?"

"She had long curly blond hair and incredible blue eyes. Her smile could captivate you. Oh yeah, and a body to worship and lips so soft they...."

"Dad! TMI! TMI!"

Jessica choked on her food. "Yeah, EJ, TMI!" She wasn't sure she could handle much more of this stroll down memory lane.

"Sorry." His rich laughter filled the room. "Just got caught up in the memory."

"Wow, Dad, you must have really liked her. Did you love her?"

"Sure did."

Jessica needed to put a stop to this now.

"Are you excited about going riding tomorrow? When was the last time you got to ride?" Jessica interjected in an attempt to change the subject. His "memory" was getting out of control.

"I haven't ridden in a while. Mom doesn't ride, so I only get to go with Dad. This is going to be so great to ride everyday."

"Sure is, kiddo. Now finish your supper so you can go unpack."

Chrissie finished the rest of her chicken, cleared her place setting and headed off to her room.

"She's a good kid, EJ, and so much like you it is unbelievable."

"You really think so? The poor kid."

"She not only looks like you, but she has your personality. Scary, very scary."

"She is a good kid, no thanks to me. I guess Chrissie is the one thing Kim and I did right."

Jessica felt a pain in her heart. At least he had a chance to be a crappy parent. The past started to creep up around her. Heart breaking memories were fighting their way to the forefront of her mind. She couldn't do this, not here, not now, not with him.

"I better get this cleaned up." She quickly rose to her feet and lost her balance falling into Ethan.

He wrapped his arms around her waist. "Easy, babe. Did you have a little too much wine with dinner?"

"I'm fine." She pulled out of his arms and started clearing the table.

"Let me help."

"No, that's okay, I can handle it myself."

"Hey, you cooked a great meal, and you're letting my daughter stay with you. I can at least help do the dishes."

"I really don't see you as the dishpan-hand type."

"Don't you have a dishwasher?"

Jessica let out a laugh at the look of distress on his face at the thought of no dishwasher.

"Why would I need a dishwasher?"

"Oh, wow, I guess you really don't." He paused and looked around her kitchen. "You aren't kidding, you really don't have a dishwasher in here."

"Nope, looks like it's the start of dishpan hands for you." She giggled and tossed the dishcloth at him. "You wash, I'll dry and put away."

"Okay, I guess I'll just get a manicure tomorrow."

Jessica's head snapped around. "A manicure?"

"Kidding."

"Thank goodness. I didn't really see you as the metrosexual type."

"So, would you like to join us tomorrow morning for a ride?"

"No, that's okay. You enjoy your time with your daughter. I know you haven't seen her in a month. You need to catch up."

"We did a lot of that today. I know how much you like your morning rides, and I would feel better if I could keep an eye on you while you're out there."

"So what you're really saying is that when I go for my morning ride, you and Chrissie will be joining me."

"Yeah, something like that."

"Fine, although, I really don't think it is necessary."

"Did you forget about the bale of hay that almost crushed your pretty little head?" He patted the top of her head.

"That was a freak accident."

"Yeah, just like everything else that has happened on this ranch."

"Alright, alright, you win. I will allow you and Chrissie to join me in the morning. Besides, I'd like to see how she handles Lilly just to be sure they will work out together."

"That is one thing I can assure you of, she's an excellent rider."

"Good. One less thing to worry about."

Chrissie emerged from the bedroom and yawned. "Dad, I'm all unpacked. I'm kind of tired. I think I'll go to bed if that's okay."

"Is it okay if your old man still tucks his little girl in bed?"

"Dad, I'm not a little girl anymore."

"Humor me. You'll always be my little girl."

"Okay, if it makes you feel better."

"So kind of you to indulge your father."

Jessica finished putting things away in the kitchen while Ethan said his good nights. She was busy drying the dishes when strong arms slipped around her waist. She almost jumped out of her skin at the feel of his body pressed up against hers. Her heart pounded in her chest as the scent of his musky cologne teased her nose.

"What are you doing?" She tried to turn and pull out of his embrace, but his -like arms wouldn't give.

"I can't thank you enough for doing this. I'm hoping it's not too late to do right by her," he whispered in Jessica's ear.

Between the wine and the way she felt being wrapped in his arms, Jessica thought her legs would buckle beneath her. She tried desperately to control her breathing so that she could speak.

"I'm glad I can help. I see how much you love her." She prayed her words didn't sound as breathy as she thought they did. Thank God he couldn't see her face because she was positive her cheeks were flushed with a lovely shade of pink.

"Tonight was wonderful and Chrissie likes you."

"That's nice. I'm glad. I like her, too." Jessica finished drying a plate and placed it on the counter, trying to remain busy.

Ethan turned her around to face him. She thought she was going to faint staring up into his green eyes. She had loved him so much when they were younger. But too much had happened. Her mind whirled.

"Thanks for dinner, too. I had no idea you were such a good cook."

"I'm not. I just have a few things I make well."

"I know there are other things you do well, too."

He lowered his lips to hers before she knew what was happening. His arms tightened around her, pulling her closer into him. Her eyes closed as her body relaxed into his and her arms instinctively wrapped around his neck. He deepened their kiss and parted her lips with his tongue. She was done for. Lord help her, she was falling.

"I want you, Jessie." Ethan scooped her up in his arms.

She couldn't answer; all she could do was moan. He started to move toward her bedroom when her brain finally engaged. "No. Please, no."

He stopped and looked at her. "What's wrong? I know you still love me."

"I'm not ready for this, and your fourteen-year-old daughter is in the next room. That alone is reason enough."

He let out a big sigh. "Okay, you're right." He set her back down, but didn't let go.

"It's getting late. I think maybe you should go."

"You're tossing me out now?" He smiled down at her.

"I wouldn't call it tossing, let's say, better safe than sorry. I don't think I could explain this to Chrissie, and I'm definitely certain you couldn't."

"You're right again. I wasn't thinking. Whose idea was it for her to stay with you?" He raised an eyebrow at her.

"A smart man who cares immensely about his daughter. Now, you better go before I change my mind."

"You mean there's a chance I could wear down your defenses?"

"EJ, I'm immune to your charms." She smiled up at him and brushed the palm of her hand across his cheek.

"I am getting to you. You do still love me."

"I never stopped. That's the problem."

A confused look crossed his face, and for a moment she saw regret in his eyes. What could she say? She wasn't the one who had walked away. She never would have left him.

"I guess I better go." He pulled her closer and leaned down to kiss her.

It was soft, yet asked for something more. He pulled away from her breathless body. She stared up at him, reluctant to let go but scared to hang on.

"Good night, EJ."

"Good night, Jessie." He kissed her forehead and slipped out the door.

She closed it behind him and fell back against it. What on earth was she doing? She was playing chaperone to his daughter and almost let him carry her off to bed. Wine. It was the damn wine. She knew better. They were not playing house now or ever. With a clear head, none of that would have happened, or would it have?

He was right, he was getting to her. Loving him had never been the issue. She forced her weakened legs to move and decided to head for bed herself.

When she snuggled down under the sheet and closed her eyes, Ethan came to torment her as he did every night since he had arrived. Only tonight she didn't feel tormented by the thoughts that filled her head. In fact, she felt peaceful and safe. There was no use in fighting it. His smile enchanted her and she opened her arms to the man who had stolen her heart a lifetime ago.

chapter 9

ETHAN SADDLED UP the horses and waited for his two favorite ladies, when they finally strolled into the stables.

"I was beginning to think you were going to sleep all day." Ethan hugged and kissed his daughter good morning.

"I guess I was more tired than I thought."

"And you, what's your excuse. You're always here at the crack of dawn."

"Toss up between too much wine and taking half the night to fall asleep." She smiled and walked past him to Sadie.

Yes. He was finally getting to her. It was written all over her face. She wasn't so immune to his charms after all. Maybe his daughter's visit would be just the thing to help him wear down those damn defenses. It certainly helped last night. Well, the wine didn't hurt, either. For the first time since he'd arrived, she didn't pull away from his embrace. In fact, she didn't seem to be interested in leaving it at all.

"What are you waiting for, Dad?" Chrissie and Jessie were mounted up staring at him.

"Oh, now you're in a hurry," he grumbled as he mounted Caesar.

"Oh, Dad." Chrissie laughed.

"Where to?" he asked Jessica.

"Let's go down to the creek bed. That's a nice ride."

"Ladies." Ethan took his Stetson and made a sweeping gesture for Jessie and Chrissie to move out ahead of him.

He opted to hang back. It gave him a better vantage point for searching the area, just in case anyone had any ideas. The hay bale was too close for comfort. Besides, he wanted Jessie and Chrissie to get to know each other. So far, so good. The two of them were chatting away like long lost friends.

Even though he didn't have proof, he had a feeling it was someone on the ranch. His gut told him there was no way someone could move about the place that easily undetected. If it was someone on the ranch, that would make his job much easier. He could narrow his search. It could also make his job more difficult because it would mean the person had easy access to Jessie. That thought made his stomach churn.

"Dad, Dad, hello, Dad!" Chrissie yelled at her father.

Her voice snapped him from his thoughts. "Uhh? What?"

"Good thing you're following and not leading." Chrissie picked on her dad.

"What? You two were clucking away like a couple of hens, certainly not interested in my two cents worth." He rode up between the two.

"That's not true. Jessie was just telling me about the ranch and how she fixed it up. What were you day dreaming about?"

"Just a case I need to solve. What's going on?"

"Jessie was telling me about the hay rides at night. She said you're quite popular. That's just gross."

"I thought you liked my singing."

"It's not your singing, Dad." She gave him a 'you know what I mean' look.

"Can I help it if I'm irresistible?" He grinned.

"Pleeaassee," Jessie and Chrissie chimed in unison.

"I hate to cut this love fest short, but I do have some work to do around this place before the boss gets mad. I think we should head back."

"Race ya. Last one to the barn has to muck stalls!" Jessica called out and kicked Sadie into action.

"Like I don't already!" Ethan yelled at their backs.

The three raced across the ranch neck-in-neck. Jessica leaned low and held tight to Sadie's mane as she ran like the wind.

In the end, she was the victor.

"Chrissie, do you want to help me cool off the horses and give them a rub down?" Jessica asked as she reined up in front of the barn.

"Sure."

Jeremy stepped out of the stables. "Hi Aunt Jess, do you want me to take care of your horses?"

"Hi Jeremy, we're fine, but you could take EJ's horse so he can go finish up his work."

"Sure thing."

"Who's that?" Chrissie asked.

Jessica saw Chrissie's eyes wander up and down Jeremy as he walked past. "That's my nephew, Jeremy. He's working on the ranch this summer."

"He's here all summer?"

"Yes." She saw the wheels churning in Chrissie's head. Great, she was interested in boys. This ought to be fun. Hopefully, her interest was only through her eyes and not any other part of her body. Jessica led Chrissie and the horses around the courtyard in front of the stables a few times, and then proceeded to give them a rub down in their stalls.

Chrissie was more interested in watching Jeremy than she was in giving Lilly a good brushing. Thank goodness he was too busy feeding the other horses and wasn't paying attention to the eyes that followed him.

"Ahhh," Jeremy yelled, jumping back away from the rattling sound. "Holy crap!"

"Dad!" Chrissie screamed at the top of her lungs.

Jessica dropped her brush as she tried to get out of Sadie's stall, and Ethan came tearing into the stables.

Jeremy stood motionless, backed into a corner.

"Oh my God! EJ, do something!" Jessica yelled.

"Don't anybody move. Jeremy, don't even breathe."

The diamond-back rattlesnake was curled up ready to strike, its rattle sounded the alarm. Ethan reached for a pitchfork.

"Jessie, my gun is in the bunkhouse, in my trunk. Go get it, and fast."

Jessica took off out of the barn as he instructed. Ethan held the pitchfork in his hands ready to pierce the hostile creature. He crept forward slowly, not wanting to startle the snake. One false move and somebody would be going to the hospital.

Like a streak of lightening, Ethan speared the snake. It hissed and tried to lurch. Jessica ran back in, gasping for air.

"Here. Oh God! What are you going to do?" She handed the gun to Ethan.

"Okay, Jeremy, you can move now. It's not going anywhere." With pitchfork in hand and snake attached, Ethan proceeded to slide the snake across the floor and out the door. "Here, Jessie, you hold the pitchfork."

"What?" she screeched.

"It can't hurt you. Hold the pitchfork."

Jessica did as she was told. Jeremy and Chrissie stood in the doorway watching. Ethan took his gun and fired one shot. Chrissie turned her head into Jeremy's shoulder. Their nemesis was dead. Adam and Aaron came running up to the stable, Scott pulling up the rear on his crutches.

"Did we hear a gun shot?" Scott asked breathless.

"Yeah, what's going on?" Aaron asked.

"That tried to take a chunk out of me." Jeremy pointed to the dead snake.

"Damn, you're lucky, dude." Adam looked down at the snake and back at Jeremy.

"Where the hell did that snake come from?" Ethan asked after he disposed of the creature.

"I was going to get feed out of the barrel. I lifted the lid, and it sprang out at me. It almost nailed me. Thank God I jumped backwards."

"The snake was in the feed barrel?" Ethan gave Jessica a look.

"Yeah, sure glad I didn't stick my hand down in there." Jeremy breathed a sigh of relief.

"Jess, ever have a problem with snakes in the feed before?" Ethan was ticked.

"Never. I suppose it's possible it came from the grain mill that way. Oh, EJ, please don't say it. I know what you're thinking." She walked back to Sadie's stall.

Ethan followed. "Jess, that was no accident. Weren't you standing in that exact spot yesterday when the hay bale fell?"

"Damn it! You think that snake was meant for me."

"Yeah, I do. Same spot, almost same time. You normally feed Sadie after your ride."

"I'm getting really tired of this. When you find out who this person is, I get first shot at them. Nobody threatens my family." Jessica turned on her heel, slammed out of the stall and stomped out of the stable.

"Dad, what's wrong? What's going on? Is your case here?"

"Chrissie, you really should go back to the lodge." He put his arm around her shoulder. He didn't need for the hired hands to find out he was the sheriff and what he was really doing on the ranch.

"Don't, Dad." Chrissie shrugged off his arm and turned to look at him. "I'm not a baby. What's going on? Is somebody trying to hurt people here?"

Ethan ushered her into Sadie's stall and lowered his voice to barely above a whisper. "Yeah, honey, they are. That's why I'm here. Somebody wants to sabotage Jessie's ranch, and I'm trying to find out who and why." Ethan took her by the shoulders. "Only a few people know I'm the sheriff. I'm working undercover. You have to promise me you'll be careful. Okay?"

"Yeah, Dad. I promise."

Ethan exited the stall. "Jeremy, are you okay?" Ethan walked over and patted him on the shoulder.

"Yeah, thanks for helping me out. Might've ended up standing there for a while if you hadn't been around."

"I'm just glad you're okay. I guess we all need to be more careful until we find out who's doing these things."

"You can be sure I will. I'll catch ya later, Ethan." Jeremy headed out of the barn with the other guys as Joe came storming in.

"What the hell is going on? I heard gun shots."

"Rattlesnake in the feed barrel," Ethan said.

"What? We've never had an issue with snakes."

"I know, Joe."

"This is getting out of hand. Nobody is safe, and Miss Jessica can't afford to have anyone else get hurt."

"I agree."

"What the hell kind of cop are you? How come you haven't figured out who's doing this, yet?"

"I'm working on it, Joe. This is a busy place with a lot of people who could be possible suspects."

"I suppose you have a point. I'm sorry, Ethan. I worry about something else happening to Miss Jessica or someone else."

"Don't worry. I'll look out for her." Ethan patted Joe on the shoulder.

※

The rest of the day passed without incident. Jessica decided to lock herself in her office. If they were after her, she was going to make it difficult. She hadn't even bothered to go to dinner. She just hoped they wouldn't end up targeting her friends and family next.

Someone lightly tapped on her office door.

"Come in."

"Sorry to disturb you, Miss Jessica, I didn't see you at dinner, so I brought you some tea and a ham sandwich. I heard about Jeremy and thought perhaps you didn't feel like dinner with a crowd."

"Maddie, thank you. You take such good care of me."

"Not a problem." Maddie placed the tray on Jessica's desk.

"I wasn't hungry earlier, but now I'm famished."

"Can I get you anything else?"

"No Maddie, I'm good. Thank you for keeping an eye on me."

"Someone has to take care of you because you're too busy taking care of everyone else. Without you, there'd be no ranch."

"That's my job."

"And this is my job. Are you sure you're okay? That cowboy isn't giving you a hard time is he?"

"Who, Ethan?"

"Yeah, I told you he has been watching you. You be careful he doesn't hurt you."

"Don't worry, Maddie, I won't give him the chance to hurt me."

"How well do you know him? You just say the word, and I'll go get Joe to throw his hunky butt out the door."

Jessica laughed. "Maddie, we've known each other forever. He even knows Laurie. We're safe, I promise."

"Okay, but I don't like seeing you stressed out, and I can tell you've got a lot on your mind."

"I'll be fine, honest."

"Okay, but if you need anything, you call me."

"Thanks, Maddie, I will."

Maddie left her alone, and Jessica sipped her tea and enjoyed the sandwich. She was lost in thought when she glanced down at her watch and realized it was time for the evening hayride. She had missed last night, and so did Ethan. She had to make an appearance so gossip wouldn't get started, especially after his display at dinner the other night.

Locking up her office, she went to seek out Laurie. She wondered if Laurie knew what happened today with Jeremy. Since Laurie hadn't come flying into her office, she wasn't sure. Perhaps she sought out Ethan instead. A small pang of jealousy poked at her heart. She finally admitted to herself that she didn't like the idea of anyone finding comfort in Ethan's arms.

Jessica wandered through the courtyard that was a buzz of activity. A group of ladies was preparing for an evening hike, and she stopped to chat.

"Hey, Jessica." Missy waived to her.

"Hi Missy, what's going on?"

"I talked to my husband today. He misses me so much. I told him how I felt about things. I was a bit of a coward because I did it over the phone, but I made it very clear things were going to change."

"What did he say?"

"He was quiet at first, but as I continued to explain to him what I wanted, he started to understand. We had the best talk. I can't wait to go home and see him."

"Missy, that's wonderful, I'm so happy for you." She hugged her.

"Thanks to you and your seminars here, I saw what the problem was and had the courage to fix it."

"I'm so glad we could help."

When Jessica finally made her way to the front porch, the wagons had already been pulled around. Laurie was standing with Ethan and Chrissie.

"Hi guys." Jessica approached the threesome.

"Nice of you to join us." Ethan picked at her.

She just smiled at him. "Laurie, can I talk to you?"

"Sure."

The two women walked over to an empty part of the porch.

"Laurie…"

"Stop. You don't need to say a thing. Ethan told me what happened. It's not your fault, and he is here trying to help us."

"I know, but what if Jeremy had gotten hurt. I couldn't live with that. This person's beef is with me, not those that I love. Maybe he should go back home to Keith."

"Are you crazy? My son is my world, and I'm not ready to give him up so soon. I know I went a little crazy on you earlier, but that was before Ethan was here. He's trying to figure this out, so it's not like you're ignoring it. I promise that if it gets too dicey, I'll send him home."

"Are you sure?"

"Positive. We're here for you. Both our lives are here at this ranch. You don't have to handle this alone."

"Thanks. I'm just glad he's okay." Jessica reached out and hugged Laurie.

"Me, too. So, how's it going with Ethan and Chrissie? I was dying to ask you how dinner went last night. After what happened with Jeremy, I thought you might want to be alone. So give it up."

"Chrissie is a great kid. She's so much like Ethan. She adores her father in spite of what he thinks."

"And what else?"

Jessica pursed her lips together in disgust at Laurie's ability to dig deeper. "Ethan and Chrissie decided to take a stroll down memory lane back to our college days."

"Oh...ouch."

"It was okay. She was curious about what her dork of a dad was like back then."

"What else happened?"

"Nothing else happened. Why do you ask?"

"Because of the flush that just spread across your cheeks when I asked says you're lying."

"I had too much wine, that's all."

"Jessica Lynn Montgomery, I am your best friend and holding out on me is against the rules. Speak woman."

Jessica sighed. "Laurie, this is getting too complicated. I can't do this."

"Can't do what, have feelings for him?"

"Yes."

"Why?"

"Because of what happened between us. Because of what always happens to me."

"Jess, people make mistakes, they learn from them and they change. You don't have to repeat the past. Why can't you give him a second chance?"

"He has a family, and I don't."

"So, his family becomes your family."

"*His* family was supposed to <u>be</u> my family. It hurts just to look at her."

"I know I don't have a clue how you feel about not having your own children, but that never stopped you from loving your nieces and nephews and even Jeremy."

"It's different."

"What happened that has you so rattled?"

"He keeps apologizing. He wants that second chance."

"Okay, so what's so bad about that? I'm sensing maybe you would actually like to forgive him and try again."

"Don't ever allow me to drink around him again."

A smirk crept across Laurie's face. "What did you do?"

"I almost allowed him to carry me off to bed." Jessica buried her face in her hands.

"You what!" Laurie squealed.

"Shhhh!"

"Sorry." Laurie lowered her voice to a whisper. "You mean you almost slept with him? Honey, you are obviously ready to forgive him."

"It was the wine."

"Yeah, use whatever excuse you want. You still love him. You know Jessica, you can be angry with Ethan for breaking your heart, but you're the one that made the choices that effected the rest of your life."

"But he's the one that started the horrible chain of events."

"And you were the only one who could stop it and you didn't. We may not be able to control what others do to us, but we can certainly control how we react. Isn't it time to put an end to this?"

"Alright, enough. Let's get this hayride on the road." Jessica walked away from Laurie, past Ethan and jumped up on the second wagon. She tried to make conversation with the women already seated on the wagon, but Laurie's words kept rattling around in her head.

"Is this seat taken?"

"No, go ahead." She closed her eyes tight and winced. Her mouth opened before her brain engaged. The lag time in her brain's ability to react appropriately was really beginning to annoy her. She was slowly unraveling. The walls she had built around her heart were beginning to crumble. She turned to look at Ethan who was getting comfortable next to her as Chrissie sat next to him.

"Nice night. Are you doing okay after this afternoon?" he asked.

"I'm fine, thanks. Are you having fun, Chrissie?" Jessica asked, hoping to engage his daughter instead of him.

"Dad and I had a great afternoon once the drama was over."

"Good. Maybe we can relax and enjoy the evening." Jessica settled back against a hay bale. Relax, yes, she just needed to relax and give her emotions a chance to settle down.

"Are you going to sing for us, Ethan?" A well-endowed brunette asked as she flashed him an inviting smile.

Jessica caught the look on Chrissie's face as she rolled her eyes.

"Absolutely, ladies. Give me a moment to ponder a tune."

Jessica leaned over to him. "I liked you better when you just drove the wagon," she whispered.

Ethan chuckled. "Jealous?"

"Not on your life."

"Okay, ladies, you might have noticed this beautiful girl here next to me..."

"Way to go, Jessica!" someone shouted out.

"Not me ladies, not me!" she yelled back to the woman on the wagon behind them.

"I was referring to my beautiful daughter, ladies. This song is for her." Ethan began to strum his guitar. He started to sing Colin Raye's 'I think about you'.

When he finished, the crowd of women roared with appreciation and applauded loudly. Chrissie threw her arms around her father's neck for a big hug and kissed his cheek. A big 'awww' sounded from the group on the wagon at the display of affection between father and daughter.

Several songs later and the wagons rolled up in front of the lodge. Jessica was busy discussing some things with a couple of her guests when she noticed Chrissie walking away with Jeremy. Ethan was helping the ladies off the wagon and hadn't noticed his daughter's disappearance.

"Excuse me, ladies, I have something I need to take of care." Jessica followed the two as they walked around the side of the porch.

She found Chrissie leaning up against the lodge, and Jeremy leaning into her. Both were deeply engrossed in their conversation.

"Hi, kids! What's going on?"

Jeremy jumped. "Aunt Jess, we were umm just talking."

"I'm sure you were."

"No big deal, right?"

"Nope, no big deal. Oh, yeah, when I introduced Chrissie today, I bet I forgot to mention that she is only fourteen." Jessica caught the nasty glare Chrissie gave her.

"Aunt Jess! I didn't know. I uhhh…"

"I know you didn't. Now you do."

"I've gotta finish taking care of the horses. I'll see you later." Jeremy was off like a shot back to the wagons.

"Shall we?" Jessica motioned toward the front of the lodge.

Chrissie stomped past Jessica. "Thanks a lot."

Jessica just shook her head and followed the girl. Obviously, she had not misinterpreted the looks Chrissie gave Jeremy earlier. Great, just what she needed: a teenager with over-active hormones. That was not part of the babysitting deal.

"Hey, Jess?"

"Yeah." She walked up to stand next to Ethan.

"I'm going to take the horses to the stables and bed them down, then I'll be back to say good night."

"Okay. We'll be here." Jessica watched Ethan head off to the stables with the horses. She noticed Chrissie sat in one of the rockers on the porch with her arms crossed.

Jessica walked over to her. "Mind if I sit here?"

"Suit yourself."

"I thought you were having a good time."

"I was."

"Was? I'm not going to say anything to your dad, if that's what you're thinking."

Chrissie's head swung up to look at Jessica. "You're not?"

"No, under one condition."

"Oh, what's that?"

"You have to promise you won't sneak off with Jeremy again. You're too young for him."

"No, I'm not." She started to protest.

Jessica cut her off with a wave of her hand. "Chrissie, do you promise?"

"Yes, I promise." She frowned.

"Good, because after your father saved him today, I don't want him to turn around and have to kill him." Jessica tried to joke to lighten the mood. "Spilt blood just isn't good for business."

Chrissie giggled. "I guess you're right. Thanks."

"You're welcome. Oh, look, here comes your dad now."

"Are you two ready to turn in?" Ethan asked as he took the steps two at a time.

"I am. It's been a long day." Jessica stood and stretched.

"Yeah, I guess I'm tired, too." Chrissie joined Jessica.

"I'll walk you two to your suite."

"That's not necessary."

"I know, but I want to tuck my little girl in while she'll still let me." Ethan put his arm around Chrissie.

"Oh, Dad." She rolled her eyes at him.

"Oh, Dad what? You'll always be my little girl so get used to it." He messed up her hair.

"Okay you two, let's go." Jessica led the way to her suite.

Ethan tucked Chrissie in bed and said his goodnights. Jessica sat in the living room waiting for him.

"I'm gonna turn in." He started for the door.

"EJ, before you go."

He stopped. "Yeah, what is it."

Jessica rose and walked over to him. "Thank you for saving Jeremy today. I don't know what we would have done if you hadn't been here."

"You're welcome."

"You have that look. You really believe it is someone here on the ranch don't you?"

"I'm afraid I do. Somebody would have to notice a stranger sooner or later. It has to be someone who works here."

"EJ, that's not good. If they work here, they have access to everything."

"Especially to you."

"You still think the snake was meant for me?"

"You ride every morning, and then you feed Sadie. First the saddle, then the hay bale, now the feed barrel. Obviously, someone is watching your every move, learning your habits."

"So, what do I do?"

"Change your habits. Don't do the same things you always do. Ride Sadie at different times, eat at different times, take different routes to go places."

"You're scaring me."

Ethan caressed her cheek and put his arms around her waist, hugging her to him. "You should be scared. This isn't a game anymore."

"Great." She rested her head on his shoulder. Her body was tired, and she leaned into him trying to sap some strength from him.

"Will you be okay?"

"I'm fine. You can go. I'm going to turn in."

"If you need me, just yell." Ethan kissed the top of her head and left.

Jessica was exhausted. She trudged into her bedroom and turned down her bed. The blood-curdling scream that escaped her lips could have woken the dead.

"Ethan!" she screamed at the top of her lungs.

Chrissie came running into her room. "Jessie, what's wrong?"

"Go get your father, now!"

Chrissie ran to the door and yelled down the hallway for her dad. Ethan hadn't gotten far and came running around the corner.

"What's wrong?" He grabbed Chrissie by the shoulders.

"It's Jessie. Something is wrong." Chrissie cried.

Ethan tore into her bedroom and found Jessie standing there crying.

He pulled her into his arms. "What happened?"

"Look." She pointed to her bed, soaked with bloody sheets, and then turned in his arms and buried her face in his shoulder.

Lying in the middle of her bed was a decapitated rat. She couldn't hold them back anymore. The sobs racked her body as Ethan held her close.

"Dad, what's going on?"

"Chrissie, go back to your room. Everything will be okay."

"But, Dad."

"Christina, I said go back to your room." His stern voice made her turn and leave. "Jess, let's go out in the living room. I'll dispose of this."

Ethan guided her to a chair and sat her down. He returned to her room, gathered up the sheets, rat and all and hurried them out the door. She couldn't look at the pile he carried.

Chrissie came running out of her room and knelt down in front of Jessica. "What happened? Are you okay?"

"I'm sorry. I must have scared you half to death. Yes, I'm fine. Your father will take care of everything."

Ethan returned to Jessica's suite. "Is everybody okay?"

"We're fine."

"Chrissie, it's okay. You can go back to bed."

"Are you sure, Dad?"

"Positive." Ethan kissed the top of her head, and she returned to her room. He knelt down in front of Jessica.

She was shaking like a leaf. "EJ, he was here. He was in my suite, in my bedroom."

"I know. It's not safe for you. We need to move you to a different place."

"And endanger someone else? I don't think so. Whoever this person is, they are not going to drive me out of my own place. I'm not leaving. I won't let them win."

"Jessie, I don't think that's a good idea."

"I don't care. I'm not leaving. End of story." She folded her arms across her chest in defiance.

"Fine. Then I'm moving in."

"What!"

"If you won't leave, then I'm moving in."

"You can't stay here."

"Damn it, I'm moving into this suite whether you like it or not. It's not just about you anymore, Jess. My daughter is staying under this roof, too."

"My point exactly! Your daughter is here. What will she think?"

"Think? She'll think I'm protecting you."

"In my bedroom?"

"Jessie, you would let me share your bed?" A smirk started to creep up at the corner of his lips. "I thought I would sleep in your other bedroom."

"I knew that," she stammered. "I mean, what will people say? They don't know I have a third bedroom. They don't know what goes on behind closed doors. I can only imagine what they will think."

"Nobody but us has to know I'm staying here. I promise I will be as discreet as possible. Do you think housekeeping will say anything?"

"Maddie would never gossip about me." She could only imagine what Maddie would think of this little arrangement. "What about Chrissie? Maybe it's not safe for her. Maybe she should go stay with Laurie."

"Ummm, that's not a bad idea. Then we could be alone."

Jessica glared at him. "This isn't funny. Is it safe for her to be around me?"

"I would never put her life in danger. As long as I'm around, I will protect you both. I don't want to be distracted worrying about her somewhere else."

"Okay, fine. You win. I don't have the energy to fight anymore."

"Now, that would be nice for a change."

She raised an eyebrow at him. "I can always change my mind."

"I guess I'll quit while I'm ahead."

"One thing."

"What's that?"

"We burn that mattress. There is no way I'm going to sleep on that thing. I'll have nightmares. We'll get a new one tomorrow."

"You got it. Do you think you can sleep?"

"I don't know."

"Why don't you go sleep in the other bedroom, and I'll stay on the couch. I want to go over your bedroom with a fine-toothcomb in the morning. I can only pray that this time they left a clue behind."

"You're kind of big for my couch."

"I've slept in worse places. All I need is a blanket and pillow."

Jessica went and retrieved the items from the closet. "Are you sure you can sleep on this?" She laid them on the couch.

"Positive. Now let's get you in bed." He put his arm around her and ushered her toward the bedroom.

"I beg your pardon?"

"Sleep, you need sleep." He pushed her into the spare bedroom. "Now crawl in."

Jessica was too tired to argue. Too much had happened, and she was drained. She settled into the bed and pulled the sheet up to her chin.

"Good night." Ethan leaned down and kissed her forehead.

"Good night, and thank you for being here, again."

"I wouldn't be anywhere else." He turned off the light and left the room.

Jessica closed her eyes. For once she actually felt relieved knowing Ethan was there to protect her. Yes, protect her. She never dreamed the one person she swore to keep out of her life would be the one she needed most in her life.

chapter 10

Jessica couldn't sleep. The clock glowed five-thirty a.m. as she slid out of bed and tiptoed into the kitchen. Ethan was snoring on the couch, looking rather uncomfortable. She started a pot of coffee as quietly as she could.

A few minutes later a pair of strong arms were placed on either side of her, pinning her to the counter. "Couldn't sleep?"

She jumped at his touch. The soft whisper of his voice tickled her ear. She never heard him walk up behind her. "Are you trying to give me a heart attack?" She turned to face him, putting her hands on his chest, attempting to put some space between them.

"I would never dream of it. Did I scare you?"

"Yeah, I guess I'm a little jumpy knowing that he was in here."

"I'm sorry."

"It's okay. I started some coffee. It should be ready soon. Did you get any sleep? You looked so uncomfortable."

"I got some. I'm hoping the bed will be more comfortable tonight."

"Yes, it will be. Speaking of beds, that is my first order of business today. That mattress is out of here. I don't need that reminder around."

"I'll help you. I really think you need to lay low for a while."

"EJ, you know I'm not going to do that. I'll be careful and I'll do what you said and change my routine, but I'm not hiding."

"I keep forgetting how stubborn you are."

"I'm sure there a lot of things you forgot."

"There are a lot I remember, too." He leaned down, tightened his arms around her waist and kissed her deeply. "I remember how soft your lips are and how sweet they taste."

She was backed up against the counter, and he pressed into her to prevent her from going anywhere as his lips consumed hers again. Her eyes fluttered shut and she let him kiss her the way she remembered all those years ago. Her arms instinctively wrapped around his neck. He was stealing her heart away. His hands roamed up over her hips and tickled her sides. She felt the steel of his hard body pressed against hers through the sheerness of her nightgown. Her knees were ready to give way beneath her.

She wanted him.

Ethan pulled away. "Coffee?"

"Uhh?" She was stunned by the sudden loss of his touch and grabbed onto the counter to steady herself.

"Coffee. Would you like some coffee?"

She stared at him for a moment until the aroma tantalized her senses and her brain registered what he was asking. He was teasing her. He wanted her to want him, and it was starting to work. "Yeah, coffee sounds good." She tried to compose herself.

"Allow me." Ethan grabbed a couple of mugs on the counter and poured the coffee.

"Can I make you breakfast?"

"First dinner, now breakfast, what next? Dessert? Perhaps a nightcap? Now we're talking." He winked, flashing her a devilish grin.

"Don't push your luck." She laughed.

Jessie cooked a couple of eggs, sunny side up and toast. "It's not as good as what they make in the kitchen, but you won't starve."

"Smells good to me. Hey, do you remember the time we went to my parents' camp and we had to fend for ourselves? You had no idea how to cook anything." Ethan chuckled.

"I don't recall you being any help." She sat down at the table.

"You're the girl."

"Where does it say it's the woman's job to know how to cook?"

"It's the world as it should be."

Jessica threw a napkin at him. "Why, you male chauvinist. So, I guess I was born the wrong sex."

"Oh, I would say your sex is just fine?"

"EJ!" She quickly rose from the table to fill her cup with more coffee. She couldn't handle the thought of Ethan picturing 'her sex'. Thank God he had pulled away when he did. She was losing her mind and control.

"Jess, in all seriousness, you've got to be careful. I know you think this has to do with the people around here thinking you're running a brothel, but that just doesn't sit right with me."

"Why not, what are you thinking?"

"Well, if people disapprove of the ranch, it's because of their morals and religious beliefs. I don't see them resorting to violence. Are you sure there isn't something we're over looking?"

"Like what?"

"Revenge. Payback."

"Who would want revenge or payback?"

"Maybe Keith or some other ticked off husband, some former guest who left unhappy."

"No one comes to mind, but I'll keep thinking."

"Hey, what's going on?" Chrissie stumbled out into the kitchen, rubbing the sleep from her eyes.

"Good morning, Sweet Pea. Did we wake you?"

"Yeah, I heard a lot of laughter. What are you two doing?"

"We're having breakfast. Are you hungry?"

"Not right now. It's way too early to eat."

"We're going to head out to the stables in a little while for a morning ride. Do you want to come?" Ethan asked.

"A morning ride? Yeah sure. I'll go get dressed."

"I should get going. I'll see you at the stables in a little while. Please be careful, okay?" Ethan rose from the table.

"I will. Promise." Jessica crossed her heart and then her fingers.

She went and got dressed herself. When Chrissie was ready, they walked out to the stables. Jessica detoured through the kitchen. Chrissie grabbed an apple to eat, and she grabbed some carrots for Sadie, Lilly and Caesar.

Ethan was waiting as usual with their horses already saddled. "It's about time you two showed up."

"Sorry. We had to get treats." Jessica held up the carrots.

"Before we go, I've gotta check on Rocky. He acted like he had an issue with his shoe."

"Do you want me to come?"

"No, Rocky is a good boy. I've got it covered." Ethan walked into the corral where the draft horses were grazing.

He patted Rocky on the neck and gently lifted the Clysdale's leg and checked his hoof.

"Is he okay?" Jessica called out.

"It looks like he has a stone under his shoe. We'll have to call the Ferrier." Ethan put Rocky's foot back down.

Ethan heard Duke let out a snort and before he could turn around to see what the problem was, Rocky, Baron, Dutchess and Dehlia were snorting and stomping their hooves in distress.

"Ethan, look out!" Jessica yelled.

"Daddy!" Chrissie screamed.

He didn't see them coming. Before he knew what hit him, Ethan was knocked to the ground by a ton of horseflesh. Huge hooves frantically stomped over him, trampling various parts of his body.

"Ethan!" Jessica scrambled over the fence as fast as she could, trying to get to his limp body. "Help! Somebody help us!"

Ethan laid face down in the dirt. He wasn't moving. Several of the wranglers came running, some to Jessica's side and others to settle the horses down.

"Oh, God, EJ! EJ, talk to me." Jessica ran to his side and dropped to her knees. She caressed his face. "Ethan, wake up. Oh, God, please be okay," she cried.

Ethan groaned and tried to move, his hands flew to his head. Blood oozed from a large gash across his forehead and covered his fingers. He moaned again, and then his hands fell to his side and he didn't move again.

Jessica ran her hands over his body to see if anything was visibly broken. She didn't see any signs.

"Daddy! Is he okay?" Chrissie cried, dropping down next to Jessica.

"It's okay. Your Dad will be okay. Why don't you go get nurse Cindy and tell Laurie to call Doc Anderson and bring the first-aide kit."

"But..."

"Please, Chrissie, go get Laurie."

Chrissie jumped up and ran to get Laurie.

"Aunt Jess! What happened? Is Ethan okay?" Jeremy asked, dropping down next to her.

"Can you guys help me get him to the lodge?"

"Sure." Jeremy and the rest of the other guys grabbed a blanket and then gently rolled Ethan onto it, so they could carry him.

Laurie came running up with Chrissie and Nurse Cindy. "Chrissie said Ethan was hurt. How bad is it? I called Jamie. She is on her way."

"Thanks," Jessica said.

"I think he'll be okay. He just got pounded pretty good by the horses. He might have a concussion," Cindy said after quickly checking Ethan over. "You can move him."

"Okay, follow me." Jessica led them to her suite.

"I'll wait for Jamie out front," Laurie offered.

"Good idea." Jessica had the guys put Ethan in her spare bedroom. Chrissie sat by his side, holding his hand.

"Daddy, wake up. Please wake-up," she cried.

"It'll be okay."

Laurie poked her head in the door. "Jess, Jamie is here."

She rose and greeted the doctor. "Jamie, thanks so much for coming."

Jessica had befriended Jamie Anderson at the local clinic when she came down with a sinus infection. Jamie was one of the attending physicians, and Jessica liked her instantly. Also new in town, the two found it easy to become quick friends.

"Jessica, what's going on?" Jamie set her medical bag down on the night stand.

"He got trampled by the draft horses. I didn't see any visible signs of broken bones, but he's got a pretty good gash on his head."

"Has he gained consciousness?"

"Not really. He moaned and tried to move, but that was it."

"Okay, let me take a look." Jamie began her examination.

"Chrissie, why don't we wait outside?" Jessica took her by the shoulder and led her out into the living room where Laurie was waiting.

Fifteen minutes later, Jamie emerged from the bedroom.

Jessica jumped to her feet when she saw her. "How is he?"

"I had to put some stitches in the gash. It doesn't appear that anything is broken, but you were correct, he does have a concussion. You're going to have to keep an eye on him. When he wakes up, if he is experiencing any pain besides a headache, has slurred speech, abnormal pupils or balance issues, bring him in right away."

"Absolutely. We'll watch him."

"He's probably going to be fatigued and nauseous for a day or two."

"Jamie, I can't thank you enough." She hugged her friend.

"Anytime, Jessica."

"I'll walk you out," Laurie said.

Jamie fit right in on the ranch and often helped them out when things were beyond what Cindy felt comfortable with. Jamie had also experienced her fair share of tragedy, having lost her husband and five-year-old daughter in a plane crash.

Jessica returned to the bedroom and sat next to Ethan. She ran her fingers across Ethan's forehead where Jamie had placed a bandage.

"You're going to be fine. Do you hear me, EJ? You have to be okay." She leaned over and kissed his cheek.

"You care a lot about my dad, don't you?" Chrissie was standing in the door, watching Jessica.

"Yeah, I do." Jessica struggled with the over-whelming emotions swallowing her up. She did care about him, more than she ever thought she would or should again.

Who was she kidding? She had never stopped caring. Yeah, she had moved on with her life, but the truth was, he had never completely left her heart. In spite of the hurt she felt, a part of her never let him go. But that didn't mean she was prepared to keep him, either.

"Why don't you sit with him?" Jessica got up so Chrissie could sit.

"Ohhh..." Ethan moaned and tried to move.

"Daddy!" Chrissie leaned over and hugged her dad.

"Ummm, hey, Sweet Pea," he groaned out and wrapped his arms around his daughter. His gaze drifted to Jessica.

"Hey there, how are you feeling?" She moved to stand next to the bed.

"Like I was trampled by a herd of horses."

"You were."

"I remember checking Rocky. What happened?"

"I have no idea. One minute the horses were fine, the next they panicked. Something spooked them."

"Chrissie, how about going and getting your dad a glass of water?"

"Okay." Chrissie jumped up and left the room.

"Jess, what spooked the horses?" His voice was a weak and shaky whisper.

"I don't know."

"This wasn't an accident." He groaned again as he tried to sit up.

"Here, let me help you." Jessica fluffed his pillows. "You think it was the person targeting me?"

"I wouldn't be surprised. Do you remember who was around the stables?"

You Still Love Me

"No, I wasn't paying attention. Why don't you just rest? We'll talk about this later." She saw his eyes start to flutter closed.

Chrissie returned with the water. "Here ya go, Dad."

"Thanks, Sweet Pea." He took the glass, sipped the water and handed it back.

"I think your dad needs to rest."

"I'll be outside if you need me, Dad." Chrissie leaned over and kissed him.

Jessica and Chrissie retreated to the living room so they could be close by in case Ethan needed anything.

"I didn't know you cared so much about my dad."

"He's a good friend and trying to help me with a problem."

"He told me someone is trying to hurt people here on the ranch. Now that they've hurt Dad, who's going to protect us?"

"We can take care of ourselves. We're strong and capable. We'll just be extra careful. Your dad is really tough, and I think he's going to get better real fast. We'll make him proud."

"I hope so." Chrissie sighed and plopped down onto the couch.

"In the meantime, I think we should stick close by so that no one can hurt him or us. What do you think?"

"That sounds good. You know he likes you, too. I can see it in both your eyes."

Jessica didn't know what to say. Feelings. What feelings? Feelings she swore she wouldn't have? She knew she was fighting a losing battle, but she had no idea her feelings were visible. If Chrissie saw them, who else saw them? She sank down into her overstuffed chair and grabbed a book. She needed to gain control of the situation. Somehow, someway, she needed to be in control again.

※

Ethan laid low the next couple of days, allowing his body a little time to heal. His head was still attached which was encouraging. He struggled to dress with his uncooperative limbs, and a groan escaped his lips as he pulled on his jeans. Bending to tie his boots wasn't much easier. He left the room to find Chrissie and Jessica eating breakfast in the kitchen.

"Good morning."

"Dad!" Chrissie jumped up and ran to hug him.

"Hey, nice to see you back among the living." Jessica smiled up at him. "How are you feeling?"

"Better. My headache is gone, and my body is almost willing to move. I guess I would say I'm feeling pretty darn lucky. Jamie came by yesterday and said I could join the living again."

"Glad to hear it."

"Any new developments since I've been out of commission?"

"No, Chrissie and I spent most of our time with you so there wasn't an opportunity, at least not if they were targeting me. Laurie and Jeremy were on their toes. Thank goodness all is quiet."

"Good."

"Maybe this person found out they hurt the new sheriff and beat feet out of here."

"We can only hope." Ethan sat down at the table with them.

"Let me fix you something to eat. Coffee?"

"That sounds great." Ethan watched Jessica as she busied herself in the kitchen. She was different. The way she had taken care of him, sitting by his bedside when he had first gotten injured, all told him she still had feelings. The last couple of days there had been no indication she was still angry with him.

"Here you go." She placed eggs, toast and coffee in front of him.

"What are your plans for today?" Ethan asked.

"I really need to spend some time in my office. I have a pile of work to do. I need to play catch up."

"Good. I won't have to worry about you getting into trouble. I should get back to the stables. I'm sure everyone is talking."

"Yeah, I think they are. According to Laurie, you've been missed immensely on the hayrides."

"I bet they'd like to play nurse maid to ya, Dad," Chrissie said with disgust.

"Ummm...I might have to think about that. Could be fun." He joked.

"Daaaddd, I don't need that picture in my head."

"Chrissie, what are your plans?"

"Laurie said I could hang with her today. I get to be her assistant director."

"Good, then I won't have to worry about you, either."

"Nope, we'll both be good." Jessica smiled at him.

"I'll see you later then." Ethan downed the rest of his coffee and rose from the table. He leaned over to hug and kiss Chrissie. Then he moved around the table and leaned down and kissed Jessica on her cheek.

Jessica looked up at him with surprise. "What was that for?"

"To thank you for taking care of me." He quickly left the room before she had a chance to comment. Time. The time was helping, and he was pretty sure he was knocking down those walls she had put up. It may only be one brick at a time, but he was making progress. There was no doubt in his mind she still loved him.

He made his way through the lodge, receiving greetings from many of the ladies. Some offered to nurse him back to health, and many asked when he would be returning to the hay rides. Apparently, they really had missed his singing.

Ethan contemplated what to do next. The horses weren't spooked by something, but more like someone. He scratched his head. Who? Who could it possibly be? He had gotten to know the wranglers pretty well and was fairly certain it wasn't one of them. He supposed it could be one of the maintenance guys or the guy who did the hiking and biking tours. They would be next on his list to befriend. He went in search of Ralph, Henry, Dusty and Norm.

chapter 11

THE FINANCIAL LEDGERS covered Jessica's desk, as she skimmed over the numbers and prepared to write checks to pay bills. She needed to step up her marketing campaign if she wanted to keep the guests rolling in. The finances seemed never ending. She wanted to add more spa features and inspirational classes, then there was continual upkeep. 'Money makes the world go round,' was an understatement.

A light knock sounded at the door. "Come in."

"Hey, Jess, what's going on?" Laurie entered and flopped down in one of the chairs in front of her desk.

Jessica put down the invoices she had been reviewing. "Just trying to make sure that at least the financial end of this ranch still runs smoothly. What's up?"

"Nothing. I saw Ethan back down at the stables. He looks all right. I'm assuming everything is okay."

"Jamie told him he could go back to work."

"You were pretty worried." Laurie leaned forward and rested her chin in her hands.

"Your point?"

"It's written all over your face."

That answered her question about whether or not Chrissie was the only one who saw her feelings. "What? Worry? I'm concerned about anyone who gets hurt on my ranch. Especially people I care about."

"Umm hmm. I thought so." Laurie nodded as a smirk turned up the corners of her lips.

"You thought so what?" She was going to play dumb.

"I know. No point in denying it any longer."

"I'm not denying anything." Okay, so maybe she did care more than she wanted. It didn't mean she had to admit to it.

"Okay, go ahead and play coy. I can see it, even if you won't admit to it."

Jessica scowled. "After what you went through with Keith, I can't believe you still believe in happily-ever-after."

"Just because you make one bad mistake, doesn't mean you have to make a repeat offense. I've learned a lot about myself these past couple of years. Speaking of repeat offenses, I almost forgot, Doris Ruppert was found rip-roaring drunk again. She almost fell off the horse she was riding. I had to send her back to her room to sober up. She is not handling her divorce well and needs more help than we can give her."

"Is she here alone or with someone?" Jessica inquired.

"Alone, but she has an adult daughter."

"Winona Sheppard is coming tomorrow. She was only supposed to do a couple of workshops, but maybe she can council Doris, at least enough to convince her to get help when she gets home."

"We certainly pay her well enough for that PhD in psychology, I'm sure she might be willing to meet with Doris once and hopefully convince her to get professional help."

"You should also call her daughter and fill her in. Anything else going on?"

"Nope, I was checking in with you." Laurie hopped to her feet and came around Jessica's desk. She leaned down and hugged her friend.

"What's that for?" Jessica creased her brow.

"I'm so happy for you. You two belong together. Always have."

"That again? Is it a crime to be concerned? The man got hurt. I'm not cold hearted."

"Whatever." Laurie waved her hand and headed to the door. "Hey, you're awfully tense. Why don't you have Tanya give you a massage? Loosen up would ya?" On that note, Laurie disappeared back out the door.

Loosen up. She was loose. Well, sort of. Maybe a massage wasn't such a bad idea. She had been rather tense with everything that had happened. Maybe a nice spa treatment was just what she needed to help her forget her troubles.

Another knock sounded at her door.

"Come in."

"Hi, Miss Jessica, I thought you might like some ice tea." Maddie set the tea down on Jessica's desk. "You've been keeping yourself held up in this office or your apartment. That's not healthy."

"Thank you, Maddie. Ya know, you're right. I have been spending too much time cooped up. I think I'm going to go and have a massage."

"Sounds wonderful. You go and enjoy. It's about time you did something nice for yourself. Call if you need anything." Maddie turned and left the room.

Jessica sipped on her tea and reached for the phone to call the spa. Tanya was available if she came over in about 15 minutes. Why not? There had to be some advantages of owning your own retreat.

Jessica finished writing a few more checks, then put away all her papers, cleaned up her desk and headed out the door. It only took her a couple of minutes to walk over to the spa. Tanya was ready and waiting for her when she arrived.

"Hi, Tanya, thank you for squeezing me in."

"Jessica, you crack me up. You're the owner of this place and you never take advantage of what you have. Honey, if I owned this place, I'd be in here every day, getting a rub down."

"The spa is for our guests. They pay to be here, so they come first. Besides, if I'm in the spa, who's taking care of the ranch? I can't have anyone slacking off." Jessica joked.

"If you don't take care of you, who's going to take care of us? Now get undressed and let me rub away all your troubles."

"If only you could take them away, Tanya. What I wouldn't give for a little peace in my life." Jessica quickly undressed and hopped up on Tanya's massage table, covering herself with a sheet.

"Come now. That hunk of a cowboy you hired has been your shadow. That can't be so bad. He can be my shadow any day." Tanya's hands started to work their magic on Jessica's stressed out shoulders.

"He hasn't been my shadow," she said defensively.

"Easy now, you're gonna undo all my work. It's okay to have a lover, sweetheart. We all wish we could have one the likes of him."

"He's not my lover!" Jessica squealed.

"Whatever you say. If he's not your lover, what are you doing with him? Cause, honey, there is only one thing I can think of that I'd wanna do."

Great, her staff all thought she and EJ were lovers. Tanya spent most of her time in the spa. If she thought that, then people must be gossiping. Tanya must have overheard some of the women talking. Jessie needed to quiet those rumors.

"He's an old college friend. He moved here and needed a job. I thought I would do him a favor. Isn't that what friends are for? Besides, his daughter came to spend some time with him. She's staying in my suite with me. Not like anything is going to happen with her around."

"If you say so." Tanya shrugged. "I can't believe he's just your friend. Have you had your eyes checked lately?"

"Tanya, I swear, we're not lovers." She knew Tanya wasn't buying any of this, and the problem was neither was anyone else. She wasn't lying, they weren't lovers. No one needed to know about their history together, including his own daughter.

"Well, there must be something wrong with you honey, cause if that man was around me all the time, I'd be body slamming him to the bed and riding him into the sunset."

"Tanya, you're killing me." Jessica laughed. The picture that formed in her head made her insides quiver.

"You relax and think about that hunk of a man. Whether he's friend or lover, he's still pretty to look at. Maybe by the time I'm done with you, you'll be ready for a wild ride of your own."

Jessica closed her eyes and let images of Ethan fill her head.

꒰ ꒱

Jessica's spirits were soaring when she joined her guests for dinner. The massage had done wonders for her, and the conversation during dinner was light and full of laughter. A few glasses of wine later, she felt more relaxed than before her divorce. In fact, she couldn't remember the last time she felt this good.

She was actually looking forward to tonight. They were having a dance, so she wandered out to the barn and was delighted when she walked inside. Kudos to Laurie who had transformed the barn into a country dance hall.

On a platform, set-up center stage, the band played a lively country song. A group of women line danced on the wooden dance floor that graced the middle of the barn. Other women sat on bales of hay stacked up in different areas, along with tables and chairs from the patio. Appetizers galore filled several large tables that were lined on one wall, and a bar sat in the opposite corner.

It was a celebration and she watched as people filed in. Everyone from the ranch would be there tonight, from guests to staff. Jessica couldn't wait to see Ethan. For once, she hoped he would seek her out. She grabbed a drink at the bar and went to sit on a hay bale.

She wasn't disappointed when Ethan strolled across the barn, with Chrissie in tow, and headed straight for her. She was, however, a little disturbed when she saw how Chrissie was dressed, or should she say undressed. Her short shorts were clear up to her little butt cheeks and her midriff bearing halter-top left little to the imagination. Jessica was surprised Ethan would allow her out in public showing her belly button and half her derrière.

"Evening, ladies." He tipped his hat to the women who sat near by.

"Evening, Ethan." they all chimed in together.

Chrissie sighed in disgust at the shameless outward adoration the women showed her father.

"Hi, Chrissie. How was your day as Assistant Director?" Jessica asked, trying to distract her from the public display the women were making.

"It was great. Laurie's job is a lot of fun. I got to help with things for the dance tonight."

"Did you help her transform this place?" Jessica asked.

"Yeah, it was really cool setting up, but hard work." Chrissie beamed.

"You did an outstanding job," Jessica praised.

"That's my girl." Ethan hugged her proudly.

"Laurie said I could help her again tomorrow. Would that be okay?"

"Sure. I'm glad you had fun." Thank heaven for Laurie because she had been too distracted to entertain Chrissie.

Ethan sat down next to Jessica. He leaned over and whispered in her ear. "Your cheeks are awfully rosy tonight. A little too much wine at dinner?"

"No, just enough wine." She winked at him. "I had a massage this afternoon, and I feel fabulous."

"You look fabulous, too." He winked back at her.

All she could do was smile at him like an idiot. What was she sixteen again? Feelings were creeping in all around her. Feelings she hadn't experienced since she met him twenty years ago. They were warm and exciting. She wanted to embrace them, but fear of losing that again made it's presence known.

"Ethan, sing us a song," someone called out.

"Yes, come on, Ethan, don't keep us waiting."

"Ladies, I would never dream of keeping you waiting." He walked up on stage and borrowed a guitar from a member of the band and started to strum. The women went crazy.

"You might know this song, ladies. I'm certainly not Michael Bolton, but here goes. It's called 'When a man loves a woman'." He gave a nod to the band, and they began playing.

"You sing it, sweetheart!" Laurie shouted from across the room.

"Honey, you can love me anytime!" another woman called out.

Jessica couldn't take her eyes off of him. There was no use denying it anymore. She was falling head over heels in love with him all over again. She adored him, had never stopped. Perhaps that's why it hurt so much, and she couldn't let go of the past. She had loved John, but Ethan had always been her soulmate. She prayed her heart would handle the road she was about to go down.

When he finished singing, he looked directly at her and mouthed the words 'I still love you'. Jessica just smiled at him. Her heart so desperately wanted to love him again, but her head was creating doubts, telling her not to be foolish, she would only get hurt again. He was trying so hard to make it up to her. He really was sorry.

She had been so determined to make it on her own without a man in her life, and she was succeeding until this mystery menace showed up.

Was Laurie right? Could fate have decided to intercede? It was true; she could have made different decisions in her life. She knew John wanted children and was willing to adopt or whatever it took to have a family, yet she only pushed him away.

Ethan wasn't the one who had stopped her from having her happily-ever-after, she had stopped herself. The whole purpose of her ranch was to help women move forward and here she was stuck in the past. She had no one to blame but herself. Maybe it was time to change the course of her life, and maybe it was time to forgive Ethan.

He sang a few more songs, a little more lively this time around, and the women filled the dance floor for some line dancing. Jessica enjoyed the entertainment except for the hay that was scratching her back.

When he finished, Ethan came to sit next to her. "Ants in your pants tonight?" he leaned over and asked as she wiggled back and forth.

"No, just hay. Seems to be irritating me tonight." She fidgeted and squirmed, trying to get comfortable and not scratch.

"Hey, I think they're playing our song. Care to do a little wiggling on the dance floor with me?" Ethan extended his hand to her.

The band played *Amazed* by Lonestar. She took Ethan's hand and wondered if the words of the song had any meaning to him. He wrapped his arms tightly around her, and she placed her head on his shoulder. She closed her eyes and leaned into him as he guided her around the dance floor, swaying back and forth. He was smooth and light on his feet. Why didn't that surprise her? Much to her disappointment, the song ended too soon.

Once again, Ethan's services were requested. This time a couple of the other guys joined him on stage, and the ladies went wild. Jessica was enjoying the spectacle until she realized they were missing a person, and she quietly got up and started to scan the barn. She noticed a few shadows off in a distant corner, so she went to explore. Sure enough, there was Chrissie with another cowboy.

"Aaron, how are you tonight?" She caught a groan of displeasure from Chrissie at being discovered.

"Hey, Miss Jessica, I'm good. How about you?"

"Good. Nice night for a dance."

Aaron still held Chrissie's hand. "Sure is."

"You are aware that you've taken your life into your own hands, aren't you?"

"Begging your pardon, Miss Jessica, I'm not following you."

"Chrissie is Ethan's daughter."

"Jessie, don't," Chrissie begged.

"Oh, I didn't know that." Aaron frowned and looked at Chrissie.

"Jessie," Chrissie whined.

"I bet you also didn't know she is only fourteen."

"Fourteen!" Aaron quickly dropped her hand and stepped away from her.

"I think that's a good idea. Come on, Chrissie, your *father* will be looking for you when he finishes singing. You have a good night now, Aaron."

"You ruined everything." Chrissie stomped past Jessica and headed to the opposite side of the barn.

Jessica followed her, thinking about what she was going to do. Chrissie threw herself into an Adirondack chair, crossed her arms and pouted.

Jessica walked over to her and knelt so she could whisper in her ear, "I know you don't understand, but please don't make me tell your father."

Chrissie turned away from her. Jessica saw Laurie sitting in another area with tables and chairs and went to join her.

"What was that all about?" Laurie inquired.

"Growing up too quickly." Jessica sighed.

"I see you are certainly enjoying yourself tonight."

"As a matter of fact, I am."

"Finally giving him a second chance?"

"Maybe." She smirked.

"Oh Jess, that's wonderful."

"We'll see. There's a long way to go to heal all the pain." Jessica squirmed in her chair.

"Yes, but Jessica, are you willing to give him a chance?"

"I think so. Laurie, I think I'm actually ready to try to forgive him." She moved back and forth across the chair like a bear against a tree.

Laurie paused and watched her. "What are you doing?"

"The hay has me itching and scratching all over. I think I'm going to go back to my suite and take a shower."

Laurie laughed. "Would that be alone or with some company?"

"Alone, thank you very much." Jessica laughed.

She rose and walked over to Ethan, who had finished singing, and sat down on the bench next to him.

"There you are. I wondered where you disappeared to."

"I'm right here. Worried?" She leaned into him.

"Always. What's going on?"

"Nothing. It looks like you were missed. I'm thinking you might have to give up your day job and come work for me permanently."

"You'd like me to stay here permanently?" He smiled a brilliant smile at her.

"I have to think of my guest's needs and you, apparently are one of them. They need their Ethan fix, as shameful as that is." She laughed.

"Oh, I see, it's all about the guests."

"Yep, all about the guests." She stared up into emerald-green pools and watched yellow flecks of light dance in them.

"I think Chrissie is really having a great time here. I can't thank you enough for letting her stay."

"Not a problem. I just hope she doesn't get sick while she's here."

"Sick? Why would she get sick?"

"Well, there's not much to her outfit. At least you know she doesn't have a bellybutton ring."

"What? She's fine. All the kids dress like that."

"All the kids, humm." Jessica raised an eyebrow at him. "I see she has discovered the opposite sex."

"What are you talking about?"

"I saw her eyeing Jeremy and a couple of the other cowboys."

"Oh, I'm sure she did. She's at that age. Thank God she's only looking and too young to do anything about it. I dread the day when that changes."

"Too young to do anything? You really don't have a clue. Lord, help this boy." She looked up toward heaven then elbowed Ethan and chuckled.

"You can say that again. Good thing I own a gun."

Jessica fidgeted on the bench. "I think I'm going to turn in. Chrissie is sitting over there." She pointed to the still pouting teen.

"Okay, we'll be along in a little while."

"Goodnight." Jessica rose.

"Goodnight." Ethan grabbed her hand and kissed the top of it.

He retuned to the stage one last time for a few more songs and then went to join Chrissie. He sank down into one of the chairs next to her. "Hey, Sweet Pea, what's going on? Are you having fun?"

"I was."

"You were? What's the matter?"

"Nothing." She paused and then looked at him. "Dad, do you like Jessie?"

"Of course I do."

"No, I mean do you really, really like her?"

"Why do you ask?"

"Because you get a funny look on your face when you're around her."

"Yeah, kiddo, I really, really like her."

Chrissie frowned. "Do you love her?"

"Would you be upset if I did?"

"I don't know. Never thought about it." Chrissie shrugged. "Do you?"

"Yeah, I do."

"She was your old college girlfriend wasn't she?"

"What makes you say that?"

"Dad, I wasn't born yesterday. You and Jessie seem really into each other, and the way you talked about your old college girlfriend, I figured it had to be her. You pretty much described Jessie. Plus, if you were as popular as Jessie says, there's no way your girlfriend would have let you be really good friends with her."

"You're awfully smart for someone your age, observant too."

"You're a good teacher, Dad."

"So it seems. Yes, Jessie was very special to me. She still is."

"Why did you break up with her?"

"I joined the FBI."

"Did you want to marry her?"

"Ohhh, that's a loaded question." He paused, thinking back. "I did want to marry her, but I didn't think I could be married and do my job."

"So you broke up?"

"Yep."

"Oh, I see. So you made a mistake marrying Mom?"

"Why would you say that?"

"You got divorced, and you still love Jessie."

"No, Sweet Pea. Marrying your mother wasn't a mistake. I loved her very much. Things just changed between us, and my job was always getting in the way. Besides, we have you, and you're the best thing that could ever happen to me."

"Your job isn't in the way now, and you have me. Plus Mom is still available." Chrissie sounded hopeful.

"Oh kiddo, it's not that easy."

"Sure it is. You said you loved Mom, and now your job won't take you away from us anymore."

"Some day you'll understand. Are you ready to turn in?" He was ready to end this conversation.

"Yeah, I guess so."

"Come on." He walked Chrissie back to Jessica's suite.

Ethan got ready for bed and then went to tuck Chrissie in. When he came out, he stopped dead in his tracks. A loud thumping noise was coming from Jessica's bedroom. His heart nearly stopped. He had never thought to check on her. What if their mystery menace had returned? What if something had happened to her? Damn, he wasn't thinking.

He quietly walked up to her bedroom door and listened. There it was again, the thumping noise. He held his breath as he turned the knob. The door was unlocked, and he slowly pushed it open as his heart beat in his throat.

He couldn't believe the sight before him. There stood Jessica, rubbing back and forth on one of the posts of her four-poster bed.

"Are you okay?" He walked into her room.

She jumped and spun around at the sound of his voice. "What? You scared me half to death, again. Please stop doing that. It's really becoming annoying. You're making me a wreck."

"Sorry. I heard a strange noise and got worried. What on earth are you doing?"

"I can't stand it. I'm itching like crazy. I took a shower, and I still itch. It's driving me nuts! I've never reacted to hay like this before."

"Come here." Ethan spun her around so her back was facing him. She was only wearing a light-weight pair of pale green baby doll pajamas. He touched her shirt, and she jerked forward. He slowly lifted it up so he could look at her back.

"Well?" she asked.

"Holy crap, Jessie, you've got more than a little itch here."

"What?" She spun around, trying to look at her back and only kept turning around in a circle.

"Stop." He put his hands on her shoulders. "You have a rash all over you. Do your legs itch?"

"Yes, but not as bad as my back."

"Alright, let me see what I can do." Ethan walked into her bathroom.

She heard him rummaging around in her medicine cabinet. "What are you going to do?"

He emerged a few moments later. "Here, take one of these."

"What is it?"

"It's a Benadryl. It will help with the itch, especially since I think you might be allergic to something. Now lay down on the bed."

"Excuse me?" she asked. "I'm not laying down on the bed for you."

"Jessie, I'm going to rub cortisone cream on your back. It will stop you from scratching yourself to death."

"Oh. Alright." She lay down on the bed.

"Can you remove your top?"

"What?"

"Your top, remove it, please."

Jessica removed her top, trying to make sure he didn't catch a peek.

Ethan chuckled as he watched her struggle with the shirt. "I've seen them before."

"So." She laid face down on the bed, her arms held tightly against her side.

He squeezed some cream into his hands and placed them on her back. His touch caused her to nearly jump off the bed. He chuckled again. "Relax, would ya? I don't bite, I only nibble."

"Very funny," came the muffled reply.

He felt her tense as he started with her shoulders and slowly worked his way down her back. Cortisone cream wasn't exactly like moisturizing lotion and didn't spread easily. He had to work a little harder to rub it all over her inflamed back. Not that he minded the extra effort, he enjoyed touching her. She was soft and silky against his calloused hands.

As his palms roamed over her back, he could feel her start to relax. His application of cream began to turn into a massage as he rubbed her shoulders and then the muscles along her shoulder blades. His hands slipped lower along her back and then down her legs. He rubbed each one thoroughly.

A soft moan escaped her lips. He leaned forward and saw that her eyes were closed, and a smile of complete pleasure graced her lips. For the first time since he had arrived on the ranch, she looked completely at peace.

He couldn't help himself. Running his hands over her body was doing things to him that he struggled to control. He wanted her. It was against his better judgment, but he had to, he just had to kiss her. He leaned forward and pressed his lips to her neck then nuzzled her ear.

Another moan escaped her lips.

He placed more feather-light kisses on her neck, traveling down her back. He saw goose-bumps form on her flesh, and she shivered.

"Cold?"

"Nope." Her response was breathless and lazy.

He ran his hands over her back again and tickled behind her knees with his fingertips. She made no attempt to stop him. He lay down on the bed next to her.

"Jessie."

She opened her eyes to look directly into his. She merely blinked at him.

He ran his finger along the side of her cheek. "Jessie, I want you."

"I know." She didn't move.

"You know?"

"I know your daughter is in the next room."

He groaned. "You know I'll behave."

"Yep." A smile crept across her face.

"Are you teasing me?"

"Maybe."

"I see. And here I thought I was doing a good deed and chastising myself for the sinful thoughts that were going through my head."

"Sinful?" She raised an eyebrow at him.

"Totally sinful. Wouldn't you love to know what they were?"

"Maybe."

"I better go before I forget that my daughter is next door. Good night, Jessie. I hope you feel better." He leaned over and kissed her cheek.

"Thank you for coming to my rescue, again."

"Anytime. I enjoy rescuing you." Ethan rose to leave.

"EJ."

He stopped. "What?"

"I'm really glad it's you who's helping me."

"I'm glad it is, too. I will figure this out."

"I know you will."

"Sleep tight." He winked and quietly left her room.

chapter 12

THE DINING ROOM was already busy as both guests and staff headed in various directions. Jessica strolled through the room and said good morning to the ladies. She was starving and eager for a cup of coffee and some breakfast.

The aroma of scrambled eggs, pancakes and maple syrup tantalized her senses, making her stomach grumble. She grabbed a cup and set it down on a table, then went to the buffet to fill a plate. She heaped it high with bacon; it was one of her weaknesses. She didn't normally eat a breakfast like this. Fruit and yogurt were usually her breakfast of choice, but today she was famished.

Jessica returned to the table and quietly watched the comings and goings of her staff and guests. A group of new arrivals was expected today, and the staff was getting prepared. Laurie walked through the dining room with Chrissie in tow and waved. Chrissie merely looked at Jessie, and then looked away. Jessica chuckled. She was not sorry she had caught Chrissie. If Ethan had found Aaron or Jeremy with his daughter, they would have been toast, burnt toast. She also didn't want to see Chrissie in a situation she wasn't ready to handle. She wasn't as grown-up as she thought she was.

"No scratching this morning?"

She looked up at the sound of his voice. "Hi." She smiled at him, her eyes roaming over his incredible physique. She never thought it was possible that a pair of jeans and a t-shirt could become the sexiest outfit on earth. Combine that with a golden tan, dark, curly locks and eyes like emeralds, and you were a goner.

"I don't see you scratching. Are you feeling better?" He sat in the chair next to her.

"Yes, much better. I still itch a little, but I took another Benadryl. Thanks for helping me out last night. I think I would have lost my mind if you hadn't put that lotion on."

"Believe me, the pleasure was all mine." He winked at her.

She could feel her cheeks grow warm at his enjoyment of rubbing lotion all over her body. "I guess I better stay away from the hay."

"Jessie, I don't think it was the hay."

"You don't?" She looked up and saw the serious expression on his face. "What else could it be? I didn't start itching until I sat on the hay at the dance."

"Are you sure you weren't itching at dinner? Did you eat something you are allergic to?"

"I guess it's possible I was itching at dinner. I really don't remember. I'm positive I didn't eat something I'm allergic to."

"Didn't you say you had a massage?"

"Yeah, but I've had massages before, and I've never had a problem. Besides, if it was from my massage, how come I don't itch all over?"

The thoughts that went through her mind made her tingle everywhere. She could picture Ethan covering her whole body in cortisone. She looked down at her plate so her face wouldn't betray her thoughts. Her loose hair fell forward shielding the blush on her cheeks from Ethan's gaze.

"I'm not sure, but I think I'll do a little checking just to be safe."

She looked up at him. "Are you trying to say that someone did this to me?"

"Jessie, there are a lot of accidental things happening around here. I don't know what to think anymore."

"That's ridiculous. Everything that goes wrong around this place isn't because of this mystery menace. I'm obviously allergic to something."

"Are you sure you can't think of anyone who'd want to hurt you or ruin your business?

"Good heavens, no."

"How about your ex-husband?"

"Ethan, John is too wrapped up in his perky new bride to give me a second thought."

"What about any of your guests?"

"My guests? Why would they want to hurt me? They are only here a week."

"Well, most of them have issues of some sort. Maybe they were disappointed in the ranch, or how about somebody's husband or ex-husband."

"I suppose that's possible." She paused for a moment, thinking hard. "There was this one woman. Her name was Amanda Antonucci. Her husband was very abusive. She was here about four or five months ago, I think. She was afraid of her husband, and he did call here a couple of times and was totally builigerent. I guess that's a possibility."

He placed his hand on her arm. "Jessie, I really think someone did something to your massage oil. Whether it was meant for you or your guests, I don't know. Let me look into this. I'm sure you're right, but I'd feel better if we were absolutely positive."

"Alright, you're James Bond, do what you must."

He leaned over and kissed her.

"What are you doing?" She jerked away from him.

"You said do what I must, and I must kiss you. Have a good day." He jumped up from his chair and left.

"Who do you think you are, Don Juan?" she called out to his retreating back.

He was too much. She was remembering why she had fallen hopelessly in love with him the first time. He had stolen her heart then, and he was stealing it now.

She finished her breakfast and decided to make some rounds around the ranch. She had been so preoccupied with the accidents and dealing with her feelings for Ethan, she had neglected her staff and guests. She needed to let them know everything was fine. The campfire tonight would be the perfect opportunity.

☙❧

Jessica pulled her sweater tighter around her as she sat by the fire, enjoying the cool, quiet, night. The majority of people were out on the hayride. After making her rounds today, she opted to attend a yoga class in an effort to keep her stress under control. She passed on dinner and the hayride, deciding quiet time would be best.

Ethan had been reluctant to leave her alone until she finally convinced him that she would be fine if she locked all her doors and windows and sat with the phone just in case someone tried something. It was ridiculous, but the only way she could convince him to leave.

Maddie had stopped by to check on her when she hadn't shown up for dinner or the hayride. God bless Maddie for always looking out for her. Even though there wasn't much of an age difference between them, Maddie had taken it upon herself to mother

her. Perhaps it was from raising four children of her own. It must come naturally to her.

It was times like this that Jessica missed her own family, especially her dad. She really needed to do something about that. They were way overdue for a visit to the ranch, and she desperately wanted to see her nieces and nephews.

Knowing that everyone should be returning soon, she had decided to venture outside to wait. Ethan would probably throw a fit, but she needed the fresh air.

The campfire area quickly filled up with people. Laurie chatted with some new arrivals, Penny, Betty and Linda, as they strolled in and made themselves comfortable.

"You missed an enjoyable hayride tonight, Jessica." Penny, a red-head with pale skin and freckles, said.

"That Ethan is a real keeper." Betty patted Jessica on the arm as she walked by.

Did everyone know about them? It didn't take Ethan long to find her and make himself comfortable in the chair next to her.

"Are you feeling better this evening?"

"Not really. I'm still worried about someone else getting hurt." She stared off into the fire.

"I'm sorry. I really hate to make your evening worse."

Her head snapped around to look at him. "What happened? Please tell me there wasn't another accident."

"No, relax. It's about your massage."

"What about it?"

"I found something."

"What could you have possibly found?" She scowled at him.

"Someone put salicylic acid in the massage oil. That's why you broke out in a rash and itched."

"Salicylic acid? Is my skin going to start flaking off?"

"No, it's actually very common. You find it in acne medicine, facial scrubs and things like that. But, if it is used in a high enough dosage, it will cause major skin irritation. There was just enough in your massage oil. You're lucky. In really high doses, you can get salicylic acid poisoning."

"That makes no sense. If it was the massage oil, then I would have itched all over," she snapped at him.

"I talked with Tanya…"

"Are you saying she did this? That's absurd. I don't believe you. Keep your crazy thoughts to yourself."

He placed a hand on her arm. "Hey, easy now, let me finish."

"Alright, finish." Her irritation with him was growing.

"I spoke with Tanya, and she told me she used two different bottles of oil. She said there wasn't much in the first and when it was gone, she changed bottles. Apparently she started with your back and then had you roll over. So I took the empty bottle and a sample from the new bottle and had it analyzed."

"You got results already?"

"It does pay to be former FBI. I kind of kept a few items that I shouldn't have, and I was able to send the samples to a friend still at the Bureau."

"So you're saying Tanya did this to me?" Jessie truly thought he was out of his mind.

"No, there is no way she is doing these things unless she is working with someone else. Tanya spends all her time in the spa. I've checked her schedule, and when she is here, she is busy. These women line up at the door for her. She doesn't have the time or opportunity to do any of this."

"Well, I certainly don't think Tanya is working with this menace. She's just not that kind of person."

"I don't think so, either. I'm not sure if it was meant for you or if this person is now moving onto your guests. May I recommend not having any more massages?"

"Don't worry, I won't." Jessica folded her arms across her chest and harrumphed.

"I'm sorry to upset you more, but I found something else out."

"I can hardly wait to hear this," she grumbled.

"I looked up your Amanda Antonucci. Guess what? She's here on the ranch right now."

"What?"

"She arrived with the last group of guests. It's even better; she's in the process of getting a divorce."

"No way, good for her." Jessica smiled.

"Jess, she's from New Jersey. Her husband has a FBI file. There is a possibility they are connected to the mob."

Her smile faded. "Oh, fabulous, can things get any better?"

"I'm really sorry. You've got to be careful."

"I'm getting sick of this. I'm tired of my life being turned upside down."

"I can see that. Maybe I could give you a massage tonight to relax you." He smiled and winked at her.

"No thanks."

"Wow, mood so bad she's immune to my charms. I might have to work on that."

"Don't bother." She rose from her chair.

"Where are you going?" He stood next to her.

"For a walk."

"I don't think that's a good idea. It's late and dark."

"I really don't care, and I don't need you following me. I mean it, just back off," she snapped.

"Hey, I'm not the bad guy here." He held up his hands as a sign of surrender.

"I'm sorry. I'm just tired of the whole situation. I didn't mean to take it out on you, I'm just frustrated." She needed some time and space. The fact he felt it necessary to stay with her made her angry that she needed protection, but glad that he was near by.

She walked toward the stables. Being with her horses always calmed her nerves and made her feel better. She had neglected Sadie lately. Ethan didn't feel she should go riding. That was something she missed terribly.

She heard a couple giggle near one of the barns. She didn't want to know and started to walk past when she took another look. No, it was not. Why that little…Now she'd really had it.

"Chrissie, is that you?" Jessica marched toward the couple. The girl didn't say anything.

"Scott?"

"Miss Jessica?"

If looks could kill, Chrissie had just knocked her dead. "What are you two doing?"

"Taking a walk, or should I say hobble." Scott joked.

"Scott, I thought you broke your leg not your brain."

"What are you talking about?"

Jessica thought Chrissie was ready to lunge and scratch her eyes out. "This young lady happens to be Ethan's daughter. Were you aware of that?"

"No, ma'am."

"Did you also know that Ethan's daughter is only fourteen-years-old?" She was in no mood to play games, she told him like it was.

"What?" Scott jumped away from Chrissie.

"I would have thought word had gotten around by now that she was Ethan's daughter. I figured that alone would be a deterrent, never mind her age."

"I haven't talked with the guys much since I broke my leg. Hey, what do you mean other guys?"

"It doesn't matter. You know all you need to know."

"Christina, I suggest you shag your suggestive little butt up to the lodge, now! Scott, I trust we won't need to have another conversation regarding this matter."

"No, ma'am. I'm really sorry, Miss Jessica. You have nothing to worry about."

"Good."

Chrissie brushed past Jessica and stomped her way back to the campfire. She stomped directly past her father and into the lodge. Jessica was hot on her heels.

Ethan reached out and grabbed Jessica's arm. "What's wrong with Chrissie?"

"What's wrong? She's a teenager with overactive hormones, and she's distracting the guys who work for me. That's what's wrong."

"What are you talking about?"

"I found her down by the stables with Scott."

"What? I'll kill him." Ethan took a step toward the stables.

This time she grabbed his arm. "Hold on. It wasn't his fault."

"What? Give me a break. She is just an innocent little girl. I can't believe you would suggest otherwise."

"Not so innocent I'm afraid. Just ask Jeremy and Aaron, as well."

"Jessie, what's the matter with you? Why would you say that about Chrissie? She's just a kid."

"Oh, wake up and smell the hormones, EJ. She's turning into a woman right in front of you. I know she's still your baby girl, but she's not a baby anymore. She's growing up." With that, Jessica stomped off herself and headed for her suite, a suite that contained one hormonal teenager she was pretty sure wanted nothing to do with her. Great. Just Great.

☙❧

Jessica tossed and turned. It was no use, she couldn't sleep. What had happened to her life? Everything she treasured was turning upside down. Damn this menace.

She slipped out of bed and paced the small span of her room. Watching TV in the living room wasn't an option because she didn't want to wake Ethan or Chrissie. Reading might work. She picked up a book and settled back in bed. Her mind began to wander. After reading the same paragraph for the third time, she snapped the book closed. That wasn't working, either.

She spotted her swimsuit lying on a chair in the corner. A swim. Perfect, just what she needed. A swim would relax her.

She put on her hot pink bikini, grabbed a towel and quietly slipped out of her bedroom and then her suite. She slowly walked down the dimly lit hallways.

All was quiet. Good.

She made her way out to the pool, shivering from the cool night air. Dropping her towel on a chair, she slipped into the warm water and relaxed against the side of the pool. The sky was clear and stars twinkled brightly. Day and night were so vastly different in the desert. It was one of the many things she loved about living there.

She swam a few laps, then grabbed an inflatable ring and quietly kicked around the pool. The water was refreshing, and her worries started to melt away. She kicked away the pent up anxiety and energy that had been building. Her thoughts drifted as she enjoyed the quiet night.

She closed her eyes as she floated, until something tickled her leg. Before she knew what was happening, it wrapped around both her legs, pulling at her. She had no time to scream before she was dragged underwater. It was a person, and their strong arms wrapped tightly around her. Terror gripped her heart, and then suddenly she was propelled to the surface, sputtering and thrashing.

"Don't you ever sneak out like that again until this person is caught. Do I make myself clear?" His deep voice echoed in the calm night air as he spun her around to face him.

Jessica came nose to nose with Ethan, and he didn't look very happy. He still had his arms wrapped around her. There was no escaping his anger.

She choked and gasped. "If this menace doesn't get me, you're going to give me a heart attack. You could have drowned me!"

"So could the person who is trying to sabotage your ranch."

She struggled against his embrace, but his arms were too strong for her to break free from. He pulled her up tight against his chest. "I'm sorry," she mumbled.

Ethan loosened his hold and pulled them both against the side of the pool. "What the hell are you doing out here at this time of night? What were you thinking?"

"I couldn't sleep. I guess I was thinking too much. I said I was sorry."

"You should be."

"How'd you know I was out here?"

"I know everything."

"Come on, how'd you know? You were sleeping. What'd you do, put a tracking device on me?" She laughed and then saw Ethan look down. "EJ, did you put a tracker on me?" She raised her arm to smack him, but he caught her hand in his.

"Easy now. No, I didn't put one on you; I put a censor on your door. I was thinking more along the lines of someone entering your room while you were sleeping. If they did, I'd know about it. I wasn't thinking about anyone leaving your room." He scowled at her.

"You've got to be kidding me."

"I thought it rather ingenious. This way we both could get a good night's sleep."

"Well, it sure took you long enough to find me."

"Oh, I found you right away."

"You were spying on me?"

He pulled her closer to him and wrapped her arms around his neck. "I wasn't spying; I was just waiting to see if our mystery menace was watching you and if they would show their face."

"You used me as bait?" She tried to push away.

He covered her protesting lips with a kiss.

She stopped protesting.

Her eyes fluttered shut as she felt her body melt into his, and her breasts pressed against his naked chest. Her fingers threaded through his wet hair while his tongue darted in and out of her mouth, playing a teasing game with her own. He slid his hands down her back to cup her buttocks, pulling her closer to him. She could feel his arousal and automatically wrapped her legs around his waist.

Ethan turned and pushed Jessica up against the side of the pool leaving his hands free to caress her body. He slid them up her side and cupped her breasts with both hands, his thumbs teasing her nipples.

Jessica's head spun, as Ethan covered her neck and collarbone in feather light kisses, sending tingling sensations through her body. She lifted her head and took his face in her hands, capturing his lips in a passionate kiss. She wanted him. After all these years, she wanted him more now than she had ever wanted him or anyone else before.

Her hands roamed over his shoulders, across his back and down his arms. His muscles quivered beneath her fingertips. He was rock hard in more places than one. Her hips began to move instinctively against him. He let out a deep moan.

"You're killing me, Jessie." His voice was raspy. "I want you now."

"Take me." She surprised herself when her response came out in a breathless whisper.

He groaned and pressed into her with his arousal. "Not here. Someone could be watching or find us."

Her voice was still breathless and full of passion when she was finally able to speak. "EJ, you're right. We can't here, we can't in my suite, and I refuse to sneak into a vacant room." She caressed his face with her fingertips.

He groaned again. "I know." Ethan held her hips still. "I guess your honor is safe for now." He kissed the top of her head.

"Lucky me." She leaned forward and kissed his lips, biting at them playfully. She wiggled her hips against him one more time for good measure.

"You're an evil woman." He stilled her hips again.

"Not evil, just a little worked up."

"You don't even know the definition of worked up, trust me." Ethan growled into her neck.

"I guess I better quit while I'm ahead."

"Unless you want me to take you right here, right now, in this pool, I would suggest it."

"Fine, have it your way." She turned to the side of the pool to get out.

Ethan placed both hands on her butt and gently caressed it while giving her a hand out of the pool. She grabbed a towel and wrapped it around her. Ethan hopped out of the pool and shook the water off.

"Come here." She opened her towel to him after noticing he didn't have one of his own.

Ethan slipped his arms around her waist, as she wrapped the large towel around both of them, rubbing it up and down his back.

"I could get used to drying off like this."

"I bet you could." She smiled up at him. "I'm freezing now. Let's go back to the room."

The two quickly and quietly made their way back to Jessica's room. They paused at her bedroom door.

"Good night." She leaned up and kissed him.

"No more sneaking out?" He cocked his head to the side and raised an eyebrow.

"I'll be good, promise." She crossed her heart.

"Okay, good night." Ethan consumed her lips in one last passionate kiss.

Jessica slipped into her bedroom and closed the door behind her. She stripped out of her bikini and slipped into her baby doll pajamas. She lay down on the bed and smiled. As if she couldn't sleep before, she really couldn't sleep now. A chuckle escaped her lips when she heard the shower running in the other bathroom. Poor EJ, it wasn't quite so easy for him to fall asleep, either.

chapter 13

ETHAN HEARD JESSICA leave early. He was tempted to follow her, but after last night, he thought perhaps she wanted a little time alone. He was trying so hard not to push. Last night he had made huge strides. As much as he wanted to protect her, he didn't want to blow it by smothering her. So, he let her go, figuring after his surprise attack, she would be more careful.

Ethan waited patiently for Chrissie to finish getting ready. Thank goodness she was an early riser and not like most teenagers who slept until noon.

Chrissie emerged from her bedroom. "All ready, Dad. I'm starving, can we go eat?"

"Must be all the fresh air you've been getting. Come on, let's go attack the buffet." Ethan put an arm around his daughter and ushered out of the suite.

They entered the dining room to find it hectic with activity. Ethan searched the room, looking for a place to sit, when he spotted Jessica at a table alone, sipping coffee.

"Sitting with your friends?"

Jessica looked up at him and smiled. "As a matter of fact I am. The place is mobbed with them."

"Mind if we join you?"

"Not at all, please sit. Laurie just deserted me."

Ethan and Chrissie sat down at the table. He sat next to Jessie, and Chrissie sat next to him.

"I'm gonna grab a plate. Someone should be around with the coffee and whatever Chrissie would like to drink." She excused herself from the table and went up to the breakfast buffet.

"Dad, what do you see in her?"

"What?"

"What do you like about her?"

"I like a lot of things about her. Why wouldn't I? She's a great person. I care about her a lot."

Chrissie frowned at him. "I don't think she's so great. Maybe you're rushing things because she was your old girlfriend."

Ethan raised an eyebrow at her. "What are you talking about? Since when do you analyze me? Did something happen between you two?"

"She's not very nice to me. I don't think she likes kids."

"What? That's crazy. She's been nice to you, and she loves kids. She has a ton of nieces and nephews."

"They're family, I'm not."

"Chrissie, I don't understand. Jessica gave you a horse to ride and pretty much free rein around this place. It was nice of her to let you stay with her; otherwise, you wouldn't have been able to come."

"So, if she had said no, you wouldn't have let me come to see you?" Chrissie scowled at her father.

"I'm afraid not."

"Oh, so she's more important?" Chrissie pouted.

"I didn't say that. I would have had to solve this case first before you could have come. I couldn't leave you at my house alone."

"She is more important, then."

He placed his hand on her arm. "Chrissie, people are getting hurt around here. You saw that yourself with Jeremy and Jessie. What kind of a cop would I be if I turned my back on that? Not only is it my job to protect people, but I also help my friends."

"I suppose, but she still isn't very nice."

"You're going to have to be more specific. I've only seen her be nice to you."

"Exactly! She's always nice to me in front of you. When you turn your back, she's mean to me."

"How is she mean?"

"She says mean things. Why do you think I have been spending time with Laurie?"

"I thought you wanted to be with Laurie because she had a fun job."

"I do, but it's mainly because Jessie doesn't have time to be bothered with me, and when she does, she's mean."

"Sweet Pea, she has a lot on her plate right now. Someone is running around her ranch, hurting people she cares about. I'm sure if she was short with you, she didn't mean it. You've gotta cut her some slack."

"Of course you'd take her side; you're trying to get her back."

"Christina, that's not true."

"Whatever, Dad." Chrissie got up, grabbed a plate and headed to the buffet.

Ethan shook his head and followed her. Teenagers.

Jessica was eating her breakfast when they sat back down at the table with full plates. She looked up at them and smiled. "So what are you two up to today?"

"My mom is coming today," Chrissie blurted out.

Ethan's head whipped around to gape at her, and Jessica's fork hit her plate with loud clank.

"What?" they said in unison.

"Mom is coming for a visit today."

"Why on earth would your mother be coming here?" A great deal of anger erupted from Ethan.

"Because I miss her, and she needed to get away for a few days to relax."

"Where is she staying?" Jessica inquired, folding her hands in front of her.

"Here, if that's okay." Chrissie batted her eyelashes at Jessica. "I saw on the computer that you had a couple of empty rooms. I didn't think you would mind."

"Mind? Of course not. Why would I mind?" Jessica choked on her food.

Ethan saw the look of dread written all over Jessica's face. Asking her to entertain his daughter was one thing, but subjecting her to his ex-wife was another.

"Chrissie, you should have asked first. That was wrong of you to tell your mother it was okay to come. Both of you should have discussed this with me first."

"Why, Dad? It's a free country, and Mom is a paying customer. She can come here if she wants."

Jessica placed a hand on his arm. "EJ, it's okay. Chrissie is right; I do have a couple of empty rooms. The two of them are welcome to share one."

"But, Jessie, this was wrong. I am so sorry. You don't have to do this."

"EJ, I said it's okay. I never turn away a paying customer." She smiled brightly at him.

He adored her. After all these years, she was still the woman he had always loved. She had a few extra scars, some very deep that hadn't healed yet, but she was still as sweet and loving as ever. She had allowed his daughter to stay because she knew how much it meant to him. Now she was going to endure his ex staying there. He knew she was only doing it to keep the peace; but still, he loved her for her kindness.

"Thank you for your understanding." He leaned over and kissed her.

"Dad! That's disgusting. You shouldn't do that in public. What are people going to think?" Chrissie shrieked at him.

"Chrissie, it was only a thank you kiss. I believe you should also be thanking her."

"For what?"

Ethan kicked her under the table. "Chrissie."

"Thank you, Jessie, for letting my mom come, even if she is paying." Chrissie jumped up from the table and headed toward the door.

"Christina!"

"EJ, it's okay. She's just a kid."

"A rude kid," he said loud enough for his retreating daughter to hear.

"It's the age. It'll get worse before it gets better."

"Lord help me." Ethan laid his head on her shoulder as she patted him.

☙❧

The van from the airport arrived, and new guests filed into the lodge. Jessica was standing at the front desk, reviewing their list of bookings, when a slender woman with short dark brown hair came up to it. She was impeccably dressed in peach slacks and a short-sleeved, cream, silk, blouse. Her suit jacket was thrown across her arm and, in spite of traveling, she looked fresh as a daisy. One of the cowboys brought her luggage in and sat it next to her.

"Hi, welcome to the WWC. How can I help you?" Jessica smiled at her.

"I'm Kimberly Kirkpatrick. I'd like to check in."

Jessica swallowed hard and stared at the woman. Oh God, this couldn't be her. Kimberly cleared her throat and stared back at her.

"Certainly, I can take care of that." The woman didn't even crack a grin at her. Oh, how special was this going to be? Jessica walked over to the computer and pulled her name up. She printed off a form. "If you would just put your signature on this, I'll have Adam take you to your room." She motioned for him to come over.

"And who might you be?" Kim signed the paper and looked Jessica up and down.

"I'm sorry. I'm Jessica Montgomery, the owner of the WWC Ranch." She stuck her hand out to shake Kim's hand. Kim loosely shook it in return. Jessica quickly dropped her hand back down to her side.

"Oh, so you're Jessica. Christina mentioned you. Could you let my daughter know I'm here and have her sent to my room? I've missed her, and I'd like to see her right away."

"Absolutely." Jessica handed Adam Kim's room key, and the woman turned on her heel and followed him out of the lobby.

"Who was that?" Laurie came up behind Jessica.

"*That* was Kim."

"Kim who?"

"Kimberly Kirkpatrick," Jessica mocked the woman's proper tone.

"Kim Kirkpatrick? Ohhh, Kim Kirkpatrick! What the hell is she doing here?" Laurie's voice relayed her shock.

"Her loving daughter missed her. Chrissie noticed we had some empty rooms and took it upon herself to invite her mom for a vacation."

"She did what? Does Ethan know?"

"Yes, and he was not too pleased."

"I should say not. What is this all about? If she missed her mother, why didn't she go home?"

"I'm not sure, Laurie, but I have a sneaky feeling that Chrissie is pretty mad I foiled her attempts to become a woman."

"She's just a kid."

"Well, Jeremy, Aaron and Scott all thought she was more woman than kid. I don't know what to say. She is just a young girl who doesn't need to grow up so quickly, but she's not my daughter to reason with. I let it slide the first two times I caught her, but not the third."

"<u>Three</u> times! Did you tell Ethan? I'm sure he'd want to know. I can't see him allowing that kind of behavior."

"I told him, but he didn't believe me. There's nothing else I can say. At least with Kim, I mean Kimberly here, if Chrissie wanders off again with someone, she can deal with it."

"If Ethan didn't believe you, do you think Kim will? What if Ethan takes it out on one of the guys?"

"I suggested to them that they share the information with each other that Chrissie is Ethan's daughter and only fourteen. If they valued their lives, they would stay far away from her."

"Good Lord, yes. Those boys are eighteen to twenty-four years-old. That would be very bad in more ways than one."

"Yes, it would. When she wants to, she looks older than fourteen."

"Oh look, here she comes again." Laurie pointed to Kim coming back across the lobby.

Kim cleared her throat. "Excuse me."

"Yes, Kim, I mean Kimberly, what can I do for you?" Jessica forced a smile.

"I need more towels, and I prefer sheets straight from the laundry so that I know they are clean."

"Certainly. I assure you that all our linens are clean, but I'll be happy to send housekeeping to your room right away. Is there anything else?"

"My daughter. Did you forget already?"

"We'll find her and send her to you." Jessica strained to keep her smile.

"You'll find her? You mean you don't know where she is?"

"She's with her dad, and it's a pretty big ranch. I'm not exactly sure where they are at this very minute. I promise we'll send her to you."

"Fine." Kim spun around and started to leave again.

Ethan and Chrissie came through the French doors off the patio. Someone was obviously watching out for her, and she silently offered a thank you.

"Mom!" Chrissie ran across the lobby and hugged her mother.

"Hey, baby girl. How are you doing?" Kim ran her hand over Chrissie's face and inspected her appearance.

"Okay, I guess." Chrissie let out a big sigh. "I'm just glad you're here."

"Don't you worry, baby girl. Now that I've arrived, I won't let that Jessica woman be mean to you any more."

"Thanks, Mom." Chrissie smiled up at her.

Laurie watched the interaction between mother and daughter with her mouth gaping open. "There is no way Ethan was married to that woman."

"Well, he was. Hard to believe, but he was." Jessica watched as Ethan approached Kim and Chrissie. Seeing her didn't seem to bother him. In fact, he seemed pretty unaffected by it.

"No wonder it didn't last." Laurie leaned over and whispered in Jessica's ear. "I just can't picture him with someone like that."

"Neither can I." Jessica shook her head.

"What was he thinking? Obviously, he wasn't when he married her."

"Maybe she wasn't always like that. People do change, as you keep reminding me. So, there you have it. I have the pleasure of dealing with Kim, too." Jessica leaned against the desk, arms crossed over her chest.

"Don't worry, I'll run interference for you. I'll keep those two so busy, they'll be begging to go home."

"Thanks, but I'll be fine. I can play nice. Kim hasn't done anything to me, and I haven't done anything to her. As for Chrissie, well, she's just a kid, and I spoiled her fun. Hopefully, she'll get over it sooner than later."

"You're a better woman than I, my friend." Laurie patted Jessica on her back.

She saw Adam coming back through the lobby. "Adam!" she called out.

"Yeah, Miss Jessica?" Adam walked over to the front desk.

"Could you do me a favor?"

"Sure, anything."

"Could you come by my suite in about fifteen minutes? I have some suitcases I need you to deliver to Ms. Kirkpatrick's room."

"Sure thing, Miss Jessica."

"Thanks, Adam. Gotta go, Laurie, there's packing to be done." Jessica flashed her a big smile, waved and left.

chapter 14

THE AROMA OF steak, mashed potatoes and gravy tantalized her nose. Jessica's stomach gave a loud grumble now that it had been awakened. She approached dinner with caution. She had not seen Kim since she had checked in and for that matter hadn't seen Ethan or Chrissie. She hoped dinner would go off without a hitch, as well as this whole visit. She was a strong woman and could handle his ex-wife.

Jessica spotted Ethan, Kim and Chrissie sitting together at a table laughing. A little pain stabbed her in the heart. It felt odd seeing him sitting there with his family. Deep breath, she could do this.

Jessica walked up to their table and laid her hand on Ethan's shoulder. "Good evening. Is everyone enjoying their dinner?" She flashed them all her best smile.

"The steak is okay, I guess, but I could use some steak sauce." Kim looked directly at Jessica.

"I'll send someone over with it."

Ethan looked up and grinned at her. "Dinner is wonderful. Chrissie wanted to have a family dinner. I hope you don't mind."

There was that pain again. "EJ, don't worry about it. You're entitled to eat with your family."

"EJ?" Kim questioned Jessica's nickname for Ethan.

"Yeah, Mom, they are old college friends," Chrissie piped in.

"Really now, how very nice." Kim looked at Ethan and then back at Jessica.

Jessica was beginning to feel extremely uncomfortable. "Yeah, that was a long time ago. I'd better go. I've got things to do. Enjoy your meal."

Ethan reached out and grabbed her hand. "I'll see you later?"

Jessica looked down at it like it was searing her flesh. "That's okay. Enjoy your evening."

She bee-lined it for the kitchen and told a server to deliver the steak sauce. Then she made her way to the opposite side of the dining room to chat with some of her new guests. Perhaps she had underestimated her resolve. This might be a little more than she could handle.

After dinner, Jessica headed for a walk down to the stables. She missed being around the horses and the peace she felt when she rode, which she did so little of lately. Jessica climbed up on the fence and whistled for Sadie, who trotted right over and nuzzled her hand.

"I thought I might find you here." Joe walked up to lean on the fence next to her.

"You found me. What's going on? Did something happen?" She hopped down from the fence as a feeling of panic washed over her.

"Relax. I was just coming to chat. You haven't been yourself. I wondered how you were doing since your friend showed up. Is he any closer to figuring things out?"

"I don't think I can do this, Joe."

"What can't you do? Run your ranch? Stand on your own two feet? Beat a menace at his own game? You're stronger than that, Jessica."

"Thanks for the vote of confidence." She smiled weakly.

"There's more than what's going on around here that's got you all worked up."

"It's nothing, really, Joe."

"Did that cowboy do something to upset you?"

"Why do you think that?"

"I see the way you two look at each other. I was young once ya know. Do I need to have a chat with him?"

"You're sweet to offer, but no."

"Alright, but if he gets out of line, you let me know. Now have a good night. I'm here if you need me." He patted her arm.

"Thanks, Joe. Good night." She leaned over and kissed his cheek.

"Hey, Joe." Laurie waved to his departing figure as she walked up to Jessica. "Hey lady, I've been looking all over for you."

"I needed some air."

"Had your fill of Kimberly?"

"I don't know if I can handle this, Laurie."

"What? Be nice to her? I know I couldn't."

"No, be with EJ."

"Jessica, don't give up already, especially because of Kim. Lots of people have exes, including you."

"You wouldn't understand. It's more than that."

"I understand that when you love someone, it shouldn't matter."

"Well, it does."

"Why don't you go back to your suite and take a hot bath. You'll feel better. I'm sure today was a bit overwhelming. You just need to relax."

"Maybe you're right. I'm really not in the mood for a hayride or hanging out at the campfire. There has been way too much togetherness lately."

"I will fill in for you. Go on, go relax. You've had a lot on your plate." Laurie pushed her toward the lodge.

"Alright, I'm going." Jessica strolled back to her suite. Alone time would be good for her. She could regroup and pull herself together. She really hadn't had time to prepare for Kim's arrival. Even worse, was that Kim didn't seem like a very nice person.

As Jessica stepped through the door of her suite, she stopped dead in her tracks. Turning around, she walked out and checked her surroundings to make sure she was in the right place. She walked back through the door and looked around.

She couldn't believe her eyes. Filling the room were bouquets of flowers. From roses to lilies and daisies, there were beautiful bouquets all over her suite. A warm glow cascaded across the room from the candles that were lit all around. She felt like she had stepped into the middle of a romantic movie.

Her gaze landed on the coffee table where an ice bucket sat with Champagne chilling in it and two glasses next to it. Two glasses? She surmised that she would not be enjoying this alone.

"You finally returned. I was beginning to worry." Ethan emerged from the bedroom hallway.

She couldn't speak. She just stared at Ethan dressed in a tuxedo. His unruly curls were slicked back, and the tux, which was obviously tailored, emphasized his broad shoulders and slender waist. He was magnificent.

"I believe there is something on your bed waiting for you. You might want to go take a peek."

She still said nothing but disappeared into her room. Her heart was racing. It had to be a dream, it had to be. She must have fallen, hit her head and was now having the most wonderful fantasy in the world or had died and gone to heaven.

She walked to the bed and was pleasantly surprised to find a sapphire blue knee-length dress. It only took her a few moments to pull herself together and get ready. She stopped and looked in the mirror, brushed and fluffed her hair, pulling it up and securing it with a clip. She really was in a romantic movie, her very own version of pretty woman. She stepped out into the living room and cleared her throat.

Ethan turned to look at her. "You have to be the most incredible creature on the face of the earth."

Jessica spun for him. The strapless creation was form fitting, pushing her breasts up until they almost spilled over the top of the dress. The bodice was adorned with small rhinestones, and the skirt was made of a rose brocade fabric that accentuated her waist and curvy hips.

"Thank you." Her voice came out as barley a whisper when she finally spoke.

"Care to join me?" He motioned for her to sit on the couch. "I thought perhaps I could show you a night out on the town in Flagstaff. When was the last time you got out and had any fun?"

She sat next to him as he poured them both a glass of champagne. He handed her a glass and raised his to make a toast. "To new beginnings."

"And second chances," she whispered and clinked her glass with his. Her head was spinning. She couldn't believe he had done all of this for her.

He leaned down and kissed her. She closed her eyes and enjoyed the soft feel of his lips against hers.

"I'm sorry, Jessie."

"Sorry for what?"

"For everything. I'm sorry Kim showed up. I can't believe Chrissie did that."

"It's okay. She's just a young girl."

"Yes, but Kim should have called me."

"Nothing you can do about it now. She's here, so let's make the best of it." Jessica sipped her Champagne.

"You are one amazing woman." He pulled her into his arms so her head rested on his chest.

"Not so amazing, trust me. I can't believe you did all this."

"I had a little help."

"That explains why Laurie came looking for me. I see you have a fellow schemer. I'll have to remember that."

"Something is missing."

"What could possibly be missing?"

"Hang on." Ethan sat her up and left the couch.

He walked over to the stereo and pressed a button. The song 'Faithfully' by Journey started to play. That had been their song in school.

"You thought of everything, didn't you?"

"I tried." He walked back and extended his hand to her. "Dance with me."

"Here?"

Ethan pulled Jessica into his arms. She wrapped hers around his neck and rested her head on his shoulders. She closed her eyes and enjoyed the feel of being safely enveloped in his embrace.

"Jessie, I wish I could take away all the hurt I caused you. If only I had realized what a fool I was for letting you go sooner, things could have been so much different."

She raised her head and took his face in her hands. "I don't know about that. A lot happened after you left and even if you came back, I'm not sure I would have forgiven you."

He stopped dancing and held her away from him. "What happened?"

"It doesn't matter."

"Obviously, it does. Why won't you tell me?"

"Because we can't go back, and I'm trying really hard to move past it."

"But still…."

She placed a finger against his lips to silence him. "We can't go back, but we can go forward."

"Really? Do you mean that?"

"I'm not saying it'll be easy, but I like having you in my life again."

"Oh, Jessie." He hugged her tight, picking her up and swinging her around.

He kissed her softly at first and then his kiss intensified. His tongue parted her lips as his hand ran across her back. A moan escaped her mouth as she melted into his arms, pressing herself closer to him. He pulled his lips away and nuzzled her ear. He placed soft kisses down her neck and across her collarbone, making her dizzy. She closed her eyes, and her head fell backwards as she reveled in the sweet sensations he was creating.

"Jessie, I want you. Let me love you," he whispered in her ear.

"Love me," was all she was able to whisper in return.

Ethan scooped her up into his arms and carried her into the bedroom. He gently laid her down on the bed and stretched out next to her. He brushed a lock of hair that had escaped her clip away from her face and ran his fingers along her cheek and down her neck.

"You are even more beautiful now than you were when we were kids." He leaned down and kissed her lips again. "You have no idea how much I regretted the decisions I made."

She placed her finger against his lips. "Shhh, I thought you were going to love me, not talk."

"Jessie, I...."

"Love me." She pulled his head down so his lips met hers.

He did regret his decisions. If he only knew then what he knew now, things would have been different. How sweet it would have been if Chrissie had been their child together.

He pulled her into his arms and ran his hands over her back and along her buttocks. His hands roamed down her thighs and slipped beneath the hem of her dress. The silky fabric slid easily up her legs and over her hips. He reached up and unzipped the dress and then lifted the strapless creation over her head.

Her purple lace bra and panties were the final trimmings on this delicious package he was unwrapping. The deep "V" of her bra offered her breasts up like a gift while the lace beckoned for him to see what lay beneath.

He slid his hands down her stomach to her panties. The hi-cut on her hips only added to the long slenderness of her legs. He moved his hands over her hips as blonde curls played peek-a-boo beneath the lace.

He had waited twenty years for this, and he was going to enjoy every moment.

He ran a finger over the swells of her breasts along the lacey curve of her bra. Beautiful full breasts that rose and fell with each breath she took. He removed her bra and cupped the voluptuous mounds in his hands, running his thumbs over her nipples.

Jessica arched up into his hands and moaned. She was incredible, all soft and curvy, everything wonderfully feminine. He continued his exploration down her body, placing kisses on her flat belly and then her hips.

She weaved her fingers into his dark curly hair and pulled his head up to hers so she could kiss him. Her hands slid down his shirt and quickly pulled at the buttons, exposing his chest. She ran her hands over the muscles in his arms and across his back. Her fingertips gently teased his flesh.

He captured her lips in a deep passionate kiss, their tongues dancing the sacred dance of love. He pulled away and captured her nipple in his mouth.

She moaned loudly. "Oh, God, EJ, take me please."

"I've waited twenty years for this. Don't rush me because I am going to love every incredible inch of you."

His hand slid down her belly and beneath her panties. He wanted to be sure he had taken her to the peak of pleasure before he found his own. She was warm and wet to his touch. He wanted to pleasure her like she had never been pleasured before. His fingers worked their magic, and she withered beneath him.

"Please, EJ, love me now." She pulled at his body. Her hand found the buttons on his pants and undid them.

Ethan pulled away from her long enough to slide out of what clothing remained. He lay back down next to her and pulled her to him, their naked bodies melting into each other.

Her hands caressed his back and down his butt and over his thighs. He sucked in his breath as her fingers wrapped around his arousal, teasing him to the point of insanity.

"I love you, Jessica Montgomery." He captured her lips in a kiss before she could protest his declaration of love.

He grabbed her hands, lacing his fingers with hers. Rolling her onto her back, he positioned himself between her legs. It was taking every ounce of resistance he could muster. He wasn't sure how much longer he would be able to hold out as she wrapped her legs around him, urging him to move. With one quick fluid movement he entered her.

It was pure ecstasy. Jessica moaned and arched beneath him. His movements were slow at first, enjoying the warmth and depth of her. He tried to control her movements, but the thrusts of her hips told him she had no intentions of waiting to find her fulfillment. Her wish was his command and his hips moved faster and faster until she screamed out her release. He quickly found his own and collapsed on the bed next to her.

Ethan pulled Jessica into his arms and held her close. He could still feel her heart beating wildly. It was better than it had ever been between them. Was it because they were older, wiser, more experienced? Or was it because he finally knew what it meant to love someone with all his heart and soul?

"Jessie, I..."

"Don't..." She placed a finger to his lips. "...ruin it."

"But...."

"Don't." She picked her head up and looked at him. "Don't ruin the most incredible experience of my life." She laid her head back down on his shoulder.

"It was for me, too." He kissed the top of her head.

"Good." She stretched her head up and kissed his lips.

"So much for taking you out on the town."

She snuggled closer to him and sighed. "It's okay, I'm not complaining. In fact, I have absolutely no complaints or cares in the world." Her fingers caressed his chest, and she yawned.

"Close your eyes and dream sweet dreams." He hugged her tight, and the two of them drifted off into peaceful thoughts full of promise wrapped in each other's arms.

chapter 15

JESSICA STRETCHED AND yawned. She lifted her head to look at the sleeping form next to her and leaned over to softly kiss his lips. Ethan's eyes fluttered open.

"Good morning, handsome." She smiled down at him.

"Am I dreaming, or are you really lying naked next to me, smiling at me?"

"It's just a dream. Someone knocked you on the head." She laughed.

"Let me see." He rolled himself over on top of her and placed kisses on her forehead, her cheeks, her lips and her neck as he worked his way down. "Feels pretty real to me."

She giggled and wiggled beneath him. "It certainly does." She raised her eyebrows at him.

"I'm a guy, what can I say. I'm happy to see you." He leaned down and consumed her lips in a passionate kiss.

She pulled away breathless. "EJ, as much as I want to explore reality with you, we have work to do. People will wonder where we are, especially your daughter." She tried to push him off her, but he refused to budge.

"Yes, we do, and I say we start right now." His kisses moved down her neck and over her breasts.

She closed her eyes and arched her back as he suckled one of her nipples. She wanted to stay more than anything, but they had already slept in by over an hour. "EJ, we can't. I need to shower." Her voice was raspy and full of passion.

"Fine." He rolled off her. "How about some company?"

She hopped out of bed and headed for the bathroom. "EJ, we'll never leave this room if you do."

"And the problem with that would be what?"

"There's work to be done, and you my dear are a distraction." She reminded him.

"You're no fun." He pouted.

She poked her head around the bathroom doorframe. "That's not what you were saying last night."

"*Memories*," he started to sing as he threw himself across the bed.

She laughed at his dramatic display. "I'll shower and then make breakfast while you shower. If you're a good boy today, I might have a treat for you tonight." She winked at him.

"I guess I can be bribed."

Jessica quickly showered, and Ethan hopped in after her. She dressed in her usual cargo shorts, golf shirt and sneakers then ran a comb through her damp hair, pulling it back into a ponytail. She chuckled when she heard his deep tenor voice coming from the shower.

"*You are the sunshine of my life…*"

She loved Stevie Wonder, and she loved being the sunshine in Ethan's life. She put in her earrings, finished her make-up, and left the room to make breakfast.

Ethan emerged from the bedroom a few minutes later. "Ummm, something smells good." He inhaled deeply. Jessica was cooking eggs on the stove when he walked up, wrapped his arms around her waist and kissed her neck.

"I could get used to this every morning."

"You could, could you?" She turned in his arms and kissed his lips. "Breakfast is ready."

"I'm starved."

Jessica placed a plate of eggs and toast in front of him. "Coffee?"

"Please. For some reason I didn't get much sleep last night." He winked at her.

Jessica fixed her own plate and also grabbed a cup of coffee. "What's on your agenda today?"

"I've got some work to do in the barn, a few leads to follow-up on, and I'm hoping to catch up with Chrissie some time this afternoon."

"Any results back from my room?"

"Only what I expected to find: prints from you, Maddie and me."

"Oh, that's too bad. I was really hopeful."

"Don't give up. What are you up to today?"

"I need to meet with Laurie about some things, and then I thought I would catch a yoga class before tackling the papers on my desk."

"Can I count on meeting up with you for the hayride?"

"Sure. With Kim here, I'll be able to relax and not worry."

"What's that supposed to mean?" He looked at her with a creased brow.

"Nothing. I'm sorry." She looked down at her plate and continued to eat.

"If you've got something to say, say it. I know Kim being here is an imposition, but I thought you were okay with everything." He put down his coffee cup and looked at her. "Is there something I should know about?"

She laid her fork on her plate. "I just figured Kim can keep an eye on Chrissie, that's all."

"Are you saying I haven't?"

She could hear the defensiveness rise in his voice. "I didn't say that. You've been busy and so have I. With Kim and her pleasant personality here, there won't be any problems and we can relax and be with each other."

"What problems? I didn't realize Chrissie was a problem, and what's wrong with Kim's personality?" He scowled.

"Come on, did you hear the way Kim spoke to me last night?"

"She asked for steak sauce."

"Since she showed up, she's treated me like the maid. Not that there is anything wrong with being a maid, but I own this damn ranch."

"I thought you catered to your guests. Each and every one of them."

"Whatever, EJ. I'm not going to argue with you." She sipped her coffee, not wanting to start a fight after such an incredible night.

"Okay, so you're not fond of Kim. What problem has Chrissie been? I thought you liked her."

"I do like her and she is a good kid, but she is also a teenage girl who has discovered boys. Whether you want to face it or not, she's not such a little girl anymore."

"What do you mean by that? Why are you finding fault with Kim and Chrissie? Is my family not good enough for you?"

"What? What are you talking about? You're twisting what I'm saying and totally missing the point."

"What point? You can only seem to find fault." He grumbled. "I'm sorry we don't all live up to your high expectations."

"Oh, my goodness, I don't believe this. We are not going to fight over this. Ya know what, I have work to do and so do you." She got up, set her dishes in the sink and left her suite, leaving Ethan sitting at the table alone.

She headed to the main lobby of the lodge. Laurie was standing in the doorway of the dining room, conversing with some of their guests. Jessica waved to her as she walked over to the front desk. Laurie finished and came to see her.

"Good morning, and how was your evening?" Laurie gave her a playful jab with her elbow.

"My evening was wonderful, can't say the same for the morning." Jessica frowned at her.

"What? Tell me about last night first."

"Like I need to tell you, 'Miss why don't you go back to your room and relax.' You know how last night was. It was incredible."

"And did you two, you know, come together?" She raised an eyebrow.

"Laurie, you're terrible."

"Well? Are you back together or what?"

"I thought so last night, but not so much this morning."

"What happened?"

"Them." Jessica pointed to Kim and Chrissie walking across the lobby to the dining room, arm-in-arm, laughing.

"Them? What did they do? Please don't tell me they had a crisis and interrupted you."

"No, they simply exist."

"Now I'm confused."

"EJ and I had a fight over them this morning. He mentioned the hayride, and I said something about Kim being around and not having to worry. That led to why I would worry about Chrissie and then Kim's charming personality, and it just got ugly. I insulted his family, even though I didn't mean to, and he had to defend them from me because, I'm too hard on them, and I'm the one with a problem."

"Are you kidding me?" Laurie placed her hands on her hips.

"I can't pretend to like Kim. She has looked down her nose at me since she arrived. But Chrissie, she's a good kid and I like her very much. She's the spitting image of EJ, how could I not. It's just hard when he refuses to see that she is growing up and doing things she shouldn't. I'm afraid she'll end up in trouble. I'm not being hard on her, I care about her."

"I understand that one. I lecture Jeremy all the time. I remind him he is too young to be a daddy."

"If EJ won't listen now, will he ever? I don't want to fight with him, and I certainly don't want to cause problems with his daughter. I know how much he loves Chrissie. I would never come between them."

"No, hon, you wouldn't."

"If he's going to freak every time I make a comment, it's not going to work. We should be able to discuss this. I think I've made a horrible mistake letting him back in my life."

"Oh, Jess, don't say that. I'm sure it's hard for him being away from Chrissie. When he does see her, he wants it to be perfect, for her to be perfect. Don't give up, yet. You two just found each other again. It's going to take a little bit of time to get into sync. You know that doesn't happen over night."

"That's true. Let's go get a cup of coffee and discuss some things. I've got a few ideas I want to go over with you and need a second opinion."

"Sounds good."

The two women grabbed a cup of coffee from the dining room and went to sit outside on the patio.

                                          ☙❧

It was late in the afternoon when Ethan strolled past the pool, tipping his Stetson to the ladies as he did. Several women called out an invitation to him to join them for a swim or anything else he might like. He just laughed and waved as he sauntered by.

"Ethan."

He looked up to see Laurie waiving at him from the patio, outside the dining room. He waved back, and then saw she was motioning for him to come and join her.

"Hey, Laur, what's going on?"

"You tell me. How was last night?"

"It was incredible. Thanks for helping me out."

"How about this morning?"

"This morning?"

"Yeah, this morning?"

"Fine, why?"

"Ethan, I love you to pieces, but sometimes you are not the brightest bulb in the bunch."

"What's that supposed to mean?" He scowled at her.

"Do you trust Jessica?"

"Of course."

"Do you think she has a good heart?"

"Yeah."

"Do you think she would hurt you?"

"Not on purpose. Where's this conversation going?"

"Why don't you believe her about Kim and Chrissie?"

"Oh, did she come tell you how awful my family is?" He couldn't believe what he was hearing. Jessie had already run to Laurie about Kim and Chrissie. What was her problem with them?

"Hold on, cowboy. She cares about you and your daughter. As for your ex, well I've had the pleasure of experiencing her myself, and all I can say is I hope she was a different person when you married her."

"Kim isn't a bad person, and neither is my daughter."

"Nobody said they were. Ethan, you're not listening."

"Oh, I think I am, and I hear you loud and clear. I've got work to do." He snarled and walked away, leaving Laurie standing with her mouth open.

What was their problem? Chrissie was a good girl, and Kim was a good mother. No matter what their differences were, she was always a good mother. Speaking of Chrissie, he was in search of his daughter so he could spend some time with her.

Ethan headed to the stables first and then the tennis courts but didn't find them. He stopped by the spa and then made his way back to the lodge. Sure enough, they were hanging out by the pool. Their paths must have crossed in his search for them. Kim lounged in a chair by the pool while Chrissie floated around on an inflatable raft.

"Hey, girls, what's going on?" Ethan came to sit on a lounge chair next to Kim.

"Hey, Dad," Chrissie called out and splashed water at him.

"Watch it. I'm your father and I can ground you," Ethan joked with her.

"Are you enjoying your stay?" he asked Kim.

"Actually, I am. Chrissie and I have been having fun. We played some tennis and had pedicures and manicures at the spa."

"This is a great place. I'm glad you're enjoying it."

"I hope I'm not cutting into your time with Chrissie." Kim leaned over toward Ethan.

"No, not at all. I've got work to do around here."

"Chrissie said you were working on a case."

"Yeah. Do you mind if I steal her for a little while? I thought we might go for a ride."

"Sure." Kim reached out and placed her hand on his leg. "Chrissie is really happy being here with you. The one-on-one time she has with you is the best thing you could ever give her."

"Good, I'm glad."

"But, Ethan, I don't think this Jessie person is a very good influence. Chrissie has been filling me in on things."

"Not you, too," he sighed with disgust. Women.

"Ethan, listen to me. Chrissie isn't ready for another woman to be in your life, and I'm not about to let her try to replace me."

"Excuse me? No one is going to replace you, but I am entitled to a personal life."

Kim reached up and caressed his cheek. "A life that should be with your family."

Ethan grabbed her hand and pulled it away from his face. "Kim, don't start. You know that's not going to happen. It's over."

"But Chrissie needs you."

"And I'll always be there for her."

"I need you." She squeezed his hand and leaned in closer.

"Kim, don't do this. We've been through all this before." He released Kim's hand and looked to Chrissie in the pool. "Hey, Sweet Pea, do you think you could spend some time with your old man?

"Sure, Dad." She paddled over to the side of the pool.

"I thought we could go for a nice ride. What do you think about that?"

"Great. I'll go change." Chrissie climbed out of the pool. She ran over, shook water all over her parents, kissed them both and ran toward the lodge.

"Why you little imp!" Ethan called out, laughing. "I'll meet you in the stables." He stood to leave.

Kim reached up and grabbed his arm. "Ethan, don't leave like this. Give us another chance. It's not too late."

He shook her hand off. "Yes, it is." He left her staring after him.

Jessica decided to catch a little bit of the warm sunshine after she grabbed an ice tea from the kitchen and headed out to the patio to relax.

She stepped outside and stopped when she saw Ethan. He was sitting with Kim, and they were laughing. Then she saw Chrissie in the pool. They were obviously joking around with her. The picture of the perfect family. He looked so at ease and happy. She saw Kim reach out and touch him then caress his face.

Her stomach did a flip-flop, and a sinking feeling washed over her. She was making a mistake, a terrible mistake. EJ had his family, and she wasn't a part of it. As much as she wanted that family, she didn't think it wanted her.

"There you are. I wondered where you were when I didn't find you in your office." Laurie walked up behind her.

"I decided to take a break." Jessica couldn't take her eyes off of them.

"Why are you lurking back here behind the shrubs in the shadows?"

Jessica nodded toward the pool. "That's why."

"Oh, I see. I tried to talk to Ethan this morning, and you're right. He wouldn't listen to a word I had to say."

"I told you. It's useless. Look at him; you would never know they were divorced. Look at the way she is touching him and leaning in when he speaks. God, why doesn't she just crawl onto his lap?"

"They're just talking, Jess. Don't read more into it. They share a child. They have to talk to each other once in a while."

"I guess."

"Trust me, I know. Although you wouldn't catch me crawling onto Keith's lap."

"Yeah, well, why is he holding her hand?"

"I'm sure it's nothing. So they have a decent relationship after their divorce. It's not unheard of. It's something you have to accept because she is the mother of his child."

"Yes, I know. Something I will never be."

Laurie placed a hand on Jessica's arm. "Don't go down that road. It's pointless. Nothing is going to change."

"I'm trying, but sometimes those feelings creep back, and they can be a bit overwhelming."

"I know, sweetie. I know." Laurie patted her arm. "But remember how far you've come. Think of all the advice we teach our guest."

"I know, but it's all about moving forward. I know I made bad decisions where my marriage was concerned, and I had resigned myself to not having children. But this, Laurie, it's taking every painful moment from my past and slapping me in the face with it. I've gotta tell ya, it hurts like hell."

"Jessie, I'm sorry. I know this is hard."

"Oh, here they come. Look natural, laugh or something." Jessica faked a laugh.

"Hey, girls, what's going on?" Ethan paused and looked at Jessica. Kim stopped next to him.

"Nothing, just taking a break from work." She felt awkward like she was sixteen all over again. This was stupid.

"Jessie, be a love and have some tea brought to my room. I'm going to relax while Chrissie is with her dad. Thanks so much." Kim smiled and walked away.

Jessica stared at her departing back. She didn't like her, plain and simple.

"Ethan, did you..." Laurie started to comment.

"Don't." Ethan's voice commanded.

"But...."

"Laurie, not now. Jessie, can I speak with you?"

She looked at Laurie and then back to Ethan. "I guess so."

"Okay, I'll catch you two kids later. Bye." Laurie waved to them and disappeared back into the lodge through the French doors of the dining room.

"I'm listening." Jessica crossed her arms in front of her chest.

"I don't want to fight, especially after last night." He reached out and caressed her cheek.

"Neither do I."

"They're my family."

"I know they are."

"I don't know what else to say."

"There isn't anything else to say. You've explained the situation loud and clear. If you'll excuse me, I've got some things to finish up." She turned to leave.

"Wait!" Ethan reached out and grabbed her arm.

Jessica stopped and looked at him. He leaned down to kiss her, but she turned her head, and he kissed her cheek. "See you at the hayride?"

"Yep. Gotta go." She couldn't leave fast enough. She was such a fool. Her heart ached. Of course Chrissie was his family, but Kim?

Would it always be like this? She wasn't asking him to take sides, but he didn't even want to entertain the thought that Chrissie was misbehaving. What kind of person did he think she was? Did he think she would just make up stories about his daughter? It was obvious how much he loved Chrissie, so why would she try to hurt him?

She was rushing things, moving too quickly. After twenty years, she was silly to think they could pick up where they both left off. Things were different. They both had lived completely different lives that couldn't be erased. She should have stuck with her original plan and kept distance between them. It wasn't too late to put the brakes on things. She felt a stab in her heart. Or was it?

chapter 16

THE WAGONS WERE pulled up in front of the lodge, and the women were eagerly piling on. Jessica saw Ethan walk out to the second wagon with his guitar in hand. The ladies would be thrilled tonight. His lack of appearance on the last couple of hayrides caused a tremendous amount of disappointment.

Jessica was ready to walk over to the wagon when Chrissie and Kim came out of the lodge. Chrissie ran to her dad, and he lifted her up onto the wagon. Kim followed behind, and he helped her up as well.

"Jeremy, the wagons are crowded tonight. Would you saddle up Sadie for me?"

"Sure, Aunt Jess." Jeremy disappeared into the barn and quickly returned with Sadie.

"Thanks, Jeremy." Jessica swung herself up into the saddle. She walked Sadie past the wagons and chatted with her guests as she did.

"Jessie," Ethan called out.

She stopped as he leaned over the side of the wagon. "You bellowed?"

"What are you doing on Sadie? How come you're not on the wagon with me?"

"Because it's crowded tonight."

Ethan looked back at the wagon. "Oh, for Pete's sake, I can't believe you're not riding the wagon because of Kim and Chrissie. Are we back in school?"

"Excuse me? There are two other wagons besides yours. If I didn't like the company on your wagon, and I wanted to ride on one, I could have picked a different wagon. It's a little crowded tonight because you're here, and for some reason, the ladies love to be entertained by the likes of you. Besides, I haven't been allowed to ride Sadie much. So get off my back." She gave the horse a squeeze and went to the front of the wagons.

Laurie sat up front on the first wagon. "Jess! What's going on?" She waived her over. "You don't look happy."

"He's a jackass."

"Ethan?"

"That would be the jackass."

"Why?"

"Because I'm not riding on the wagon with him, and he thinks it's because of Kim and Chrissie."

"Is it?"

"No! Am I the only one that can see all these women on the wagons?" She was getting irritated, now.

"Sorry."

"You should be. Besides, since our mystery menace has shown up, I haven't been able to ride like I'm used to. Sadie needs some serious exercise. Really, I swear it's the truth." Jessica crossed her heart and held her fingers like a Girl Scout.

"Okay, I believe you."

Ethan didn't feel like singing for the ladies, now. He couldn't believe how Jessica was behaving, especially after what they had shared last night. He truly believed she was falling in love with him again. He felt it, he was positive about that.

"Come on, Ethan, don't make us wait."

"Make them wait for what?" Kim asked, giving him a sideways glance.

"They find my voice enchanting."

Chrissie leaned over to add her two cents worth. "Mom, it's disgusting the way these women act."

"I see that," Kim whispered back, pursing her lips together in disgust.

"What shall it be tonight, ladies?"

"Anything you sing, honey, is fine!" someone yelled out.

Ethan chuckled. "Okay, how about a little Garth Brooks." He began strumming his guitar.

He loved to sing and play, so entertaining the ladies wasn't so bad. During his career with the FBI, it came in handy. Most of the time he found it was easy to take his guitar with him. Playing always relaxed him, which was helpful when things got a little dicey. He sang a few tunes, and the ladies went crazy. It didn't take him long before he had them all singing *Friends in Low Places*, including Chrissie and Kim.

When the hayride was over, he helped all the ladies off the wagon. He searched the crowd of people, looking for Jessie, but she was nowhere to be seen. His heart started to race. She was probably in the barn with Sadie. He couldn't over react every time she stepped out of his sight.

He made his way around to the campfire. People were settling in, and some of the guys had taken over the entertainment.

He found Kim sitting in one of the Adirondack chairs, looking rather bored.

"Kim, where's Chrissie?"

"I thought she was with you?"

"Why would she be with me? I was helping the ladies off the wagon? Weren't you watching her? She was just with you on the wagon," he snapped at her.

"Ethan, she's fourteen. It's not like she's a toddler."

"I know, but with everything that is going on around here, I like to know where she is."

"Is it dangerous here?" Kim was on her feet, her hands planted on her hips. "I knew it! That woman *is* trouble."

"No, I don't think it's dangerous for Chrissie. I think they're only after Jessie, but still."

"They're only after Jessie? Ethan, what have you done by bringing our daughter here?"

"Kim, don't go crazy on me. I would never put Chrissie in harms way."

"I suppose dead rats in your bed isn't in harm's way?"

Ethan spun around and glared at her. "*Do not* do this now. We need to find Chrissie."

"Fine, I'll go look for her," Kim said.

"You go check your room, and I'll look around here."

Ethan searched around the campfire, no Chrissie. He walked through the lodge, still no Chrissie. Now he was starting to get nervous. He asked a couple of people if they had seen her, no one had. Now he was becoming frantic.

He headed to the stables. The light was on in the barn and he burst through the door. "Chrissie!"

"It's just me." Jessica peeked her head over Sadie's stall door.

"Have you seen Chrissie?"

"No, why?"

"I can't find her. She disappeared after the hayride."

"You don't think something happened to her, do you?" Jessica hurried out of Sadie's stall.

"I don't know. She's not in the lodge or around the campfire. Nobody has seen her."

Jessica went up to him and placed her hand on his arm. "Don't worry, she hasn't been gone long, we'll find her."

"You'll help me look for her?"

"Of course I will. I'll go this way toward the bunkhouse, and you go through the other barns. Make sure you check the hay lofts."

"Okay, fine."

Ethan took off running, calling out Chrissie's name. A soft glow illuminated the bunkhouse as Jessica walked up on the porch and peeked in the window. She quickly turned and ran back the way Ethan had went.

She was breathless from running. "EJ, I found her."

"You did? Where?"

"In the bunkhouse."

"The bunkhouse? Why the hell is she in there?"

She grabbed his arm. "Ethan, don't do anything stupid."

He took off at a run. His long legs got him to his destination in seconds. He quietly stepped up on the porch and peered in the window. Laying on one of the bunks was his daughter and one of the wranglers.

He was going to kill them both.

He burst through the door. "Christina Kirkpatrick, get your ass back to that lodge before I beat you silly!" he bellowed.

"Oh, my God!" She screamed when Ethan barged in. She pulled her blouse together and started buttoning it up.

Jessica came running up behind him as Chrissie pushed past both of them, tears streaming down her face.

"What the hell do you think you were doing with my daughter?" Ethan approached the young man with purposeful strides and grabbed him up off the bed by the front of his shirt.

"Your daughter? I didn't know..." the young man stammered.

"Ethan, easy. He said he didn't know." Jessica tried to pull him off Brian.

Joe came running into the bunkhouse. "What the hell is going on here? Let the boy go."

"I don't believe him." Ethan growled through clenched teeth.

"Ethan, who in their right mind would mess with your daughter if they knew it? Think about it." Jessica reaffirmed what Brian had said.

"She is only fourteen. What is the matter with you?"

"I didn't know, Ethan, I swear. She came on to me. She didn't act young." Brian turned interesting shades of gray.

"How dare you blame your behavior on an innocent little girl? What kind of a man are you?"

"She didn't act so innocent."

Ethan pulled his fist back ready to let it fly when Joe grabbed his arm. "Hang on cowboy, he said he didn't know. Miss Jessica is right. No guy would touch your daughter if they knew. Now let the boy go."

"Ethan, don't do this! You haven't been listening. You won't listen to anybody. It's Chrissie. I keep trying to tell you," Jessica pleaded.

Ethan threw Brian down on the bed. "If I ever see you near my daughter again, I will beat you within an inch of your life."

"Don't worry, it'll never happen again," Brian stammered.

"You're such a jackass," Jessica yelled at Ethan and then ran out of the bunkhouse.

Ethan started to go after her, but Joe stopped him. "Listen son, I don't usually stick my nose in Miss Jessica's business, but there is obviously something between you two. She's been moody and distracted ever since you arrived. I know it has to do with more than just the reason why she said you're here."

"Joe, you're right, this isn't any of your business. This is between us."

Joe placed a firm hand on Ethan's shoulder. "Let me set you straight, cowboy. I love her like she's my own daughter and if you hurt her, you'll be the one being beat within an inch of your life." With that said, Joe left the bunkhouse.

Ethan stared at his retreating back. He wanted to go after Jessie, but realized he had a daughter he needed to deal with first.

chapter 17

ETHAN WAS FURIOUS for more reasons than one. With long purposeful strides, he marched his way back to the lodge and directly to the room where Kim and Chrissie were staying. He pounded on the door.

"Christina!" he bellowed.

Kim opened the door, and he barged past her. Chrissie was lying on the bed, crying. "Ethan, what on earth is going on? What did you do to our daughter?"

He stopped in his tracks and spun around to look at Kim. "Me? What did I do? Why don't you ask <u>your</u> daughter what <u>she</u> did?"

"She told me that Jessie was trying to turn you against her, and apparently, it's working. What horrible lies is she filling your head with about our daughter?" Kim stood definitely with her hands on her hips.

Kim's words echoed in his head. It hit him like a wrecking ball slamming into a building. Jessie hadn't done anything except try to open his eyes. She wasn't doing it to be mean, but because she cared. She was trying to protect Chrissie because she was too young to understand the consequences for her actions. He had been blind to what was happening before his very eyes. His blood started to boil. God, what a jackass he really was.

"Jessie hasn't done anything but try to look out for our daughter, which is more than I can say for the two of us."

"I beg your pardon? Our daughter was fine until she came here to be with you and that woman. She runs a ranch for women with a lot of men running around. What kind of things is she condoning here, anyways?"

"Kim, you know nothing about Jessie or this place, so don't go acting all self-righteous. She's trying to help women who are just like you. Women with issues."

"What! How dare you?"

"How dare I?" He raised an eyebrow at her. "What exactly did our daughter tell you?"

Chrissie wailed louder from the bed.

"She said that Jessie was telling you lies about her and some of the cowboys that worked here. She said Jessie was trying to make you think she misbehaved so you would be angry and send her away. Obviously, it's the truth."

"Kimberly, I saw with my own two eyes our daughter lying on a bed with one of the wranglers. He is twenty-two-years-old! He's a man! Do you think Jessie forced Christina to do that? Do you?"

"Well, it's no wonder she is behaving like this with the way the women act around here. I'm sure they taught Chrissie a few things. The displays they put on for you alone put objectionable ideas in our daughter's head."

"Kim, please."

"Okay, so maybe she didn't, but he was obviously trying to take advantage of a little girl. He's sick and should be fired. You're the Sheriff. Arrest him for statutory rape!"

"Kim, give me a break. Apparently, she's also tried to cuddle up to Jeremy, Aaron and Scott as well. Would you like me to arrest them, too?"

"Who told you that? Jessie?"

"Kim, I don't even care about that. The fact is, I saw Christina with my own eyes, and that's not okay."

"Ethan, I don't believe you."

He turned away from Kim. "Christina, you're grounded. You are not to leave your mother's or my sight. Do you understand?"

Chrissie nodded her head and sniffed.

"Why were you with that boy?"

"Because I liked him, but Jessie spoiled that."

"What about those other boys?"

"She ruined that, too. I wasn't doing anything wrong. We were only talking."

"Is that why you don't like Jessie, because she caught you?"

"You're obviously taking her side. You like her better than me and Mom. She made it sound worse, like I was doing bad things, but I wasn't. She's a liar, and she hates me."

"Chrissie, that's not true. We both know Jessie isn't the one lying. You're my daughter, and I love you, but I'm not going to tolerate this."

"You don't love me, you love Jessie. You should talk, Dad, you just want to get her into bed!" Chrissie yelled and ran into the bathroom, slamming the door and locking it behind her.

"Christina!" he bellowed.

"Is that true, Ethan? What have you been doing in front of our daughter?"

"This isn't about me. This is about her total lack of respect and unexceptable behavior!"

"Ethan, leave her alone. We'll discuss it in the morning."

"Fine, but *we will* discuss it." He slammed out of their room.

That went just peachy. Now to dig himself out of the other hole he had created. He figured he would find Jessica in her suite. Thank goodness she had given him a key because he was pretty sure she wouldn't let him in right about now.

When he entered the suite, he found it completely dark. That wasn't good. He went to Jessica's room and tried the door. It was locked. Now why wasn't he surprised?

He tapped lightly on the door. "Jessie, it's me, please open the door."

No response.

He tapped again. "Come on, Jessie, open up. I really want to talk to you."

No response.

"Jessie, I want to apologize for being a complete and total jackass."

Still no response.

Okay, fine. He would wait for her in the morning, and then he would talk to her. Perhaps in the morning, she wouldn't be so mad at him.

chapter 18

JESSICA TIPTOED OUT of her room as quietly as she possibly could. She was sure Ethan would be on her heels in seconds thanks to that stupid sensor. If she moved fast enough, perhaps she could be in public before he got to her. She literally ran out the door.

She hurried down the hallway, checking over her shoulder to see if he followed her. No Ethan. Good. That's the way she wanted it. She headed to the dining room for some coffee and breakfast.

She walked in and stopped. To her surprise, there was Ethan and Kimberly already sitting at a table in the far corner of the room, just the two of them with their heads together. She was right, this wasn't going to work. She blinked back the tears that wanted to run down her cheeks.

What a fool she had been. She actually opened her heart to him for a second time, and once again, he broke it. Obviously, being with Kim and his daughter again reminded him of the family he left and the family he wanted back. She couldn't blame him for that, only chastise herself for letting him into her world again.

"Aunt Jess! Aunt Jess!" Jeremy came yelling into the dining room.

Ethan looked up and saw her standing there. Damn, she was busted. She spun around to answer Jeremy and saw the panic-stricken look on his face.

"What's wrong?" She grabbed him by the shoulders.

"It's Mom, come quick! She's collapsed!" he yelled breathlessly.

Jessica went tearing down the hallways with Ethan right behind her. She burst through the door of Laurie's suite.

"Where is she?"

"In her room."

Jessica found Laurie wrapped in her bathrobe, lying on her bed with her eyes closed. Jessica ran to her side.

"Oh God, Laurie, what's wrong? Answer me." Jessica shook her lightly.

Laurie opened her eyes. "They stung me, several times, there was more than one," she gasped out.

Jessica spun around to find Ethan standing next to her. "What stung her?"

"Bathroom," Laurie whispered.

Ethan and Jessica went charging toward the bathroom. Ethan stopped her at the door.

"Wait. We don't know what we're looking for, and I don't want you getting stung, too."

"What could have stung her, bees?" Jessica poked her head in the bathroom and looked up toward the ceiling.

"What the hell?" Ethan was looking at the towels lying on the floor. "Did that just move?"

Jessica followed his gaze. "Yes! I just saw it move again."

"Okay, stand back." Ethan pushed Jessica back, and he slowly lifted the towel off the floor. "Holy Christ! Look at that." Ethan shook four creatures from the towel.

"Scorpions? That's what stung her? How the hell did scorpions get in here to sting her?"

"Jess, these aren't just any scorpions, these are striped bark scorpions, and they're poisonous. You better call the doctor, quickly."

Jessica ran into the bedroom and grabbed the phone and called Doctor Anderson's cell phone. "Jamie, it's Jessica, we have a problem. Laurie has been stung by scorpions."

"What! Where was she?"

"In her room."

"Her room?"

"I'll explain later."

"Okay. How many times did she get stung?"

"Several and, Jamie, they are striped bark scorpions."

"That's not good. We have to make sure she hasn't gone into anaphylactic shock. Is she having trouble breathing, abdominal pain, vomiting?"

"She's in and out of it. Her breathing is very shallow, almost like she's having an asthma attack. She's curled up in a ball, so I'm not sure if her stomach hurts."

"Jess, you need to call an ambulance, now. I'll meet you at the hospital. Until the ambulance gets there, try to clean the areas where she was stung, put cool compresses on them and see if you can get some Tylenol into her. If you have an Epi Pen, use it."

"Okay, I'll call right now. Thanks, Jamie." Jessica hung up the phone and then dialed 911. She gave them the address and what had happened. They were on their way. "Hang on, Laurie, we're gonna get you some help."

Jeremy stood by the bed. "Is she going to be alright?"

"Yep, go get the first aide kit at the front desk. We need the Epi Pen in there. Hurry."

Jeremy took off at a run. Ethan came into the bedroom, holding a jar with a lid. The ugly little creatures crawled around inside it.

"I'm sure the doctor will want these."

"EJ, somebody did this on purpose, didn't they?"

"I'm afraid so. Laurie, honey, can you hear me?" Ethan knelt down beside her bed. She opened her eyes and looked at him. "Laurie, I need you to help me. Where were the scorpions? How did they sting you?"

"My towel." She gasped. "They were in my towel."

Ethan stood up and looked at Jessica as a tear ran down her cheek. He reached out and patted Laurie's arm. "Laurie, honey, you're gonna be okay."

Jeremy came running in the with the Epi pen. Jessica grabbed it. Laurie winced as Jessica stabbed her in the leg with it. It wasn't long before they heard the screech of the sirens. Jeremy dashed out to show them were to go. The EMTs rushed in and quickly loaded Laurie onto the stretcher and were out the door.

"Jeremy, you ride with your mom. I'll follow you in the car," Jessica said as Laurie was placed in the ambulance.

"Let me drive you," Ethan offered.

"No thanks, I'll be fine."

"Let me rephrase that. I'll drive you to the hospital. No argument, let's go."

Jessica didn't say a word. She headed to her Envoy and tossed Ethan the keys. Before they left, Ethan saw Joe coming across the courtyard.

"Ethan, what the hell is going on now? Why was the ambulance here?"

"Someone put scorpions in Laurie's towels. She got stung several times."

"Scorpions! How the hell did that happen?"

"That's a good question? I'm taking Jessie to the hospital to be with Laurie and Jeremy."

"This is out of control."

"I need you to do me a favor while I'm gone. Can you poke around to see if you can find out who has been near Laurie's suite, either last night or this morning?"

"You've got it, anything to help catch this son-of-a-bitch."

"Thanks, Joe." Ethan patted him on the shoulder and hopped into the Envoy.

They rode to the hospital in silence. Jessica's mind was swirling. Someone had tried to hurt Laurie, maybe even kill Laurie, all because of her. A tear ran down her cheek. She couldn't stand the thought of someone she loved being hurt because of her. She wiped the tears away with the back of her hand.

Jessica found Jeremy sitting in the waiting room of the emergency department. She slid into the chair next to him and patted his leg. "She's going to be okay. I promise, she is going to be okay."

"I know, Aunt Jess."

"Did you see Doctor Anderson?"

"Yeah, she was waiting for us."

"Good, she'll make sure your mom is in good hands." Jessica got up and started to pace around the waiting room. The sterile smell of the hospital assaulted her nose and made her stomach churn. She hated hospitals.

How had things come to this? She loved her new home and new life. Her employees were her family. She was happy until some judgmental person decided to take it all away from her. Now she was not only losing her home, her business and her friends, she was losing her heart. Her life was a disaster. Things couldn't get much worse than seeing her best friend lying in a hospital bed.

"Hey, want some coffee?" Ethan walked up to her and handed her a cup.

"Thanks."

"Laurie will be fine."

"I know she will, but that doesn't make it all right."

"I know."

"Jeremy, Jess, Ethan." Doctor Anderson stepped out of the room they had taken Laurie into.

"Jamie, how is she?" Jessica walked over to her.

"She's going to make a full recovery. We're giving her some antihistamines and corticosteroids along with some Albuterol treatments. We need to keep her overnight to make sure that everything is under control, but she should be fine."

"Oh, thank God!" Jessica hugged Jeremy. "I told you she would be okay."

"We're going to move her to a private room."

"Can we see her?" Jeremy asked.

"You sure can. She's very tired and needs her rest, so don't stay long. You can probably go home and come back around dinner time."

"Thanks." Jeremy headed into the room to see his mom.

"Jamie, thanks so much for rushing here."

"Not a problem, but Jess, how did she get stung by those scorpions?"

"She said they were in her towel."

Jamie raised an eyebrow at her. "First Scott, then Ethan, now Laurie. What's going on?"

"Jamie, you don't even know the half of it."

"You mean someone is still trying to get you to close down the ranch? I know the Mayor has been pretty vocal, acting like he's so morally righteous, but I can't believe someone has listened to him enough to actually sink to this level."

"Yeah, I know. Can you believe that people are that blind? Ethan has been trying to figure out who is behind this nightmare. It's obvious that nothing immoral or illegal is taking place on my ranch. I'm running a legitimate business."

"Well, I hope he figures it out soon because I don't want to see anyone else from your ranch here."

"Neither do I. Thanks again, Jamie." Jessica hugged her friend and went to check on Laurie.

ॐ

Jessica didn't know what to do with herself when they arrived back at the ranch. She retreated to her office, but only managed to stare at the papers on her desk.

A knock sounded on her door. "Come in." She looked up to see Maddie poke her head in the door.

"Miss Jessica, are you okay? I heard about Miss Laurie. Is she going to be alright?"

"Yeah, thank goodness." A tear ran down her cheek.

"Oh, now don't you cry." Maddie came around her desk to pat her on the shoulder.

"It's all getting to be too much," Jessica sniffed.

"What about your handsome cowboy? He's got some pretty broad shoulders to lean on."

"He's part of the problem. I won't be using his shoulders for anything."

"How about I bring you some tea? That might make you feel better."

"Oh, Maddie, you're so sweet. You're always looking out for me. I think I'll pass. I'm going to take a ride on Sadie. Riding always makes me feel better."

"Well, if you change your mind, you let me know."

"Thanks, Maddie, I will."

Jessica left her office and headed to the stables by way of the kitchen. She needed a few carrots for her girl. She filled her pockets and stepped outside onto the patio. There she saw Ethan sitting with Kim and Chrissie, his perfect family.

She stared at the threesome, and her heart sank to her toes. She didn't have anything left in her. She was done fighting. It all became very clear, and she knew what had to be done. She fought back the tears that wanted to spill from her eyes. It was going to kill her, but she had no choice. No one else was going to get hurt.

She swallowed back the tears and marched over to Ethan's table.

"Jessie, everything okay?" Ethan looked up at her.

"It's going to be. I wanted to tell you I am no longer in need of your services."

"Which services would those be?" He winked at her.

She frowned at him. "Your investigative services. There is no need for you to continue with your investigation."

"What? Jessie, it isn't safe with that person running around."

"Exactly. I surrender. I'm putting the ranch up for sale. They can have it. Losing the people I love isn't worth it."

"You can't be serious. You're just upset over Laurie."

"You're damn right I am upset, but I'm totally serious. So I would appreciate it if you would get your things and get off my ranch." She spun around and headed to the stables, leaving Ethan to stare at her retreating figure with his mouth gaping open.

It was no use. Between fighting to keep her ranch and fighting with him, she couldn't hold back the tears that were now streaming down her cheeks. She couldn't get to Sadie fast enough.

Ethan was completely distracted now. How could she sell this place, it was her life? He had to focus. He needed to deal with his daughter first, and then he would convince Jessie she was wrong.

"Chrissie, I hope you understand how your mom and I feel." Ethan held Chrissie's hand.

"I guess."

"We both love you very much, but we are never going to get back together."

"Why not? Because of Jessie?" Chrissie pouted.

It was Kim's turn to interject. "No, Chrissie. Jessie had nothing to do with why Mom and Dad aren't together any more. A lot of things happened, and we grew apart."

"That's because of Dad's job. He doesn't have that job anymore."

"Chrissie, that doesn't matter. People change. It's just not going to work." Kim reached out and held Chrissie's other hand.

"But, Mom, you still love Dad."

"Oh, Honey, your dad and I had a very long talk. Yes, I do still love him. He gave me the most precious gift in the world, but that doesn't change why we separated. Daddy made me see that."

"It's because of Jessie. Dad loves her. It's all her fault."

"Sweet Pea, you'll always be our little girl, and we will always love you. That is never going to change. We're just going to love you apart." Ethan tried to reassure her.

"Fine."

"Is that why you gave Jessie such a hard time? Were you trying to make me not want to be with her so I would go back to Mom?" Ethan squeezed Chrissie's hand.

She nodded.

"Christina, that was wrong." Kim scolded.

"I know, but I wanted Dad with you, not her."

"Christina, was Jessie really mean to you?"

Chrissie's head sank further. "No."

"I didn't think so." Ethan frowned. He was more angry with himself than Chrissie because he hadn't believed Jessie. He seemed to be pretty good at being a first rate idiot where she was concerned.

"Christina, you made me think things about Jessie that weren't true. That's wrong. You caused a lot of trouble and hurt people." Kim lifted Chrissie's chin so she could look at her face. "Thank goodness your dad set me straight about her. Jessie sounds like a nice enough person, and I was wrong about her."

"I'm sorry, Mom. Jessie really is nice."

"It's not me you owe the apology to."

"I'm sorry, Dad. I was afraid that if you were with Jessie, you wouldn't have any time left for me."

"I don't think I'm the one your mother is referring to. And, Sweet Pea, you don't ever have to worry about me finding time for you. I've got room for both of you in my life."

"I guess that means I owe Jessie an apology."

"Yes, you do."

"Okay, Dad. I just didn't want Mom's feelings to get hurt."

"Oh, sweetheart, you don't have to worry about me." Kim brushed a strand of hair away from Chrissie's face. "It's okay if you like Jessie. In fact, I hope you do if your dad likes her. I want you to feel comfortable spending time with him and, if Jessie is in his life, I want you to feel comfortable around her too."

"Are you sure? It doesn't seem right. I don't want to hurt you."

"You're not. I hope someday I'll find someone and that you'll like him, too. That doesn't mean you'll love your dad any less. It's okay for you to like Jessie and spend time with her because you will always be my little girl."

"Really? You don't mind if I like her?"

"Yes, really."

"Thanks, Mom." Chrissie jumped up and hugged her mother. "Am I forgiven, Dad?"

"Come here, Sweet Pea." Ethan opened up his arms wide, and she ran into them. "You still need to go and make up with Jessie."

"I will, Dad, I promise. Actually, I really like her. I'm sorry I was such a brat."

"It's okay, I still love you. We all make mistakes." Boy didn't he know that one. Too well, he was afraid. "Speaking of Jessie, I think I better go and stop her from selling the ranch. Will you gals be okay?"

"We'll be fine. Go find her and explain things." Kim nodded toward the stables.

"Thanks. Thanks for understanding." He winked at Kim and headed off to find Jessie.

chapter 19

JESSICA FUMBLED WITH the saddle as she wiped away the tears that continued to fall. Sadie was restless and stomped her feet impatiently, eager for their ride. Jessica led her from the barn and swung herself up into the saddle. She squeezed Sadie's sides, and they were off.

Her heart was so heavy. She was losing everything she had worked so hard for. Where was she going to go? It certainly wouldn't be back home. That would be admitting defeat. Besides, she had no interest in running into John and his new bride. It couldn't be here either, not just because of the Mayor and the town's people, but because EJ would be too close.

EJ. The tears started to flow harder. She had known better, sworn up and down she wouldn't allow him to hurt her again, yet here she was. He had conquered her with his charms, even though she had tried desperately to fight her feelings. She had loved him, had always loved him. She laughed out loud. In spite of the pain in her heart, she never stopped loving him. Maybe that's why she had never been able to let go of the pain. It was a constant reminder of him. By hanging onto the pain of the past, she was hanging onto a small part of him.

She needed to pull herself together. She could sell the ranch and start over somewhere else. The question was, where?

The sound of thundering hooves caused her to turn in the saddle to see who was coming. She groaned when she saw Ethan headed straight for her.

"Can't you just leave me alone?" she snapped at him.

"Jessie, what's wrong with you? Why are you selling the ranch?"

"You're kidding, right?"

"No, I'm so close to figuring this out."

"I'm done, EJ. If someone wants me to close my ranch so bad they are willing to stoop to hurting the people I love, then I surrender. They win, EJ. No more, there isn't going to be anyone else getting hurt."

"But Jessie…"

"Stop." She held her hand up to quiet him. "My mind is made up. My best friend is lying in a hospital bed because of this menace. There is nothing you can do to change my mind."

"What about us?"

She blinked back the tears that wanted to fall. "I told you I no longer need your services. There is nothing to solve. I'm calling a real estate agent as soon as I get back to my office."

"I wasn't referring to that, and you know it." He leaned over and grabbed Sadie's reins so he could pull her closer.

"There is no us."

"But, Jessie, I love you."

"I don't know what you want me to say."

"How about I love you, too? I know you do."

"It's not going to work. I can't do this. I'm sorry I made you think otherwise." She tried to pull Sadie's reins free from him.

"Jessie, I was a jerk yet again. I'm sorry."

"So am I." She yanked on the reins hard, pulling them out of EJ's hand, kicked Sadie in the side and took off toward the stream.

"Jessie, wait!"

All she wanted was to be alone and take one last look at her home before she gave it up. But no, he just wouldn't leave her alone. Why? He didn't love her, he loved his family, a point he made very clear. She wasn't going to fight with him, and she wasn't going to make him choose.

The tears streamed down her face, and she slowed Sadie because she couldn't see. She heard a bang then felt a sting in her arm as Sadie bolted sideways. She lost her balance and found herself falling. She landed with a thud, her head finding a rock. What happened? The pain went from stinging to throbbing. Everything started to go fuzzy and then black. She was sinking, sinking into the darkness.

chapter 20

"Jessie!" Ethan screamed and kicked Caesar into action. He reined up next to Jessica and jumped from his horse. He cradled her limp body in his arms. Blood was soaking her blouse and trickled down the side of her face. Damn, he should have never let her ride off. Help, they needed to get help quickly. He reached for his cell phone, but it wasn't there. Damn.

Ethan checked her body. Someone had shot her in the shoulder. He tried to wipe the blood that trickled down her cheek. She must have hit her head when she fell.

He laid her back down on the ground and rose to grab Sadie's reins which he'd tied to the horn on his saddle. He steadied Caesar and gently lifted Jessica up across the saddle. This wasn't going to be easy. He hoisted himself up behind her and then pulled Jessie into his lap so he could hold her and ride at the same time.

He ripped a piece of his shirt and tried to apply pressure to the gunshot wound in an effort to stop the bleeding. It was useless. He was failing miserably. The blood was drenching them both. Ethan urged Caesar forward, going as fast as he could and still hanging onto her. They were farther away from the ranch than he thought. She was losing so much blood. A feeling of dread set in the pit of his stomach. He had seen his share of gunshot wounds and was scared to death she was going to die.

He hung onto her as tightly as he could and urged Caesar even faster. They needed help, now. Ethan breathed a sigh of relief when the lodge came into sight.

He rode up to the front door, screaming their arrival. "Help, someone help me now! Call 911! Someone call 911!"

Several guests came running out of the lodge. He slid off the horse and pulled Jessica into his arms.

Joe came running up the driveway. "Ethan, what happened?"

"She's been shot. Someone call an ambulance."

"I called, Ethan, she'll be okay," Aaron said.

"I need towels so I can try to stop the bleeding."

Joe ran into the lodge and emerged with some towels. "Here. She's going to be fine, Ethan. You have to believe that."

Jessica's pale limp body lay on the front porch as Ethan desperately tried to save her life. He felt so helpless. It seemed like an eternity before the ambulance roared up the driveway. Paramedics jumped out and began working on Jessica.

"Is she going to be okay?" Ethan asked.

"We're not sure. She's lost a lot of blood, and her pressure is dropping. It looks like she took a blow to the head. We've got to get her stabilized. Will you be riding in the ambulance?"

"Absolutely." Ethan hopped into the back.

The ambulance screeched back down the driveway, sirens blaring. Ethan held her hand and prayed. They had to be in time. He couldn't lose her, he just couldn't.

"Hang in there, Jessie. We're almost to the hospital. You're gonna be alright, do you here me? I love you, Jessie, please don't leave me." Ethan kissed her hand as a tear trickled down his face.

They were closing in on the hospital when Jessica's heart monitor flat-lined. "We're losing her! Her pressure is bottoming out," yelled the paramedic. He grabbed the defibulator to shock her heart. "Stand clear."

"Damn it, Jessie! Don't you dare die on me, not now," Ethan ordered her as if he could command her to live.

The ambulance pulled up to the Emergency room, and everyone jumped out. The paramedics ran along side the gurney, calling out her condition to the doctors. They raced her into a room with the heart monitor still crying out the monotonous beep.

A nurse stopped Ethan at the door. All he could do was peer in the small window as the medical team surrounded her bed.

This was all his fault.

He should have never let her take off by herself. He shouldn't have put up with her fussing. He should have dragged her back to the lodge whether she liked it or not.

"Ethan?"

He turned around to see Doctor Anderson standing there. "Jamie."

"Ethan, what happened?"

He saw her eyes grow wide as they roamed up and down his bloodstained clothes. "It's Jessie, she's been shot. She flat-lined in the ambulance. Jamie, she can't die." Ethan struggled to hold the tears back.

Jamie placed her arm around him. "Come and sit. I'll check on her." She disappeared and a few moments later, reappeared in scrubs. She entered the room where they had taken Jessica.

Ethan sat in the chair with his head hanging in his hands. Thoughts of Jessie swirled around in his mind, and he closed his eyes. It was wonderful to see her again. He couldn't believe she was back in his life, and he couldn't believe how overpowering his feelings for her still were. He had never stopped loving her. She had fallen back in love with him, he was sure of it. Making love to her again was the most incredible experience of his life. Without a doubt, he knew she was his soul mate.

Then he screwed it all up.

Even if he hadn't believed her, he still should have kept a better eye on Chrissie to discover the truth himself. He knew better. He was a cop, for godsake. Once again, he had hurt her. Something he seemed to be good at doing. But it was all a big misunderstanding that he wanted to fix, if she would let him. She had to. Now that he had her back, he couldn't live without her.

Jamie came out and sat down next to Ethan. She placed a hand on his leg.

He looked up at her and saw the grim expression on her face. "It's bad, isn't it?"

"They're taking her into surgery. She ruptured her brachial artery and lost a lot of blood. The bullet is still lodged in her scapula. They need to remove it and repair the damage it caused. Then they're going to do an MRI to see if there is any swelling on the brain from her fall. What happened, Ethan?"

"She decided to sell the ranch. She was really upset and went for a ride. I followed her, which upset her even more. She took off by herself. I should have stopped her, Jamie. Before I knew it, there was a shot. I raced in her direction. Just as I got there, I saw her fall off Sadie. She hit her head on a rock when she fell."

"Who the hell is doing this to her? Why would anyone want her to close down her ranch? I've heard rumors, but people can't seriously think she's running a brothel or anything like that."

"You'd be surprised what people in a small town believe, especially if someone keeps telling them what to believe."

"You know who's behind this?"

"I have an idea, but I need a little more proof. If I could just get the irrefutable proof, this would all be over, damn it."

"Ethan, it's not your fault."

"It sure doesn't feel that way. Will she be okay?"

"I don't know. She lost so much blood and is very weak. Only time will tell. Here they come now." Jamie stood up and walked over to the gurney. "Could you give him a quick minute?" She motioned for Ethan to come over.

He looked down at Jessica. She was void of all color, the life drained out of her. He leaned down and kissed her lips. "I love you, Jessie. Come back to me." He stepped away as they wheeled her off to surgery.

Ethan didn't know what to do with himself as he waited. He walked, he paced, he sat and then finally wandered into Laurie's room to check on her. He poked his head in the door and saw that she was awake.

"Hey there, how are you feeling?" He walked over to stand beside her bed. She looked pale and was still on oxygen.

"I'm better. My God, Ethan, what happened to you?"

He looked down, totally forgetting that he was covered in Jessica's blood. "It's nothing."

"You look like hell. What happened?"

"You need to rest. Don't worry about it, I'll come back later." He turned to leave.

"I'm gonna hurt you in a minute if you don't tell me who's blood is all over you. What happened?" She started to gasp for air.

Ethan returned to her bedside. "Easy now." He brushed her hair away from her face.

"Don't patronize me."

"It's, Jessie. She was hurt, but she'll be fine."

"Hurt? If that's her blood, she's more than hurt." Laurie started to get out of bed. "Where is she?"

"Settle down. I said she'll be fine." Ethan nudged her back into the bed.

"Ethan, you're lying to me. Out with it. I was poisoned, but I'm going to be fine. I'm not dying. What happened?"

"She was shot."

"What!" Laurie tried to sit up again.

"Please don't get upset. They'll toss me out."

"I can't help it. How bad is she? From the looks of you, it can't be good." Laurie started to cry.

"She's in surgery, but Jamie is here and she's going to make sure Jessie is okay." He could kick himself for stopping in to see her. He could only imagine what he must look like covered in Jessie's blood. Not exactly the best medicine for Laurie.

"Ethan?" Jamie poked her head in the door.

"Any word?" Ethan felt his heart racing in anticipation of her answer.

"She's out of surgery and in recovery. She's going to need her rest. Why don't you go home? I'll stay with her tonight."

"I don't know, Jamie."

"It's an order not a request. You can't do anything for her right now. Go change your clothes and get some rest. I promise if there is a change, I will call you."

"Okay. I'll go." He turned his attention back to Laurie. "See, I told you she would be okay."

"I didn't hear Jamie say that."

"You read too much into things. You need your rest, too. I'll bring Jeremy with me in the morning."

"Okay."

Ethan leaned down and kissed her cheek. "Stay out of trouble, would ya?"

"Awe, you're no fun. I kind of like you coming to my rescue. Although, being stung by scorpions is a little on the dramatic side."

"I see you haven't lost your sense of humor. Now, behave yourself." Ethan winked at her and walked out of the room.

He was emotionally drained. Two trips to the hospital in one day was more than anyone should have to handle. He needed a hot shower and a nap. Then he'd return to sit by Jessica's bedside.

chapter 21

ETHAN OPENED HIS eyes and looked at the clock. He blinked twice. It couldn't be. He was only going to lay down for a few minutes after his shower. The clock read six a.m. He quickly rose, dressed and headed for the hospital.

When he arrived, he found Jamie asleep in a chair in Jessica's room. He gently nudged her shoulder. "Good morning," he whispered.

"Hi." Jamie yawned and stretched. "What time is it?"

"It's around seven. How is she?"

"She's stable, but has a low grade temperature that we want to keep an eye on."

"Thanks for staying with her."

"I wouldn't be any place else."

"Why don't you go home and get some sleep. That chair couldn't have been very comfortable."

"No, it wasn't. I'll be back later. Call me if you need anything or if there is a change in her condition." Jamie gave Ethan a hug and left.

Ethan pulled the chair beside Jessica's bed and took her hand in his. He softly kissed it. She looked so fragile hooked up to all the tubes and monitors. He still felt an overwhelming amount of anxiety about her condition. Laurie was right; no one had actually uttered the words that she was going to be okay.

Jessica moaned and tossed about in the bed. He stood and leaned over her. "Jessie, can you hear me? It's Ethan."

Her head rolled from side to side. "No, please don't." She moaned again.

"Jessie, babe, what are you talking about?" He brushed her hair away from her face. She felt like she was on fire. Her fever must have spiked.

"No, don't leave me."

Ethan's concern grew because of the distress he heard in her voice. She was obviously upset. "Don't worry, babe, I'm not going anywhere." He pushed the nurse's call button on Jessica's bed.

It was only a moment before a nurse entered the room. "What seems to be the problem?"

"She appears to be in distress. She's tossing and turning, calling out. She feels like she's burning up."

"Well, let's take a look." The nurse walked over to the bed, checked Jessica over and took her temperature. "Her fever has risen. I need to call the doctor."

"Is she going to be okay?" Ethan stood next to the nurse.

"I can't say right now. The fever could be a sign of infection. Let me go contact the doctor."

"What about all her moaning and thrashing around? She's obviously in distress. Is she in pain?"

"It's probably the fever, but we'll let the doctor confirm that." The nurse left the room.

Ethan brushed his fingers along the side of Jessica's cheek. Her face was damp to his touch. She moaned again. He pushed the hair that clung to her cheek away from her face.

"Help me," she mumbled.

"I'm here, Jessie. I'll help you." He took her hand in his. How the hell was he supposed to help her?

"No, not the baby." She thrashed her legs and tossed her head from side to side.

"What baby?"

"Please, not the baby." Her voice was barely a whisper.

"Shhh, it's okay, Jessie. I'm here." He went to the bathroom and grabbed a cold washcloth. He came back and wiped her face.

The nurse returned to the room with the doctor, and they asked Ethan to leave while they examined Jessica. The look of concern on the doctor's face only added to Ethan's anxiety about her condition. He went to a pay phone and called Jamie to tell her what was going on.

He wandered down the hall to Laurie's room. She was sitting up in bed watching TV.

"Well, don't you look better, Little Miss Sunshine." Ethan strolled over to her bed and kissed her cheek.

"Hey, Handsome. I feel much better. I think I'm going to get out of this place soon."

"That's wonderful."

"How's Jessie? When Jamie stopped by she said she made it through surgery, and she was resting."

"She spiked a fever. The nurse had to go get the doctor. They are examining her now as we speak."

Laurie reached out and grabbed his hand. "Ethan, what else is going on? I can see it in your face. You're not telling me everything."

"She was restless, tossing and turning in the bed. She kept calling out."

"Calling out? What did she say?"

"She kept saying no, not the baby."

"Oh." Laurie looked away from Ethan.

"What baby, Laurie?"

"It must be the fever. Maybe she is delirious."

"Maybe she is, but she was in terrible distress, and I think you know what she was talking about."

"Ethan, I can't. This is between the two of you."

"Laurie, don't do this to me. If you know, tell me."

"I can't." Laurie closed her eyes tight.

"Did she lose a baby?"

Laurie nodded.

"Is that what broke her and John up? She told me she couldn't have children."

Laurie shook her head.

"For godsake, Laurie, would you just talk to me? If you know something, tell me. What if something happens to Jessie?" Ethan was trying to control his growing frustration. "I can't help her if I don't know what's wrong."

"Ethan, it's not my place to tell you. I'm sorry." Laurie squeezed his hand.

"Fine." Ethan left Laurie and returned to Jessica's room. The doctor had changed her IV antibiotics and said all they could do was wait and see. He felt confident that they had caught the infection in time, and she would be okay.

Ethan sat down in the chair next to her bed. He closed his eyes tight. A horrible feeling developed in the pit of his stomach. Something awful had happened after he left. Jessica wouldn't tell him, but she wouldn't let go of it, either. He prayed with all his heart he was wrong.

"Please don't tell me you lost our baby." He opened his eyes and looked at Jessica.

A tear trickled down his cheek as he sat in the chair, by her side for what seemed like forever. Jessica stirred in the bed.

Ethan jumped to his feet and caressed her face. "Jessie, can you hear me?"

Her eyes slowly fluttered open. "Ethan?" she whispered.

"Yeah, babe, it's me." He grabbed her hand and kissed it.

"Where am I? Water. Can I have some water?"

Ethan poured a glass and put the straw up to her dry lips. "You're in the hospital."

"What happened?" She tried to sit up and winced in pain.

"You were shot."

"Oh." Her eyes fluttered shut.

"Should I go get a doctor or nurse?"

"No, I'm okay. Laurie. How is Laurie?" She tried to rise again.

"Easy now. She's fine. She's busy worrying about you."

"Thank goodness." She relaxed against the pillows and closed her eyes, falling back to sleep.

Ethan stayed by her side until she awoke a few hours later. She was sore and thirsty but coherent.

"You scared me half to death," he said, caressing her cheek.

"I'm sorry," she whispered.

"Don't ever do that again. I'm getting to be an old man. I don't know how much my poor heart can take."

"You're heart is fine." She closed her eyes.

Ethan took her hand. "Jessie, I think I know the secret you've been keeping from me." He knew now wasn't the time, but he needed to know the answer, even though he was pretty sure he already did.

"No secrets," she whispered.

"I know about the baby."

Her eyes opened, and she stared at him. "The baby."

"Yeah Jessie, I know about the baby. Were you pregnant with our child when we were in college, weren't you? Did you lose our baby? Is that what happened after I left?"

Tears trickled down her cheek as she nodded.

"Why didn't you tell me?" Ethan brushed the tear away with the back of his hand. It felt like someone had just stabbed him in the heart and punched him in the gut.

"I was going to tell you the night you got back, but you broke up with me before I could."

He was finding it hard to breathe. The pit in his stomach was growing. Was he going to be sick? "What happened to the baby?" The chair by her bed caught him as he fell back into it.

"I was distraught and ended up at my grandfather's farm. I was on one of the horses. My eyes were stinging with tears. I didn't see the wall, and the horse hesitated. I fell and lost the baby."

"I don't know what to say." Ethan rested his head in his hands. The emotions that came raging to the surface were suffocating him. They had lost a child. Their child. No wonder she hated him. What she must have gone through, and he wasn't there for her.

"I'm sorry, Ethan. I should have told you a long time ago."

"You never had any more children."

"Later on I found out I couldn't have children. Apparently the doctor who took care of me at the time of the fall wasn't a very good doctor."

"Jessie, I am so sorry. I had made so many promises to you, and we had so many dreams together. Then I left you to pursue my own dreams and to hell with us. I'm so sorry. I should have been there for you." A tear ran down his cheek. "I wish you had told me."

"Don't say you would have stayed. It wasn't in your heart, or you would have."

"I'm even more of an ass. Now I understand why you weren't happy to see me. How can I ever make it up to you?"

He sat in the chair and rested his head on her stomach. He let the tears flow freely. Tears for their unborn child, tears for the mistakes he had made, and tears for the hurt he had caused her.

chapter 22

ETHAN FINALLY ALLOWED Jamie to convince him to go home. Jessica's fever was under control, and the antibiotics they had given her were doing their job. Jessica slept, and there was nothing more he could do at the hospital, but there was something he could do back at the ranch.

The person who was harassing Jessica was going down.

When Ethan returned to the ranch, he headed to Jessica's room so he could have some time to digest what he had learned about their child and make a plan for bringing down the person behind the attacks.

Ethan entered the room to find Maddie cleaning. He startled her when he entered.

"Ethan, what are you doing here?"

"I'm getting some things for Jessica at the hospital," he lied. He didn't want anyone knowing he was searching for evidence.

"Oh, how is she?"

"She's going to be fine."

"Thank the good lord." She made the sign of the cross. "I was terribly worried about her. I'm just finishing up. I'll be out of your way." Maddie finished dusting, packed up her cleaning supplies and quickly left the room.

Ethan sat down on the couch and started going over everything in his head. Piece by piece, he reviewed what he knew. Then the light bulb went on. Of course, why hadn't he thought of it earlier? It had been right there in front of him. He jumped up and went in search of Joe. He found him in the stables brushing down one of the horses.

"Joe, I need your help."

"Sure, Ethan, what's up?"

"I need a master key."

"Okay. What for?"

"I need to check out some rooms."

"Sure. Follow me. Miss Jessica keeps one in her desk."

Ethan and Joe retrieved the key from Jessica's office.

"Do you need my help?" Joe asked.

"No, I'm good. Any word on Laurie?"

"Yeah, Jeremy said she's coming home today."

"That's great. I'll catch up with you later." Ethan left Jessica's office and headed to the wing that housed some of the employee rooms. He had been positive that it was someone on the ranch; only he had been looking in the wrong direction.

He let himself in the various rooms and started going through the drawers and closets. Sure enough, it didn't take him long to find what he was looking for. Way back in a drawer, he found a bottle of salicylic acid, exactly what he found in the oil from Jessica's massage. That wasn't all. He pulled out a rag and unwrapped a bloody knife; one he was pretty sure was used to decapitate a rat. The lab would prove that.

Ethan gathered the evidence and was ready to leave the room when the door opened.

"What the hell are you doing?"

"That's exactly what I'd like to ask you." Ethan held the bottle and knife out in front of him.

"What are those things?"

"Don't play dumb with me. I suspected that it was someone on the ranch. Whoever this person was, they moved around freely. Then it all made sense. Who has access to the Spa, Jessica's room and Laurie's room? Who else, but housekeeping. I know it's you, Maddie."

"You don't know anything." She crossed her arms in front of her chest defensively.

"Maddie, I have the evidence. I found it in your dresser. Now, why don't you tell me who you're working with?"

"I'm not working with anybody. Someone must be trying to frame me."

"Come on, I believe that you could have cut the girth on Jessie's saddle and spooked the horses that nearly trampled me. You obviously put the acid in Jessie's massage oil and decapitated the rat and most likely put the scorpions in Laurie's towel. What I don't buy, is that you dismantled the bolts on the wagon, lurked around up in the hayloft and put the rattlesnake in the feed barrel. I certainly don't think you would shoot Jessie. Now if you want to take the fall for attempted murder, that's fine by me."

"You can't prove anything."

"I can prove enough." Ethan caught a glimpse of a photograph on her night stand. "Nice photograph, Maddie. You have a good-looking family. I'm sure they'll be proud of their convicted mother." He picked up the photograph and looked at the family picture more intently. He couldn't believe his eyes. Now it all made sense. "Your son would do anything for his mother."

"Leave him out of this!" she cried.

"So you're gonna take the fall for your son? You're a good mother. Attempted murder carries a pretty long sentence," Ethan said sarcastically.

Maddie started to sob. "Adam is a good boy, I swear. He's only twenty. He did what he was told to do. He wasn't supposed to try to kill Miss Jessica. He was only supposed to scare her."

"I thought you might see things my way. I knew it was one of the guys, but I couldn't find any evidence. None of those accidents left me a clue. Why, Maddie? I thought Jessica was good to you. You're a single mom. You of all people should understand what she's about, what this ranch is about. Why would you tell Adam to do those things?"

"Everything would have been fine if you hadn't showed up on the ranch. She would have closed her doors weeks ago. It would have never come to this. I'm not saying another word." She sat down on the edge of the bed.

"Not a problem." Ethan walked over to the phone and called the station. He asked for a squad car to come and pick her up. "Maddie, you are under arrest. You have the right to remain silent. Anything you say can be held against you in a court of law. You have the right to an attorney. If you give up that right, one will be appointed to you. Do you understand these rights as they have been read to you?"

"You'll be sorry you did this," defiance surfaced in her voice.

"Is that so? How am I going to be sorry?"

"Larry will take care of you." Her hand flew to her mouth and covered it.

"Larry? Maddie, why don't you tell me about Larry and his role in all of this?"

"I want my lawyer."

"I'll let you call a lawyer, but if there is someone else involved, you had better speak up because you and Adam are going to be doing a little bit of time. Now if you cooperate, I'll tell the judge to go easy on both of you."

"Larry Hamilton," she blurted out.

"Larry Hamilton?" Ethan wasn't sure he heard her right. "You mean Lawrence Hamilton our Mayor?"

"Yes." She hung her head and stared at the floor.

"Why on earth would the Mayor have you do this? Does he have something on you?" "Of course not. I'd do anything for him. I love him!" She closed her eyes and winced.

"Is he your lover, Maddie? Why, he's a married man, how ironic. I knew he was rather outspoken about Jessie's ranch, but I had no idea how outspoken. I assume he's the one that has been filling the town's people's heads with crap about her. Why?"

Maddie shrugged at him.

"Maddie, you've been very cooperative. If you know more, you need to tell me. He must have a motive for wanting her to close down the ranch."

"There is a developer who wants this land, and he's willing to pay a lot of money for it, but Miss Jessica wouldn't sell the ranch to him. The developer wants to build expensive homes for people who want to get out of Flagstaff. He told Larry he could have a cut."

"What's in it for you?"

"I love him. He's going to leave his wife, and we're going to be together and have a wonderful life. I can finally help my children. They can have the life I couldn't give them by myself."

"Maddie, you've been most helpful." Ethan shook his head. Of course she believed Larry, she really loved him or at least the promise of a better life. "Let's take a walk." Ethan escorted her out of the room and headed to the main lobby of the lodge. He sat Maddie down on one of the sofas in a semi-private area.

He asked one of the other cleaning ladies if they would go get Joe in the stables.

He quickly appeared. "What's going on, Ethan?"

"Joe, Maddie has been a very busy lady. She's the one who's been trying to sabotage Jessie. I've called for a squad car to come and pick her up. She's going to be having some company, so don't let them leave until I get back."

"What? No, not Maddie." Joe looked down at her. "What's the matter with you, woman? I thought you cared about her. Jessica has been good to you. How could you, you ungrateful witch."

"Shut-up, old man," she hissed at him.

"I'll leave you two to chat." Ethan headed straight to the bunkhouse.

No one was around, so he searched it one more time. The last time he turned up nothing. This time he wasn't disappointed. In a box under Adam's bed, buried under some of his gear, was a Smith & Wesson revolver. It was a .22 magnum, the same caliber as the bullet that hit Jessie. He grabbed a pillowcase and wrapped the gun in it. More evidence. Now he needed to find Adam.

Ethan returned to Jessie's suite and retrieved his Glock 24 from his gun case in the dresser drawer. He tucked it into the waist of his pants. If Adam had shot Jessie, who knew what else he was capable of? Ethan bumped into one of the housekeepers and inquired about Adam's whereabouts. She thought she had seen him going on his break. Ethan headed to the maintenance area where there was a break room.

Ethan approached the area quietly. There were people inside. First he saw Roy, one of the maintenance guys, and Aaron.

Then he saw Adam. Hopefully this would end without a fight. He took a deep breath and entered the room.

"Hey, guys, what's going on?"

"Nothing, Ethan, how's Miss Jessica?" Aaron inquired.

"She's going to be just fine."

"That's good. We were worried about her," Roy interjected.

"In fact, she's going to be better than fine when I tell her who's been causing her all the trouble around the ranch."

"You figured it out?" Aaron asked.

"I sure did. There won't be any more problems or people getting hurt."

"That's a relief. After what happened to Jeremy, I've been damn careful in the stables."

"No need to worry anymore, Aaron. Isn't that right, Adam?"

"That's great news." Adam started to inch himself closer to the door.

"It was Maddie, and she had a little help."

"No way, not Maddie. She was always so nice. She's like a mother to everyone. Who on earth helped her?" Roy asked.

"Who helped her, Adam?"

At that moment, Adam bolted for the door. Ethan didn't miss a beat and sprang on him with the force of his entire body propelling him. He flattened Adam at the door. Adam struggled to push Ethan off him. He flipped over and tried to shove Ethan from his body. Ethan took one swift swing at Adam's jaw, and the struggle ceased. Aaron and Roy stood in shock at the display in front of them. Ethan rose and dragged Adam to his feet.

"You're lucky I don't beat you within an inch of your life for what you did to Jessie. Let's go. Your mother is waiting for you, so you can enjoy the ride to jail together." Ethan shoved Adam out of the break room, reading him his rights as he did.

The patrol car waited for them in front of the lodge. One of the deputies took custody of Adam. Maddie was already waiting in the patrol car.

"Guys, take their statements. I'll be stopping in after I take care of something. I believe we're going to have one more person joining us." Ethan informed his Under Sheriff what was going on and instructed him to go pick-up the mayor.

Ethan headed for his pick-up truck. He couldn't wait to get to the hospital and tell Jessica she had nothing left to worry about.

❦

Ethan entered Jessica's room to find her and Laurie chatting away. Laurie was dressed and ready to go home.

"Hello, Ladies." He entered the room and swept his hat in front of him.

"Hi, Ethan, you really do like being the dashing cowboy, don't you? Why are you all smiles?" Laurie grinned at him.

"I have fantastic news."

"What's that?" Laurie asked.

"Your mystery menace has been caught. Or should I say menaces."

"What?" Jessica sat up more in the bed.

"Ethan, that's wonderful." Laurie rose to hug him. "Who was the bastard or should I say bastards?"

"Maddie and Adam."

"What! Not Maddie, are you sure, Ethan?" Jessica's voice echoed her doubt.

"Positive. I found evidence in her room, and then she admitted to it."

"I don't understand. She was so good to me. She was like a surrogate mother."

"That's what made this so hard. I never suspected her."

"When I think back, I guess it makes sense. Maddie was always checking on me. She seemed to know where I was all the time. Oh God, I told her exactly what she need to know and played right into her plan. I just can't believe it." She covered her face with her hands.

"She wasn't alone. Adam helped her. I just couldn't put my finger on who, then it made sense when I walked into your suite and she was there cleaning. Maddie had access to everywhere: your room, Laurie's room, the spa. Adam picked up where she left off. He was the one that shot you."

Jessica looked up at him. "Why? What did I do to them?"

"Adam did it for his mother, but Maddie did it for her lover."

"What! She had a lover?"

"Yeah, she did it for her lover and the promise of a better life."

"I thought I gave her a better life," Jessica whispered.

"Who's her lover, Ethan?" Laurie asked.

"Are you ready for this? It's Lawrence Hamilton."

"Our Mayor?" They both squealed.

"Yep. Jessie, you never told me a developer wanted to buy your ranch."

"That was over a year ago. I told him no and don't come back, end of story."

"End of story?" Ethan raised an eyebrow at her.

"Yeah, I swear. I suppose my 'don't come back' was a little more colorful than that, but I made my point. I haven't heard from the guy since." She crossed her heart.

"Apparently, he enlisted Mayor Hamilton's help. If the mayor got you to sell, he would give him a cut of the action."

"Wow, I can't believe that. I thought Maddie had a good life on the ranch. I thought she was happy." Jessie shook her head in disbelief.

"I guess our mayor promised her a better life than you could offer for her and her family," Ethan replied.

Jeremy poked his head in the door. "Are you ready, Mom?"

"It looks like my ride is ready to leave. I'll catch you kids back at the ranch." Laurie leaned over and hugged Jessica good-bye and then kissed Ethan on the cheek.

"I'm so glad she's okay." Jessica sighed as Laurie left the room.

"Me, too. How are you feeling?"

"I'm fine. A little sore, but fine." She winced as she tried to move her arm.

"A little more than sore I would say. But I'm glad you're better. Hopefully, you'll be able to go home soon."

"Yeah." She looked down at the bed and fidgeted with her blanket.

"What's wrong? You have nothing to worry about now. You don't have to sell the ranch."

"It's not that simple."

"Sure it is. You were going to sell because someone was hurting the people you love. Your problem is solved."

"Do we have to talk about this now? I'm really tired."

"Of course not. Did the doctor say when you might go home?"

"Maybe tomorrow."

"That's fantastic. I'll come and get you."

"That won't be necessary."

"Jessie, what's wrong?"

"Nothing. Jeremy will come and get me. I'm sure you want to spend some time with Chrissie before she leaves. Plus, you no longer need to stay at the ranch. Maybe you should take Chrissie to your house. I'm sure she would like to see it before her trip is over."

"Are you tossing me out?" He took her hand in his.

She pulled her hand away. "Your job is done, and you did it well. Thank you." She looked away from him and stared out the window.

"Damn it, Jessie, when are you going to forgive me?"

"I've forgiven you."

"Then when the hell are you going to believe that I'm not gonna leave you. I swear, baby, I'm never gonna leave you again. So go ahead, push all you want, but you're stuck with me."

She looked down and fidgeted with her blankets unable to look him in the eye. "Please, Ethan, you need to go," she whispered

"Fine. If that's how you want things, I'll go." He leaned over and kissed her cheek.

"Thanks, I appreciate it."

Ethan left her room. She was leaving because of him, he could feel it. He had started to crumble her walls, and now she was building them up again.

Was it because of the baby? Now he knew how much it had hurt her losing the baby and never being able to have another. There was no doubt it was his fault. But she had started to come around, maybe even forgive him. She had let him in again. What happened?

Whatever the case, it was apparent she didn't want him in her life now. Maybe that was the best thing he could do for her. If he was out of her life, maybe she could move on and finally heal.

"Ethan! Wait up!"

He stopped when he saw Jamie rushing down the hall. "Hey, Jamie, what's up?"

"I was going to ask you the same thing. How are things at the ranch?"

"Good. I found and arrested the people behind all the accidents."

"That's wonderful news. Who was it?"

"Long story short, it was Maddie and her son. Apparently Mayor Hamilton put her up to it because he and a developer wanted the land."

"What! Jessie must be heartbroken. She thought the world of Maddie. Thank god this ordeal is finally over. Jessie must be relieved."

"Yeah, I guess." Ethan stared down at the floor.

"Ethan, what's wrong. The problems at the ranch are solved, and Jessie is going to be fine. Maybe now you two can finally be together."

He looked up at her, tears trying to fill his eyes. "Jess isn't interested in being together. A lot has happened. I thought I could make it up to her, but apparently I can't. Maybe she is right. Letting her go is probably the best thing for her."

Jamie placed a hand on his arm. "Ethan, you can't give up on her."

"Jessie is very serious. I can't make her want to be with me. I'm done, Jamie."

She hugged him tight. "Oh, Ethan, I'm so sorry."

He pulled free from her grasp. "I've gotta get back to the ranch and get Chrissie. I'll talk with you later. Thanks for everything you've done." Ethan quickly walked away before his heart broke into a million pieces.

chapter 23

Jeremy helped Jessica out of the Envoy and into the lodge. All of the staff and a large number of guests were gathered for her arrival and cheered when she entered the lobby. A large banner read 'Welcome Home, Jessica,' and there were balloons everywhere. The outpouring of love and support overwhelmed her. She was still a little weak, so Jeremy suggested she go sit on one of the sofas in the great room.

Jessica chatted with her staff and some of the guests. She started to feel tired and was ready to head back to her room when Kim and Chrissie walked up to her. She wasn't sure if she was ready to deal with them.

"Jessie, I'm glad you're going to be okay. Thank you for letting me and Chrissie stay here. We're heading home today." Kim stuck out her hand to shake Jessica's.

Jessica was surprised by Kim's gesture. "Thanks. Have a safe trip."

"If you don't mind, Chrissie wanted to speak with you before we left."

"Sure."

Chrissie sat down next to her. "Jessie, I'm sorry you got hurt."

"Thanks, I'm going to be okay."

"I'm also sorry about how I behaved. I was a brat to you, and I'm really, really sorry. I only did it because I was afraid that if my dad liked you, he wouldn't have room for me anymore. I thought if I got Mom and Dad back together, I wouldn't lose him. I really am sorry, and I hope you can forgive me."

"Oh Sweetie, you never have to worry about losing your dad. He loves you very much. Thank you for explaining things. I appreciate you being grown-up enough to tell me. Of course I forgive you."

"Jessie, I really do like you and so does my dad. Please don't be mad at him. He's not too bright sometimes and needs a little help understanding when he's wrong. I messed up things between you."

"I'm not mad at him, but I don't think we'll be together."

"Jessie, I also told my mom and dad some things about you that weren't true. It really wasn't his fault, it was mine. He loves you, Jessie. He seemed happier with you than he has been in a very long time. If you can forgive me, you can forgive him, I'm sure you can."

"I wish it were that simple, Chrissie."

"It is. I've heard you tell that to the ladies here. Forgive and move forward. Besides, if you and my dad were together, I thought maybe if I wasn't a brat anymore that maybe you would like to borrow me as a daughter. I really loved being here with you and my dad."

A tear ran down Jessica's cheek. She was overwhelmed by what Chrissie was saying. A kid who just wanted to make sure she didn't lose her dad. Could she forgive him again?

Her heart ached. Was it ready to take that chance again? Laurie's words echoed in her head. She was the one responsible for her actions, and she was the one facing the consequences. They had come so far. She was tired of hurting and tired of running from what she wanted most. Forgive and move on. Was it possible to put the past behind them and move forward? Was it possible for her to have her happily ever after?

Yes, she wanted more than anything to forgive him. She wanted the life she had always dreamed of with him by her side. He truly was the love of her life.

"Please, Jessie, forgive me and my dad. I promise you won't be sorry." Chrissie stood up and hugged Jessica.

The tears were now flowing freely. "Chrissie, I think I would love to borrow you as a daughter. Maybe next time you come to visit, we'll have a lot more fun."

"Does that mean you're going to forgive my dad?"

She wiped away the tears. "Yeah, I think I would like to. I'd really like to have you both in my life."

Chrissie waved for her mother to come over. "Mom, Jessie is going to give Dad another chance."

"I'm glad for you. He really does love you. Jessie, I owe you an apology myself. I feel horrible for judging you when I didn't have all the facts. Please accept my apology."

"Apology accepted."

"Thank you." Kim reached out and shook Jessica's hand.

"Do you know where Ethan is?"

"He said he had some packing to do, and then he was going to take us to the airport."

"Thanks, Kim. You two sit tight. I'm going to go find him."

Jessica mustered up all her strength and went to the bunkhouse first. It was empty. She checked the chest were Ethan had kept his things. They were gone. She felt her heart sink to her toes. She had been horrible to him, telling him to get out of her life more than once. What if he had actually listened to her? She headed back to the lodge. Her strength was quickly getting sapped. Well, she got what she asked for. He really had left her. The tears streamed down her cheeks.

She swung open the door to her suite and made her way to the spare room he had occupied. It was empty, and his things were gone. She was feeling weak, tired and heart broken. He really was getting out of her life. Her chest tightened as the ache hit her heart. What had she done? For once in his life he actually did what she asked of him. The tears started to stream down her cheeks. She leaned against the wall afraid that her knees would give way beneath her.

After all these years of heartache, after all the advice she had given others, she was too damn stubborn to get out of her own way. Fate had given her another chance at true love, and she blew it. He really was gone. Her breath caught in her chest as she tried to hold back the sobs that wanted to escape.

She pushed herself away from the wall and headed toward the door. On her way past her bedroom she stopped abruptly when she heard a funny noise. She poked her head around the corner to peer in the room.

"What on earth?" She couldn't believe the sight before her. She wiped the tears from her eyes. Was she really seeing what she thought she saw?

He looked so adorable, sound asleep on the bed in her room. His legs were crossed at his ankles, and his chest was bare. A bouquet of red roses rested across his lap. She hated to wake him, but his snoring was a bit much. She gently shook him.

His eyes fluttered open. "It's about time you got here." He yawned.

"What do you think you're doing?" She tried to hide the grin that started to creep across her face as she ate him up with her eyes.

"I think I'm waiting for you to shag your injured little butt home." Ethan yawned again.

It had to be the sweetest and sexiest thing she had ever seen in her life.

"Here, these are for you." He handed her the bouquet.

She inhaled the sweet fragrance of the roses.

"I see you're happy to see me." A smile tugged at the corners of her lips. Her eyes roamed over him coming to rest on the unsubtle bulge in his khakis.

"Yeah, what can I say?"

"What if I'm not happy to see you?" She tried to frown and crossed her arms in front of her, walking around the bed, sizing him up. The beat of her heart raced, and her blood was heating up at the sight of him. She wanted to toss herself into his arms and kiss him like he had never been kissed before.

He rose from the bed and came to stand in front of her. "I'm an eternal optimist. I had faith you would come. Plus I was hoping you wouldn't be able to resist my charms."

"Of course I would come, I live here. What makes you think I came here looking for you?"

"Oh, I don't know, maybe the fact that I'm totally irresistible and you'd give in sooner or later." Ethan wrapped his arms around her waist and pulled her to him. "Hey, you've been crying. What's wrong?" He wiped the smudge marks from her cheeks.

"Oh, just a little emotional today," she sniffed.

"You thought I left, didn't you."

She looked down at his chest. "Maybe."

He lifted her chin so she had to look into his eyes. "I meant what I said. I know you still love me, and I'm never leaving you again. You're stuck with me for life, even if that means I have to be a farm hand on your ranch just to be close to you. I'm not leaving."

Jessica was unraveling quickly. Looking at him was one thing, but feeling his naked chest against hers and the hardness of his arousal pressed against her was too much. She wrapped one arm around his neck.

"You should be resting." Ethan picked her up in his arms, carried her over to the bed and gently laid her down on it. He stretched out next to her. "Jessie, I'm so sorry for how I behaved. I was completely deaf and blind where Chrissie was concerned."

"It hurt to know you thought I would tell you lies about your daughter. I know how much you love her. I would never deliberately hurt you."

Ethan ran a finger down the side of her face and across her lips. "I know. I wanted my visit with her to be perfect; I wanted her to still be my baby girl. I am so sorry for my stupidity."

"Chrissie told me the truth, how she lied to you and Kim. That was very grown up of her. But what's going to happen in the future? You completely dismissed me." Jessica ran her hand over the muscles in his chest and enjoyed feeling them flex beneath her touch.

"I promise to be a rational father and respect what you have to say. I should have known better. I should have listened to you and then kept an eye on Chrissie to see for myself what she was up to. It won't happen again, I promise."

"I'm sorry, too. I was so stubborn and didn't want to hear a thing you had to say. I let all the hurt from the past get in the way."

"I guess we both have a few things to work on." Ethan leaned down and kissed her. "You need to get your rest."

"I'm fine." She caressed his cheek.

"You're not fine, you were shot. Now, let me tuck you in."

"Only if you tuck yourself in with me, I don't want you to leave." She pulled him closer, and her hand ran over his shoulder and down his arm.

"Jessie, you delectable little morsel, are you teasing me?"

"Who said anything about teasing?"

"Woman, I have incredible willpower, but you're really testing it."

"Make love to me." Her voice came out barely a whisper.

"You just got out of the hospital. You shouldn't over-do it."

"I'll let you do all the work." She ran her hands over his chest and down to the waistband of his pants.

"I don't want to hurt you." He leaned down and kissed her.

"You won't," she whispered.

He let out a low growl and then carefully removed her arm from the sling, as his fingers worked on the buttons of her blouse. He helped her ease out of it as his hands caressed her skin, and his lips left feather light kisses on her naked shoulders. "I love you, Jessie."

"I love you too, Ethan." She moaned.

"Does that mean you're not going to sell and stay here?"

"I've been thinking about that."

"And?" He continued to shower her in kisses.

"I was thinking that perhaps I could win the town's people over by having a family day a couple of times a year. We could make it like a carnival. There is plenty to do here. Maybe even make it a fundraiser and pick different charities. Then they would get to know me and what the ranch is about. We could even promote some of the local shops to our guests." She closed her eyes and enjoyed the feelings he was creating inside of her.

"We?"

"Well you are the Sheriff, and I would need someone to do crowd control."

"Crowd control, huh?" Ethan's hands slowly roamed over her breasts and stomach, careful not to cause any pain to her bandaged shoulder.

"Is that a problem?" Her voice came out husky. She was finding it hard to concentrate on what he was saying. Ethan was causing wonderful sensations to flow through her body, and she quickly forgot about her fatigue, and the dull ache in her arm.

"Not at all. But I was thinking of something a little more permanent."

"You want to keep singing?"

"Only if it's a private performance for you."

"That might be kind of nice." She stretched up and nipped at his lips.

"Does that mean I can stick around?"

"You better. You have a lot of years to make up for."

"Jess, about the baby…"

She placed her finger to his lips. "Shhhh, I'm ready to let go. Maybe we can heal together."

"I love you so much."

"Stop talking and show me." She pulled him toward her.

Ethan gently rolled her onto her back. He started at the top of her head and began kissing every inch of her. She moaned and wiggled beneath him.

He raised his head and looked at her. "I'm not hurting you am I?"

"No," she said shyly.

"Come on, out with it. If I'm hurting you, I'll stop."

She saw the concern on his face and caressed the side of his cheek. "I want you so badly that if you're going to take your sweet time, I don't think I'll make it."

Ethan laughed a rich, hearty sound. "You are the most delectable creature I know, and I do plan to take my time. I'm going to love every sweet inch of you and, when I'm done, I'm going to do it all over again, and again, and again." His head bent down, and he nipped at one of her breasts.

"Ethan!" She wiggled again beneath him.

"Get used to it, because I plan to love you like this for the rest of our lives."

"Is that so?"

"Yeah." Ethan consumed her lips in a passionate kiss and finished what he had started. There would be lots of making up to do tonight, and every night, for the rest of their lives.

❧❦

Jessica lay in Ethan's arms, her head resting upon his chest. "Oh, my gosh, Ethan, I forgot about Chrissie and Kim. Weren't you going to take them to the airport?" Jessica panicked and sat up in bed. What time was it? She could see that it was still daylight. She had gotten so wrapped up in making love with Ethan, she forgot she had left Kim and Chrissie sitting in the lobby.

"You're right. I guess I got a little carried away." He rolled over to look at the clock. "We still have a little bit of time. I'm sure they occupied themselves while they waited." He sat up and nipped at her good shoulder.

"We better get dressed and go meet them." Jessica carefully slid out of bed, grabbed her clothes and dressed with a little help from Ethan, which almost made them later than they already were.

In spite of his grumbling, he followed her lead. "Hey, come here." Ethan stopped Jessica before she walked out the door.

"What's the matter?"

"Would you come here for a moment?"

Jessica closed the door and walked back to him. "What?"

Ethan wrapped his arms around her and pulled her to him. "This is for real, right? I love you and you love me, too, right? I didn't get trampled by horses again and this is all just a dream."

Jessica looked up into his green eyes that sparkled with gold flecks and laughed. "Are you being insecure?"

"When it comes to you, I'm not sure what I am."

She stretched up on tiptoe and kissed his lips. "Yes, Ethan, this is for real. I love you, and I want a future with you, the way it was always meant to be."

"Okay, you may go." He smacked her on the butt as she turned to leave.

The two lovebirds quickly made their way to the main area of the lodge, walking arm-in-arm. They searched for Kim and Chrissie until they found them drinking ice tea and lemonade on the patio.

Chrissie was the first to spot them. "Dad. Jessie." She jumped up and ran to her dad. "Is everything all better? Did you fix things?" she whispered in his ear.

"Yeah, Sweet Pea, everything is all fixed." He bent and kissed the top of her head.

The threesome joined Kim. "We're ready to leave whenever you are, Ethan. I'm sure you have things you need to do." Kim gathered her things.

Jessica walked over to Kim. "Are you okay with this? It must seem weird, doesn't it, seeing Ethan with someone else?"

"I'm fine. We've been over for a few years now. I know you'll be good to my daughter when she comes to visit, and I think you will make Ethan happy. I'm glad for him."

"Thanks, Kim. That means a lot, especially because of Chrissie. I know how important she is to Ethan, and I know he doesn't want to miss a thing."

"Alright, ladies, it's time to go so you don't miss your plane." Ethan grabbed their bags and loaded them into Jessica's Envoy.

Chrissie chattered their whole ride to the airport. They didn't have much time to spare when they arrived and their flight was called.

Ethan hugged Chrissie. "Now you promise to be a good girl for your mom?"

"I promise, Dad."

"You promise not to tell any more lies and cause trouble?"

"Yes."

"I'm gonna miss you."

"I'm gonna miss you, too, Dad."

"Okay, Sweet Pea, be good. I love you."

"Love you, too." She hugged her dad tight and then walked over to Jessie. "Take good care of him, he needs it."

"I will. You just be good so you can come back soon."

"I will." Chrissie hugged Jessica good-bye.

"Have a safe trip," Ethan called out to Kim who waved good-bye to them.

Ethan walked over to Jessica and kissed her deeply. "I guess it's just you and me now. I think we need to head home so we can work on all that making up I have to do."

"Good idea, because your penance is a steep one and will require a significant amount of effort on your part." She waved good-bye to Kim and Chrissie.

"Steep you say?"

"Yep, and I think it's going to involve a life long sentence." Jessica wrapped her good arm around him.

"Come on, love, let's go home." Ethan put his arm around her shoulder.

"Home. I like the sound of that. Lead the way, babe."

Coming in June 2012

Fancy Pants

As the Vice President of Sales & Marketing for JRH Engineering in New York City, thirty-five year old **Rebecca Eastwood** has traveled around the world, working side-by-side with her boss, the company president. After falling in love with him, she is devastated to learn he is still married and not divorced as he claimed. Not willing to be "the other woman", she returns to Upstate New York to the safety of her family and begins to heal her broken heart. While visiting her family she rediscovers her childhood past time of horseback riding and a man who was her sympathy prom date almost twenty years ago.

Single dad, Ben Dupre, is a successful Veterinarian, horse rancher and devoted father to his five-year-old son. When Miss Fancy Pants steps out of her BMW in her high-heels and silk blouse, he knows she's going to be trouble, but the biggest surprise is when he realizes the scrawny teenager he took to the prom has now become a sensuous woman. He is less than thrilled when Rebecca inquires about private riding lessons, but how can he say no to an old friend, even when his gut warns him against it. He might be drawn to her physically, but he has no interest in a relationship after being hurt badly by his ex-wife. He can't let go of his anger and mistrust of women, but in his heart he is lonely and wants to give his son the mother he longs for.

Rebecca equally has no intention of complicating her life by becoming involved with a cowboy who has a son, even if he takes her breath away. When a series of events keeps throwing the two of them together, their mutual attraction for each other begins to take over until Rebecca's ex-boyfriend darkens Ben's doorstep, unwilling to let her go. Working their way through misunderstandings and overcoming old fears, the two finally find what their hearts' desire most.

Also coming soon
Wayward Wives Club Series
Book 2   Horsin' Around
Book 3   No More Lies

To read about upcoming books visit
www.reginaedwardsdrumm.com

Regina Edwards Drumm calls home on 15 acres in Upstate New York. She shares her life with her wonderful husband Bill (who often inspires her heroes), her two beautiful stepdaughters, and a couple of lovable beagles who are more like her children than dogs.

Regina grew up in Upstate New York and in spite of the winters, she wouldn't want to live anywhere else, unless of course it was an island in the Caribbean. She grew up in a large family with wonderful parents, two sisters and two brothers. She is the baby of the family and adores all of her older siblings, even though they bossed her around when she was younger.

Writing in some form has always been Regina's passion which is what lead her to a career as marketing professional and romance author. Pursuing her dreams and seeing them come true is what life is all about.

To learn more about Regina Edwards Drumm and her books, visit her website at www.reginaedwardsdrumm.com

Made in the USA
Charleston, SC
28 April 2015